ADMIT TWO

KB FISHER

First Edition: June 2023

Paperback ISBN: 979-8-9880200-0-4
eBook ISBN: 979-8-9880200-1-1
Library of Congress Control Number: 2023906982

For CARISSA—
*a reader of drafts, a thoughtful critic, but most of all,
an amazing wife*

Acknowledgments

I am most indebted to my wife, Carissa, for discussing ideas when I was stuck, and for reading each and every chapter as I wrote the original draft. Your support and willingness to lend an ear has made my writing process far more enjoyable.

I also thank my amazing editor, Dylan Garity. You've helped to take my first novel from what I hoped was good to beyond my wildest dreams. Somehow, you always know exactly what my writing needs. And for that, I am grateful.

part one
THE ARTIST

Chapter 1

Jackson Square was clearly visible from the third-floor balcony of the French Quarter suite. The sweetness of powdered sugar and beignets wafted from an adjacent fire escape as sunlight scattered in shades of blue, plum, and orange across the rooftops. It filled Mariana with warmth as she smiled and closed her eyes in the crisp sunset.

Lifting the bottle of merlot from the bucket of melting ice, she was careful not to let the water fall to her gray dress. She wanted to appear perfect for Antoine when he arrived.

Mariana poured herself a glass, filling it to the brim to account for her overly stressful week of work. "Half for now and half for . . . now," she mumbled to herself.

Her phone vibrated, sending itself into a slow spin on the table. It was Antoine.

"Well hey, you," she said, making her voice as seductive as possible. "When should I be expecting you?"

"Give me about ten," he responded.

She'd been hoping to hear more of a playful tone in his voice, considering this would be their first time together in months. But Mariana knew how hesitant he'd been to be with her previously.

"Okay, don't keep me waiting," she continued, playing up

her sensual Southern drawl.

This weekend together with Antoine was everything if she was going to convince him to leave his wife and start a new life with her. She couldn't afford to waste a moment.

Walking inside, Mariana began laying yellow rose petals to rest, one by one, across the king-size bed. Then she lit a small, lone candle next to the headboard—hardly enough light to make her silhouette dance across the ceiling.

If Mariana was going to truly captivate Antoine, she needed to slip into something more inviting. She kicked off her black high heels as she walked across the hardwood floor toward the bathroom, slipping the strap of her dress down past her tanned shoulder.

The fabric fell to the floor as she stole a brief glance at herself in the mirror, running her hand over her throat and clasping the silver necklace. Her husband had given it to her for her birthday the year before, when they visited the French Quarter together—the last genuine time they'd spent alone.

Was it too late to salvage her marriage?

Her attention darted back to making herself presentable for Antoine. At least now, she had a chance with someone who would build a future with her.

She removed her bra and slipped on a black lace camisole top. Matching silk panties were the only other piece of clothing she kept on.

Mariana reclined on the bed, facing the door, her heart beating faster thump by thump. She couldn't recall the last time her husband had made her feel as she did now. Like she was on a first date, out past curfew.

Before she had a chance to reminisce any further over unwanted memories, the doorknob turned.

Her face contorted, eyebrows bowing, as Antoine crossed the doorway—with another man half a stride behind.

The man held a pistol pressed tightly against Antoine's lower back, and sweat poured down from his eyebrow, dripping from his chin. To Mariana's eyes, it seemed almost in slow motion.

Chapter 2

amien Baptiste eased the door shut behind himself, keeping the polished, steel .45 pressed firmly against Antoine.

"Sit," Damien ordered.

Antoine took a slow seat in the chair at the table that was positioned in front of the bed. He glanced outside to the wrought-iron balcony and saw the iced bottle of wine and empty glass, finished by Mariana. He imagined for a fleeting instant what could have been.

"Antoine, what the hell is goin' on?" Mariana asked with a slight crack in her voice.

"Hush," said Damien. And she did.

She instantly noticed that Damien was a man of important stature, one with a confidence not to be tested. His tall, muscular build towered over her as she sat upright in the bed with her arms wrapped firmly around her legs.

Her eyes moved to Damien's black, clean-cut beard, his slickly combed hair, and his round, tortoise-brown glasses. She felt he was well put together for the occasion.

Damien's focus was now fully fixed on Mariana, but the gun remained on Antoine. Damien's right arm was fully sleeved in black and gray tattoos—a picture-perfect juxtaposition to the light glaring off the polished pistol.

"Lie down," he ordered Mariana at barely more than a whisper.

Her eyes rolled to the side as she turned her head just an inch to see Antoine's reaction. Antoine quickly stood, moving toward Damien with clear intentions.

Before he could react, Damien had him pinned against the wall. The pistol was pressed so deeply to his throat, he could hardly breathe.

"Don't even," Damien said, his voice soft but unyielding. "This is your last chance."

Antoine slowly walked backward to the chair and sat down, shaking with both anger and apprehension, not sure what more he could do to save himself and Mariana.

Damien's attention shifted back to what small persona of a woman was left on the bed. Her body was shuddering in pure terror.

"Lie. Down," Damien repeated. "I won't ask again."

She eased back with her legs hanging over the edge of the mattress, her arms fixed to her chest. Damien climbed on top of her, straddling her stomach. He ran a slow index finger from her navel up to her breasts.

His eyes were drawn to her necklace. The silver chain with a fleur-de-lis attached at the end rested right down the center of her chest, sitting at the base of her sternum.

He picked up the pendant with his left hand, placing it delicately between his fingers. Then he wrapped the chain around his hand, taking his time, until there was no longer slack. The metal began to twist and pressed against her smooth skin on the other end.

His hand sat open, molded against the top of her throat. His grip added more pressure than what was already present from the tightened necklace.

Damien's weight shifted entirely to his left arm, until Mariana could no longer grab an ounce of air. Her arms thrashed, and she attempted to shift her head toward Antoine in one last attempt for help.

She failed.

Antoine stood from the chair, and before he was even upright, Damien's thumb pulled back the hammer on the pistol. He stopped in his tracks.

"Try me," Damien said. He knew cutting off blood flow wasn't enough on its own, and she was too close to reaching a breath. He leaned with greater purpose.

Shade by shade, Mariana's lips shifted color. A subtle lilac began to appear through the ever-so-light layer of nude lipstick. Her eyes flooded until Damien's face was nothing more than a muddled blur.

Her body trembled, one last time, in an attempt to draw a single breath from somewhere. Anywhere.

Damien recognized the look.

A minute later, Mariana's eyes remained wide, but no longer for the same reasons. Her arms were again pressed to her chest but now motionless, along with the rest of her body.

He leaned in close, until his lips all but kissed her ear, then turned his head to Antoine. "You tell *me*—was she worth it?" Damien whispered as he unraveled the chain necklace from his hand and gave the man a slow, wide grin.

Chapter 3

Asher stood next to Antoine's body. It sat upright in the chair, situated at the foot of the bed and facing Mariana's naked corpse, which looked as if she were clenching her chest in dread.

"Murder turned suicide?" said Cassandra, Asher's partner.

"Maybe," he replied.

Asher Huxley, the lead investigator of the New Orleans Homicide Unit, had been on the forensics team for nearly two decades, but he'd only been leading the homicide unit for the past two years, since 2020. He recognized that scenes like this, opportunities of this sort, were pivotal career moments on which he needed to capitalize if he were to keep his job. His track record since being promoted wasn't the best.

Asher had a certain swagger about him—a certain "it" factor, a confidence. His brown hair was just long enough to touch the base of his neck, and currently was pushed behind his ears, curling at the ends. He was never clean-shaven, always managing to maintain a five-o'clock shadow. His signature aviator sunglasses hid the fact that his tired green eyes echoed both a lack of sleep and the need for even more coffee than the multiple cups of black syrup he regretted downing every morning and evening.

Antoine's arms lay perfectly flat on the chair's arms, and his head was bent down to the right, staring at Mariana as if the sight of her was his last. A clean, single entry point atop his left temple ran to an exit hole on the right and down to the floor, only the exit more closely resembled an exploding metal can with ragged pieces of flesh stripped back, about five times larger than the entry.

"A .45 ACP can really do some damage," said Cassandra.

"Sure. It's not the cause of death that interests me though." Asher's tone grew concerned. "It's how they're dressed—or not dressed, I should say."

Mariana's body was indeed stark naked. She was lying on her back, her head facing Antoine's body, which was at the foot of the bed. Antoine, on the other hand, was fully clothed.

"Any reason you can think of as to why she would be naked on the bed, but he isn't?" Asher asked.

"Maybe she wasn't on the bed to begin with. Maybe she was changing, was killed, and then someone moved her," Cassandra suggested.

"Or he got dressed after killing her."

Asher's attention turned to the fact that Antoine's arms were laid perfectly on the arms of the chair. He knew such a position was highly dubious given a suicide, and he wasn't the only one noticing aspects of the scene that didn't fit.

"Asher," one of the analysts called. "What do you make of this?"

The pistol was positioned on the floor directly below Antoine's left hand, leaning against the leg of the chair. The serial number on the right side of the pistol, above the skeletonized trigger, was filed down, clean and intentional.

Asher crouched with one arm poised on his knee. "Well, this isn't the first time we've seen this. It could be stolen, and/or someone doesn't want us to trace it."

"Sure, but an Ed Brown?" Cassandra said. "You know how much one of those goes for?"

She was right. The gun wasn't any old Ed Brown pistol. It was a Classic Custom. The five-inch 1911 was anything but subtle. The highly polished, serrated slide complemented the diamond pattern engraved into the cocobolo wood grips. The trigger was skeletonized with three holes stacked, one above the other. The mainspring housing was even checkered. The pistol was not new, however, but aged, with all the imperfections and character of a wine bottle shuffled around the basement cellar for decades—a surface scratch here, a blemish in the polish there.

"Far more notes than mine," Asher said begrudgingly. Although Asher loved his sidearm—a matte-black, three-and-a-half-inch Rock Island 1911 that sat perfectly in the four-o'clock position of his back—he was also a fan of the .45.

Cassandra placed her hand on Asher's shoulder and leaned her head toward the corner of the room, signaling him for a private word. When they got there, she rested against the wall with both hands in her pockets, clearly frustrated and bewildered.

"So," she began, "we have two victims who apparently were not coming or going together, a male victim who was pretty good at killing himself *before* sitting down ever so properly, and a murder weapon with no serial number? I'm glad everything is falling together."

Asher could see the exasperation across her face.

"Why don't we call it a day," he said. "The rest of the crew can wrap everything up. The scene isn't goin' anywhere."

"No, but maybe *we* can go somewhere," she whispered.

Chapter 4

Asher held open the door for Cassandra, and they walked toward the elevator. They always received less-than-flattering looks from the unit whenever they left together, but the fact that they were "partners in crime" was the evident excuse.

Cassandra pushed the down button on the elevator and leaned against the wall, staring a hole through Asher as he stood in front of the sliding doors with his arms folded.

"What?" he said. "Do I have something in my beard?"

"Nope. I just can't help but wonder what's goin' through your mind on days like this when we have no idea what we're looking at, and you suggest leaving early. Makes me wonder what, or who"—she smiled—"is on your mind."

The elevator chimed, and the doors opened.

Asher couldn't help but notice Cassandra's figure as she walked in front of him. He certainly didn't mind when she wore form-fitting, black slacks like the ones she had on today. *If there was ever a girl next door, that's it*, he thought.

The two stood across the elevator from one another. The suspended box was lit but dim—dark to the point one could have described it as candle-lit. Neither of them needed to say a word to know what the other was thinking.

Cassandra was light skinned with dark brown hair that

contained the slightest touch of red, though it was hidden in most light. Her hazel eyes often stood out against her regular choice to opt out of makeup, but it suited her well. She went simple, with no jewelry other than two holes at the end of her left eyebrow that hinted at a straight barbell piercing, a piece of jewelry she wore when not on duty. She had no attachments, either—uncomplicated.

Asher liked simple and uncomplicated.

She walked the two short steps toward Asher on the other side of the elevator and grabbed his hand with a single index finger.

"Cass," he said softly. He'd begun using the shorter, more personal nickname in private not long ago. "What are you doing?"

The elevator sounded again. End of the ride.

Xavier, one of Asher's best techs on the forensics team, was waiting on the first floor as the doors opened. "Y'all busy? I can come back later," he said with a smart-ass tone Asher couldn't help but appreciate. The man towered over them, his short black hair and brown skin glistening from the day's heat.

"Busier than you, apparently," Asher responded with a grin. "You better get up there before they enjoy your absence even more."

Then Asher and Cassandra walked toward his car.

She admired how satisfied he was driving an old '67 Vette to work every day, a car that was—much like Asher—a work in progress. She knew he was also of the simpler kind.

"Well, you better get home to the wife," she said with a smirk. "No one likes a cold dinner."

Chapter 5

As he walked through the front door of his home in the Garden District, Asher could smell the aroma of fresh shrimp, tomato, and onion. Shrimp creole was his favorite, and Sofia made it better than anyone.

Their home was located on Coliseum Street, not far from Lafayette Cemetery No. 1. It was a small, single-story cottage, what some in New Orleans would have referred to as a shotgun home—rather narrow, but long from front to back. The black, wrought-iron fence and white house blended nicely with the antique feel of the neighborhood.

"Do I smell what I think I smell?" Asher asked as he walked into the kitchen.

"Exhaustion and a burnt roux? Damn straight," Sofia responded sardonically.

Asher loved his wife's attitude. Sarcasm was one aspect of their marriage they appreciated in one another. It kept them both on their toes, kept their relationship lively.

He noticed she was dressed more sensual than usual for cooking in the kitchen. She was barefoot and wearing the black, shorter-than-short shorts he loved. On top of that, she was braless, in one of those white T-shirts of his that swallowed her petite frame. Her long, blond hair flowed to the side of her neck and down in front of her shoulder.

He hugged Sofia from behind and instantly felt better about the absolute mess that had been his day.

"You're dressed quite perfectly for an awfully normal evening," he said.

"*Normal?* You mean you forgot," she snapped in response.

"Of course not. I never forget days like . . . this."

The look on her face said it all. At that moment, one second too late, he realized it was date night—an evening they set aside every other week for them to devote time together and work on their relationship, a suggestion put forth by Asher's very own psychologist.

"Ash, we talked about this. We're doing this for *both* of us. The least you could do is acknowledge it."

"You're right. You're absolutely right. I'm sorry. Let's finish dinner, sit down, and have the evening to ourselves."

The inside of their home had a refined, Southern style to it, with an all-white kitchen that was open to the dining room, separated only by an island. The whole space led into the living room, which was bordered with inset bookshelves.

They sat across from one another at the dining room table, next to the stunning bay windows that opened outside to the pecan tree in the front yard. The emerald grass was littered with brown shells.

"So, how was your day?" he asked.

"Uneventful. The lab's really been struggling with funding lately. We're trying to collect some more preliminary data to submit another grant to the National Science Foundation."

Sofia was an associate professor of marine biology at the University of New Orleans. She'd first met Asher while working as a tech on the forensics team, not long after he joined the unit.

Soon after, she realized the job wasn't for her and returned to college for graduate school to earn her PhD. Academia had always been her first love.

"Is that really what you wanna talk about?" she asked. "My day?"

"No, but I figure it's better than jumping straight to the obvious. My anxiety got the better of me at work, if that's the response you're looking for. I ended up leaving early."

He dropped his fork like it was burning and clasped his hands in front of his face, his elbows balancing at the edge of the table. His whole body tensed, and his ears began to ring with a pitch that would have made the deaf cringe. He despised acknowledging or talking about his anxiety while trying to eat; it was hard enough as it was, attempting to eat while nauseous.

"You okay?" Sofia asked. "Is there anything I can do?"

She noticed the sweat beginning to pool on his forehead and race down the side of his face, as if the beads of water were sprinting to the finish line of his beard.

He pictured the blood spatter across the floor and wall of the hotel room from earlier that day.

"No, I'm fine," he responded.

The truth of the matter was that Asher needed to fight this battle himself. There wasn't anything Sofia could say or do to ease his pain.

He'd been formally diagnosed with generalized anxiety disorder after a bout of debilitating attacks following his promotion to lead detective. A combination of medication and cognitive behavioral therapy with his psychologist brought him back to square one, where he managed to function well enough to show up for work. He loved his job, after all, in spite of everything.

Sofia slid around the table next to him and put her hand on his leg. She felt his body quivering.

"Hey, I love you," she said. "We're gonna get through this together, no matter what it takes."

After a moment of silence, all Asher could do was stare at his plate.

"I think I need to call it a night," he said.

He stood up and walked down the hallway and into their bedroom, closing the door firmly behind himself.

Sofia sat at the table for the better part of an hour, thinking of anything she could have done or said differently. She missed sleeping together. Nights had become a crapshoot, not knowing if she was sleeping on the sofa, in the bedroom, or elsewhere completely. Frankly, she was tired of not understanding his behavior, while being eager to help him all the while.

Chapter 6

The next morning, Cassandra rang the doorbell, hoping Asher would answer and not Sofia. The last time she and Sofia had spoken, it was unnerving. The woman clearly didn't approve of their relationship, although that was all anyone saw—a *working* relationship. For whatever reason, Cassandra simply knew Sofia wasn't a fan.

Sofia opened the door enough to see her, standing with coffee and a bag of breakfast in hand.

"Can I come in?" Cassandra asked as she lifted the coffee into view.

"Sure," Sofia said reluctantly. "Asher's in the back."

Cassandra walked to the sunroom in the back of the house, where Asher was relaxing in his hammock, soaking up the morning sun that cut across the neighboring trees.

"Delivery!" she announced. "Doughnuts and coffee. One French cruller and a large coffee, stripped black and bitter as hell."

"Talk dirty to me, why don't you."

"Man, what happened to *you* last night?" Asher looked more than a bit rough. "You either got hit by a train or need to get laid, or both."

"Nope, just need a bigger bed."

Sofia walked in and sat at the wicker table next to the hammock. "So, what y'all got goin' on today? Any new cases I should know about?"

"I'll take these to go," said Asher.

He rolled out of the hammock, coffee in hand, and grabbed his much-needed doughnut from Cassandra. "We should get going," he said as he walked out of the room.

"Hey, Cassandra," Sofia whispered.

The two women waited in silence for a moment, making sure Asher was out of earshot. They looked at one another as Sofia prepared to say what they both knew was coming.

"Asher been acting any differently at work lately? Last night was supposed to be our date night, but I couldn't get two words out of him. He mentioned leaving a case early," Sofia said.

"Yeah, we're working a murder-suicide. He wanted to duck out as soon as possible after we got the basics. We're actually heading back there now."

"I wanna make sure he hasn't said anything to you at work that maybe I should know about. He just hasn't been the same lately."

"Sofia, whatever you two have goin' on at home is none of my business. And quite frankly, whatever happens at work is between Ash and his colleagues. If he wants to discuss work with you, that's *his* business, not my job." Cassandra didn't feel like hiding her bitterness. "And what exactly do you think he's telling me at work?"

"Look, I'm only trying to figure out what's goin' on with my husband. He acts differently around you than he does with me."

Asher peeped his head around the corner with his eyebrows raised, looking at Cassandra. "You coming, or we stickin' around for lunch too?"

"I'm coming, I'm coming," she said. Without another word, he backed out of sight.

"As far as I'm concerned, Asher and I discuss what we need to in order to do our jobs. If you have a problem with that, maybe you should take it up with your husband." With a faux smile, she grabbed her coffee and stood up to leave.

"Don't forget your doughnuts," Sofia snarled.

"Asher ate the only one. You don't mind throwing that bag away, do you?"

Cassandra found him near the front door, and they walked out together to her car.

"Hey," she said as he walked around to the passenger side. "If there's anything you need to talk about, maybe a reason why we cut out early yesterday, or anything that's goin' on at home, you know we can talk, right?"

"What, about something other than this bitter-ass coffee you got me?" he said with a wink.

Cassandra could only grin, knowing she'd buy him another at lunch.

Chapter 7

It was the end of a long day at work, with both of them trying to piece together the rest of the homicide scene they'd left early the previous day. As Asher approached the porch, he knew there was much to discuss at today's session, not only about his work but also the relationships in his life that had only become more difficult by the day. He rang the doorbell.

"Ah, good evening, Asher," Justin said with a smile. "How are we today?"

Justin was always well dressed and clean cut. His blond, wavy hair and black-framed glasses were perhaps on the more cliché side of what one might picture from a psychologist, but he was far better dressed than most in the profession—a three-piece suit, a silk knit tie, and on especially fancy days, a pocket square to top it all off. Working from home didn't dissuade Justin from making an appearance.

"Good, good, and you?" Asher said.

"Oh, I'm doing fine. Have a seat."

Asher had begun seeing Justin two years prior, shortly after the anxiety attacks began. He didn't open up to many people, much less complete strangers, but he knew he needed to garner professional help if he was going to do his job effectively.

If there was one thing Asher liked about the sessions, it was the setting. Justin worked out of his home and always ensured that his clients felt as if it were their own—a fresh pot of coffee, a recliner and sofa, dim lighting, a fireplace, and the general wide open space, made full by the echo of conversations off the hardwood floors of the antebellum-style home.

Asher sat in the recliner, Justin on the sofa.

"So, tell me. How have things been?" the therapist began.

Asher chuckled and nodded. "Yeah, well, stressful. Between work, Sofia, and Cassandra, I don't know where to start."

"Cassandra? That's new. What about her?"

"Well, as you already know, she's been my partner for several years, but things have been getting a bit more personal lately. I mean, we haven't crossed a line or anything. We just seem to connect on more of a personal level than I expected, or more than most colleagues might. It's nice."

"And how does that fit into the rest of your life? Your marriage?"

"It doesn't," he said, letting his disappointment leak into his voice. "Cassandra and Sofia don't exactly click, and the two of them have opposing personalities. It sucks, because I need both of them around, but things with Sofia have been borderline intolerable."

"Really? Intolerable, or not ideal?"

"Intolerable," he said with conviction. "It's one thing to struggle with anxiety. It's a whole other ballgame for someone to try and fix you when they have no idea what you're goin' through. It's bad enough to be faced with an absolute nightmare every day, but then I have to listen to Sofia ask, day in and day out, if she can help without ever really asking what I go through, or why I feel the way I do."

"Let's go back to one thing you said there," Justin said.

"You mentioned you're faced with an absolute nightmare, every day. What does that mean, exactly?"

"Well, imagine waking up knowing from that moment, until the time you fall asleep, you no longer have complete control over your own mind."

The moment of silence that followed Asher's words was interrupted only by the crackling of fire and the shadows cast by the orange flames, jumping rapidly from wall to wall.

Asher turned his head to Justin, waiting for a response.

"Well," the man finally said, "I think it's important for us to acknowledge that one part of living with anxiety is knowing you may not always be able to control what pops into your mind, but we can work toward controlling how you respond to it. The question is, how can you overcome that realization and move past it?" He folded his hands in front of his chest. "Like I explained at the beginning of our sessions, there's two ways we can tackle this. One, we can try to understand the underlying *cause* of your anxiety; two, we can develop ways for you to practically *handle* it, a form of cognitive behavioral therapy, which we've already touched on. So, what do you think makes you anxious to begin with?"

Asher's hands began to sweat. He felt the microscopic assaults in each and every muscle fiber as they began to tense and tremble in synchrony. The fact that each bead of sweat was clearly visible along his forehead only made matters worse. He started to become nauseous, sure the room was growing ever so slightly smaller with each passing second.

"Well, my mother, one of the only people I've ever truly cared about, being murdered when I was a teenager surely hasn't helped me. Not then, not lately. I basically have no one I can turn to when things at home don't go as planned."

"You really don't talk about her much. Maybe that tragedy is something you still carry with you. What about your father, Mauricio?"

"We were never all that close. He left not long after she passed away, said he had his own problems to deal with and staying around would only make things worse."

Asher's heart began to beat quicker and more intensely, skipping a beat every so often, robbing his air and making his breathing more labored than it already was. He drew a larger breath, hoping to bring himself back to reality, anywhere really other than his current prison, detained by his own physiology.

His eyes were fixated on the fireplace, the salmon and sapphire flames bouncing as he stared with absolute, unblinking focus.

"And what do you think about that—his decision to leave after your mother died?" Justin asked.

"I think it's fucked up," he responded without breaking his concentration. Individual flames popped in unison from the logs.

"And do you think there's anyone now who can, maybe, be that person for you? Someone who can . . . not replace your mother, but be someone you can rely on when things get rough at home?"

Justin could clearly see Asher's death grip loosen from the arms of the chair as his patient drew one more deep breath and then looked him in the eyes. Justin smiled as he saw a grin beginning to show its face from the corner of Asher's mouth. Finally, he was getting at something new.

Chapter 8

amien sat outside in the far corner of Café Du Monde's patio with his legs crossed, looking at the newspaper. He was drinking from his cup of sugar and creamer, splashed with a touch of coffee. The rain misted the paper he was pretending to read, causing him to inch his chair closer to the table.

His eyes were glued to Ulises and Rosalie, who sat at the center of the café pavilion, arm in arm while eating their beignets.

Damien's mouth bent and frowned at the way they flirted openly in public, as if they had not a care in the world. The two laughed uncontrollably while Ulises wiped the powdered sugar from Rosalie's mouth. Damien just glared from a distance, crushing the empty creamer cup with his hand until it was a mere crumpled mess.

He couldn't help but think about the fact that Ulises should have been at work, running security at the New Orleans arena, and Rosalie at the firm, working on her new case. Or better yet, they could have been waiting at home for their spouses to return from a hard day's work. But they weren't. They were here, enjoying each other's company.

Continuing to shift in his chair, Damien crossed his left leg over his right, his right leg over his left. His hands ran backward through his greasy hair, adjusting his glasses up, then down.

Watching them reminded him of his younger years, when his father and mother used to take him on long walks through the French Quarter. His parents had played with one another like they were teenagers falling in love for the first time.

Damien's favorite memory was when they would pull the classic "swing the kid between the two of us" move while walking down the old cobblestone roads. His mother and father were richer in love than anyone he had ever seen before.

One evening in particular came to mind.

Not long before his father died, late in Damien's teenage years, the three of them had the perfect evening together. They were eating dinner at The American Sector—the restaurant of the World War II Museum. His parents sat next to one another at a corner window, the light cutting across the table but flawlessly missing their faces. Damien was sitting across from them.

His parents would always cut up in public, no matter how quiet the place, while feeding one another and cracking jokes about Damien being the third wheel to their epic city adventures. He smiled nonstop with his parents—in this case, maybe a little too much, as the three of them struggled to eat between their gut-wrenching bouts.

It wasn't the same, though—the picturesque view of his parents dodging the evening sun while feeding one another— compared to Ulises and Rosalie acting out these ridiculous laughs under false pretenses.

Something cut through Damien. His stomach churned and twisted as he rolled his eyes and stood from the table. He thrust his chair backward into the metal rail behind him. Without breaking his gaze, he grabbed his newspaper from the table and began walking toward the pair.

He was grinning from ear to ear as he approached, the newspaper tucked tightly under his arm. Then he rested his hand on Ulises's shoulder from behind and squatted down beside the man with his arm around him, uncomfortably squeezed between them.

"I am *so sorry* to interrupt," he said with the biggest grin, "but the two of you just made my day. I haven't seen a couple as happy as y'all in years. Please, I have something for you."

"No, no, no," Ulises contended. "Really, that's very nice, but we're okay."

"Nonsense." Damien chuckled. "I insist."

He reached into the pocket of his sports coat and pulled out a ticket.

"Here, a dinner reservation for two. I'll never use it, and I couldn't think of a couple more deserving from what I can see."

"Are you sure?" Ulises asked in disbelief.

"Of course. My plans got canceled long ago."

Rosalie's eyes lit up as Ulises showed her the free meal ticket for two to The American Sector.

"We've been wanting to eat there, but we've never been able to afford it," Rosalie said. "We really do appreciate it."

"Absolutely. The two of you deserve it," said Damien. Then he walked out into the evening rain.

Chapter 9

Cassandra pinned Asher against the front door, her body pressed against him. His hand grabbed the back of her head, her mouth pressed tightly against his as they kissed fervently.

"Please," she said gently, her voice yearning for more.

Asher turned around and unlocked the door. She wrapped her arms around him from behind, running her hands down his chest and into his pants.

"Damn, at least let me open the door." He laughed.

Asher closed it behind himself as Cassandra pushed him back against the wall. He untucked her blouse as she began to remove his belt and unbutton his pants—he was already hard.

She dropped her skirt to the floor. Removing his shirt, he grasped her thighs just below her ass, picking her up and carrying her to the sofa. Her legs were wrapped tightly around his waist as he laid her down onto her back.

He kissed her neck, slowly running his tongue down between her breasts, all the way to her stomach. Her fingers ran through his hair as she moaned. He looked up as she tilted her head back and to the side, closing her eyes.

"Asher, *please*," she repeated.

He ran his tongue up and across her left nipple as he cupped her right breast.

Then he sat up and grabbed her thighs, pulling her closer. She grabbed him between the legs and guided him toward her.

Asher inched forward, pushing himself inside her. He let out a slow, satisfied sigh. Then he leaned into her and grabbed the arm of the couch behind her head as she ran her nails down the top of his back.

"Please, don't stop," she begged. *"Please."*

He loved the encouragement, the way her eyes begged for it.

"Asher, please. Asher!" Sofia yelled while shoving his shoulder, waking him up from his evening nap. "You plan on helping with dinner? You've been passed out since you got home from therapy."

"Sure," he responded with a visage of pure disappointment. "Perfect timing."

Chapter 10

efore Asher and Sofia had a chance to cook dinner, a knock came at the door. "Open up! NOPD! Let's go, open up!"

Asher ran to the front of the house, more confused than ever.

"Damn, brother," Xavier said as Asher slung open the door. "What the hell took you so long?"

Asher smirked. "You know how it is, man. You get woken up from your nap only to be put to work."

"You got a minute?"

"Yeah, come in. What up?"

They sat on the couch. Xavier placed a manila folder onto the coffee table in front of Asher. It was overflowing with crime scene photos.

"Hey, Xavier," Sofia called from the kitchen. "Can I get you anything? Coffee maybe?"

"Thanks, girl," he shouted back. "How about some of that French Market you keep stashed above the stove?"

"You got it."

Sofia loved Xavier. He was, without a doubt, one of Asher's best colleagues, and he always made her husband light up when he arrived unexpectedly.

Asher and Xavier couldn't have been any more different physically, but they were gravely alike otherwise. Xavier was by no means little. Standing at six foot one, 225 pounds, he put Asher's physique to shame. To Asher and Sofia, though, he was one large teddy bear.

"So," Xavier began, "I looked a bit closer at the photos, and one thing in particular stood out. You notice anything strange about the ones of the table out on the balcony?"

Asher looked at three of the shots of the crime scene for a moment, striving to come up with something meaningful. Perching his chin on his fist, he glanced over at Xavier with a bewildered look.

"That's where you come in, right?" Asher asked cynically.

"Damn right, baby. Why is there only one wine glass on the table? These two are a couple, right? Who drinks alone when they're with their significant other in New Orleans?"

"Yeah, but that could be anything. Maybe he didn't drink, or maybe things got heated and went south before he had a chance to pour a glass. There's a million reasons for why that could be the case."

"Sure, but I did some more digging. The two are, from what I can see, completely unrelated. They aren't married to one another, not even formally dating."

Asher glanced at Xavier out of the corner of his eye. "Well, *that's* a useful piece of information."

Sofia placed the coffee onto the table. "Take it slow, now. I don't wanna be babysitting you two bouncing off the walls at 2 a.m. again."

"Yes, ma'am," Xavier said with a smirk. He turned back to Asher. "And get this. Both of them *are* married, just not to each other. They live with their spouses, both right outside of downtown."

"Well, Cassandra is gonna love this one," Asher added. "One more piece that doesn't fit."

"Cassandra? Hey," Xavier said in a faint tone, leaning in close to Asher while looking over his shoulder for Sofia, who was already gone, "what's up with the two of you anyways?"

"Boy, get away from me," Asher joked as he pushed Xavier's shoulder. "I've told you and everyone else in our unit multiple times, we're colleagues. Besides, what's it to you?"

"Well, we better call it a night. Nothing more to discuss here," Xavier teased.

"That's what I thought."

"Hey, just be careful. Don't do anything I wouldn't do."

They burst into a mutual fit of laughter as Sofia stared at them from the kitchen, her smile brightly burning.

Chapter 11

The following day, Mariana's body lay stiff and pale white on the metal gurney. She was covered below the neck, but the bruising and ligature marks around her throat stuck out like a sore thumb.

Agnes, the city's chief medical examiner, was carefully scouring the body, looking for any tell-tale signs of what precisely had taken place. She knew the surefire way of helping the case was to take her time. In particular, she was focused on the marks around the woman's neck.

The morgue was secluded in the basement of the examiner's building. Asher felt a chill run over his body; the hair on his arms stood erect once he crossed the threshold, pushing open the heavy, metal door. This visit was no different than every other. The stark lighting, frigid temperatures, and smell of formaldehyde washed over him.

Walking to the examination room always sent his nerves into overdrive. He would break out into a cold sweat as he made his way around corner after corner, hardly able to make out what was near the end of each seemingly never-ending hallway. Luckily, Agnes practically lived in the exam room, so he knew exactly where to power walk to.

"Well, what do we have here," Asher said as he moved behind her. "I thought a princess was best dressed in a gown, not a lab coat."

"Ha, well I suppose you need a word with my supervisor, then," she retorted. She would've stuck out her tongue if it weren't for the mask she was wearing.

She was holding a scalpel in her right hand and a cigarette in her left. Such methods were one reason Asher enjoyed working with her. She knew what it took to get the job done, even if it meant alternating between a contradictory mask and cancer stick. Her carefree attitude and rebellious fashion certainly didn't match her attention to detail and endless knowledge of her field. Her worn clothes and dreads originally made Asher think she was someone who paid little attention to the intricacies of her job. That was just surface level, though. To the contrary, over the years, he had discovered that she was relentlessly detail-oriented.

"Please, tell me you have some good news," Asher said.

"Well, that depends. You wanna know the cause of death or the new discovery?"

"Discovery?" He let each syllable of the word linger. "Please, do tell."

"Well, as I'm sure you already know, the girl was strangled. So it's not really a matter of how, but what."

"From what we could tell at the scene, it was some sort of wire."

She nodded. "And you're right. At least, in part."

Agnes pulled down her mask and took a long drag from her Marlboro Red, then pointed to Mariana's neck with the scalpel. "Notice anything other than the so-called wire marks?"

He carefully leaned over the body, sure not to let his leather jacket touch the gurney. "You mean, other than the ridiculously deep lacerations?" he asked. "Not really."

"Well," she said while flicking the ash of her cigarette into a tray on the counter, "that's an awful lot of bruising up the neck for being strangled with such a thin wire."

"Sure, but being strangled with anything is gonna cause a bit of bruising, no?"

"True. However, this type of bruising is something we see fairly often with strangulation from someone's hands. I don't think it was merely a wire."

He shrugged. "So what are you saying?"

"To be honest, all I know at this point is it wasn't just a wire, and the wire was really a necklace. You see the laceration marks?" She pointed with the scalpel. "There's a pattern similar to a thin chain. I'd say she was strangled with her own necklace, then finished off with someone's bare hands."

"So, where's the necklace?"

"That's a good question."

"Okay, well what about him?" Asher gestured to Antoine's body.

"I haven't gotten to him yet," she said. "But I have a feeling he won't disappoint."

Chapter 12

The next evening, it was pouring rain, and Sofia could barely see the road. The individual drops of water collided with the windshield so loudly, she couldn't hear herself think.

Kenney Seafood was the best place to buy fresh seafood, although it was just outside of town and across Lake Pontchartrain in Slidell. It was about a thirty-minute drive, but it was worth it. Sofia had the perfect dinner planned for her and Asher—gumbo.

She darted in from the car, soaking wet; there'd been no way to avoid it. Upon one's entry to the building, an eight-foot, white shark hung from the ceiling of the shop, surrounded by nautical artifacts—trawling nets, crab traps, life vests. A generous display of fresh shrimp, fish fillets, and whole trout were on ice for purchase behind the counter's glass display.

"Hey, how's it going," she said in greeting to the short, bearded man behind the counter. "Y'all have any twenty-six thirty shrimp? I need about three pounds."

"We sure do," said the gentleman.

As he was weighing the shrimp, Sofia noticed out of the corner of her eye someone standing awfully close to her. She glanced over for a split second, careful not to draw attention to herself.

"Hi, how are you?" the man asked. "You know, the shrimp are even better if you buy the smaller ones, believe it or not."

It didn't even take her a second to notice how handsome he was. The slick hair, the shimmering eyes, even the tattoos. All of it made her wet.

"Well, thank you," she responded. "I'll be sure to go that route next time."

"Mind if I ask what you're cooking?"

"Seafood gumbo," she responded with bright eyes. "It's my favorite."

"Good to know."

"And you? What are the soft-shells for?" She gestured at the bag in his hand.

"Oh, nothing," he said. "I just have this unhealthy addiction to fried soft-shell crabs on the first of the month."

"Sounds like a party."

"Here ya go." The man behind the counter handed her the clear bag of shrimp. "Three pounds."

Sofia and the other man made their way to the register across the room. He was sure to remain behind her so he could get at least one good look at her before she left.

She turned around to see if he was still there. And he was, in all his tatted glory, that beaming smile on his face.

"So, I gotta ask," he said. "There's *no way* all three pounds are just for you."

"Actually"—she hesitated—"they are. I've been known to get quite hungry."

"What a coincidence. You know, the same thing happens to me."

Sofia chuckled. She brushed her hair from over her eyes in a subtle gesture, making her view that much clearer.

"And?" she asked.

"And, what?"

"What, you don't expect me to ask the same question? Four crabs, all to yourself?"

"Oh, right." He laughed. "Big boy can't eat alone, huh?"

"Of course. I just think of two crabs each as the perfect serving, you know, unless you're a *big boy*, I guess."

Sofia finished paying, and the clerk handed her the change. "Have a good night."

"Be sure to have a good one," Sofia said to the gentleman as she turned to walk out the door. "At the most, I recommend stopping after three," she said, biting her lip.

The guy paid too, then started to make his way out as well. He knew, however, not to follow too closely. He had her in the bag thus far.

"Hey, Damien," the guy from behind the counter called out. "Don't forget your shrimp. You know those crabs ain't gonna be enough for the two of you."

Chapter 13

sher was already home when Sofia walked through the door, groceries in hand. The blank stare and sodden clothing immediately registered with him as the reason for the slammed door.

"The weather's bad, huh," he said while taking the bags from her hands.

"Yeah, it's really coming down."

He sensed something was off, between the taut expression on her face and her unwillingness to help with the overflowing bags. She walked out of the kitchen and went straight to the living room, where she sat on the couch.

Asher left the groceries behind and followed her. He stood to the side, staring at her, just barely in her peripheral vision.

"Can I help you with something?" she asked in a harsh manner.

"Yeah," Asher said, "no help with anything? I'm on my own?" He shrugged.

"You're a big boy. Is there something you *need* help with?"

He didn't get it. All the concern and compassionate attitude he had seen over the last few days had apparently vanished into thin air. They glared into each other's eyes in dead silence for what seemed like an eternity. Finally, she shrugged.

"Guess I'm the designated chef for the night then," Asher

said as he turned around and marched back into the kitchen. "Good. To. Know."

Poor okra. The damn fruit hadn't done a single thing to Asher.

All Sofia could hear was what sounded like punches being thrown in the kitchen as he slayed the tiny green tubes. Each drop of the knife was a deafening thud of blade against the cutting board, loud enough to drive her batshit crazy.

"Is there something you wanna get off your chest?" Sofia scolded as she stormed into the kitchen. "From what I can tell, the fucking okra got the death penalty."

"Yeah, it sure has. As a matter of fact, it's fucking Al-Qaeda."

He threw the knife across the counter and into the backsplash. "You wanna tell me what it's all about—the attitude and lack of caring all of a sudden?"

"What, I can't come home and relax every once in a while?" she yelled, loud enough to really get his attention. "Look, I don't know what's goin' on with you lately, but something's gotta change."

"I told you once already, I'm fine. We've had this conversation before. I just need some time to myself every now and then."

She shook her head. "Well, I tried to give it to you the other night, and all you could do was gawk at me. Look, I'm willing to help, but this is a two-way street."

"Sorry," he said. "Between work and therapy, it's all just been crashing down."

"I get that."

Asher could tell something more was on her mind. Her brow lifted subtly, and she twisted her mouth to the side.

"Can I ask you something? Don't take it personally?"

His eyes bent in confusion. "I guess."

"Well, I've noticed that you . . . you and Cassan—"

The doorbell rang, resonating throughout the house.

They looked at each other, gazes filled with bewilderment and simultaneous accusation. Neither was expecting anyone.

Asher walked at an eager pace toward the door, wondering what in the world Sofia could possibly need to know about Cassandra. Whatever it was, he wasn't looking forward to the conversation, even if she didn't need him to "take it personally."

When he opened the front door, he saw no one.

"Who is it, babe?" she asked.

"Nobody. Were you expecting someone?"

"No."

Approaching from behind, Sofia looked over his shoulder and out to the vacant porch.

He bent down and picked up a bouquet of red roses, looking back over his shoulder and staring into Sofia's eyes.

"You sure about that . . . *babe?*"

Chapter 14

The following morning, Asher marched up the brick steps of the large, five-story building on South Broad Street and through the double doors at the top. He smiled and nodded graciously to the officers behind the lobby counter as he proceeded through the metal detectors and toward the bank of four elevators. As he barely managed to keep his morning coffee from spilling while juggling his briefcase, Cassandra pushed the button for him.

"You made the mistake of ordering espresso again by the looks of it," she said.

"It's always a mistake, but that's no reason to avoid it." He smiled.

"You ready for this?"

Today was the first day of questioning Patrick, Mariana's husband. These were the less-than-exciting days for Asher, as he never felt fully in control while examining witnesses and others related to cases.

The elevator chimed, and the two squeezed in just barely before the doors closed. Very rarely were they ever alone.

Cassandra decided to take full advantage and move in a bit nearer.

"So, it looks like you had a bit of a rough one." She spoke gently.

"You could say that. Sofia and I had somewhat of a strange evening. What's your take on sending someone flowers to their home?"

She turned her head sideways in confusion. "Sofia?"

The elevator sounded. Asher was taken aback by how quickly she moved away from him, as if to ensure they weren't seen within any reasonable distance of one another. The doors opened all too dramatically.

Asher could see Patrick sitting in the lounge, awaiting his arrival in silence.

"How are we today?" he greeted Patrick. The man jumped to his feet to shake Asher's hand. "Shall we get started?"

He ushered Patrick into an interrogation room between his and Cassandra's offices. The unit didn't care to tell the loved ones of homicide victims it was such a room, but in fact—at least in Asher's mind—everyone was a suspect until he could prove otherwise.

"So, can we get you anything?" he asked politely. His number-one rule was to always begin so nice that it was almost cliché. Give them exactly what they wanted and expected from law enforcement.

"Coffee, perhaps? It's been a long one," Patrick said.

"Sure thing," Cassandra said. "Cream? Sugar? We've got it all."

"Both, please," he said while settling into the cushioned, rolling office chair.

Asher noticed the grin on his face. It was unnerving, someone appearing so nonchalant after receiving notice of their spouse's murder.

He bypassed the option of sitting altogether and took up real estate on the edge of the table instead, a mere two feet from

Patrick.

"So, just to jump right in, we wanted to meet with you briefly to touch base and see if there's any information you can give us regarding your wife's passing," Asher started. "I know this is all rather sudden, but time is important with this sort of thing. We hope you understand."

"Sure, I wouldn't expect anything less." Patrick spoke clearly, his hands folded in a formal pose at the edge of the table. "I'm assuming there's at least something good you can tell me, some sort of lead you have."

"Actually, that was more so our expectation," Asher said with a hint of hesitation. "You'd be surprised how often spouses and loved ones have information investigators don't have so early on in cases like this."

Patrick gave a slow nod with a dissatisfied scowl.

"What I'm really interested in figuring out, Patrick, is who *this* is."

He slid a black-and-white photograph of Antoine in front of Patrick, the picture nearly falling into his lap.

"As of yet, all we have is his name. No family relations, no occupation, nothing. Any ideas?"

"Nah. Don't even think I've seen him before, to be honest."

"Well, if there's any information you come up with, or anything you can remember, feel free to give us a call," Asher said while leaning over the picture, clearly violating Patrick's personal space.

"Is there something else you're forgetting to ask, Detective?" Patrick questioned.

Asher held the man's gaze, not sure whether Patrick was intentionally being a smart-ass or if it might just be the air of such tight quarters in a cold police building.

Suddenly, he felt the espresso kick into overdrive as the pins and needles shot from his shoulders into his fingertips and from his thighs into his feet. The room began to tilt and spin as his stomach churned and his eyes jerked back and forth involuntarily. He knew what was happening.

Patrick stood slowly, sliding his chair back into the white, cinderblock wall. "So, you mean to tell me you dragged me all the way down here to show me a picture of my dead wife's lover and suggest I should 'give you a call' if something comes up." Somehow, his voice remained calm even as he was an inch from Asher's face.

Asher didn't know left from right in that moment, but by the time he realized what had happened, he had Patrick pinned against the wall with his forearm, hand on his pistol.

Cassandra entered the room, holding the man's coffee, then slammed the door shut behind herself. "Ash!" she yelled. "Asher!"

Asher wasn't the type to relinquish his position, whether he was right, wrong, or beaten six ways from Sunday. He leaned back an inch at a time, then released the pressure from Patrick's throat, placing his hand onto the cold, solid brick next to the man's face. Casually, he slid his other hand from his pistol around to his belt buckle, where it rested below his stomach. "Like I said, give us a call."

"You're fucking crazy," Patrick stammered, shuffling to the door as if taking his first baby steps.

Asher's gaze never faulted—rule number two.

Chapter 15

"**M**y office, *now*," Cassandra barked at Asher. She never had any power over him, and she surely wasn't his superior, but he listened to her without fail. He knew one of the best qualities in a law enforcement relationship was complete and utter trust, and to him, that meant not resisting.

"What do you think you're doing?" she started in on Asher. "You think Pierre's gonna let shit like that slide right now? Do you?" she said while moving her head in line with his, refusing to break eye contact. "*Do you?* Cause it won't."

Pierre was their boss—and the chief of the homicide unit. Everyone in the precinct looked up to Asher, not because of his ability to do his job but because of the way he carried himself. Pierre, however, was Asher on steroids; the two butted heads on more occasions than not.

"Would you chill?" Asher said. "He hardly even notices what in the hell we do around here. You really think he gives a shit?"

On cue, Pierre burst into the room, bouncing the solid oak door off the wall.

"Congratulations, dickhead!" he shouted at Asher. "Now the one and only person who's willing to talk to us about these two victims is pressing charges against us for your inability to keep your hands to yourself."

Asher always felt that the chief's outbursts were comical. Right now, Pierre was so outraged he was drooling. The detective couldn't manage to keep his sunflower seeds in his mouth he was trying so hard not to laugh. He was practically choking to death while being scolded.

"Oh, you think it's funny, do you?" Pierre continued to shout. "I'll tell you what's funny is you working traffic duty on Bourbon all of Mardi Gras week. Keep tryin' me, numbnuts. You two better get your shit together and make some headway on this, or you'll *both* be lookin' at traffic time."

The boss shut the door behind him as hard as when he'd entered the room, only this time it stuck.

"What, I can't help it," Asher slurred to Cassandra as the sunflower seeds slipped between his lips.

She, meanwhile, couldn't help but smile at the way he handled the tough situations.

Immediately, though, she noticed everyone on the floor peering through the dimly lit blinds of her office. All too often, her and Asher's work was the drama of the department. She closed the blinds and leaned against the windowsill.

"Hopefully, we hear a bit more from Agnes sometime soon. Pierre's patience isn't gonna hold much longer," she said.

"Yeah, let's hope the rest of the unit doesn't come down on us before we find out who's behind this."

Right then, Pierre made a second and unexpected entrance, causing Asher to spill his spit cup of empty seeds across the desk. "Oh and by the way, Antoine's wife, Camille, was interviewed last night, and we got nothin'. So let's quit the tip-toein' around and get some shit done, huh."

$$Chapter\ 16$$

sher arrived home knowing he needed to revisit the information from Xavier to make some headway before Pierre became more of a problem than he already was. He tossed his briefcase onto the floor next to his guitar, then collapsed into the corner chair.

His home office was part mancave, part music studio, part crime scene investigation. The neutral tones of everything—the gray walls, the matching furniture, the amber and black Paul Reed Smith guitars—all of it depicted the type of man Asher had become, an individual who craved no one's attention but basked in the material world on occasion for his own pleasure.

He kicked his feet up onto the ottoman and grabbed the folder of photos off the end table, clicking on the overhead lamp. The room was lit only dimly, by the small lamp and a mere two beams of light forcing their way through a single crack in the blinds.

Asher no longer drank, had never smoked, never really had much of a vice at all, other than his incessant fixation with puzzles—the puzzles of human existence and death. As the great philosopher Gregory House once put it, "Saving lives is just collateral damage."

He shuffled through the same photos Xavier had shown him a couple nights prior. Asher had seen a number of murder-suicides before, but two aspects of the photos in particular ignited his curiosity: the position of Antoine's body and the pistol.

While it was possible, the likelihood that someone could shoot themself in the head and have their hands fall perfectly flat on the arms of a chair was suspect at best. This, in combination with information from Agnes on the missing necklace, created somewhat of an anomaly, which excited Asher.

Homicide investigators loved anomalies.

Second, the serial number on the pistol was shaved down. Although this wasn't unusual, it was an odd occurrence to be found on such an expensive 1911. However, even that wouldn't be so unexpected if it had been taken from somewhere, or someone, that could tip off authorities if identified. Perhaps the key to finding the suspect was identifying the pistol. Such a point seemed obvious, but Asher knew it wouldn't be a shoo-in.

His plan was to work backward and search all records of firearm theft in the city so he could determine what, if any, 1911s had been lifted over the prior five years. From there, he could determine which cases matched the pistol from the scene and if the owner was either a person of interest or happened to know Mariana or Antoine.

This small but useful plan was enough to scratch the proverbial itch for the night, allowing his mind to wander to matters of equal importance. For example, how he could not for the life of him figure out the final lick to "Little Wing." He couldn't be too hard on himself, though. After all, Stevie Ray Vaughan was only the greatest guitarist who ever lived.

Leaning forward, he grabbed the Singlecut 594 from the guitar rack, his latest addition to the collection that fed his obsession. As he settled back to get started with teasing apart the riff, he remembered one of the final moments he'd spent playing guitar with Mauricio, who had skipped town following the funeral of Asher's mother.

Although he didn't remember much of the day itself, or the details of her passing, which his father kept to himself, he did recall an overwhelming sense of helplessness while carrying her casket to the hearse. At the time, he drowned himself in music and played the guitar as a means to escape the impending sense of abandonment.

If there was one consistent aspect of Asher's life that he knew would always be there, waiting amid the chaos, it was the music.

Chapter 17

Damien admired his collection of 1911s. He'd had them for many years. Each one appeared to have its own story, and many were older than Damien himself.

The WWI model was his most prized part of the collection. Being able to hold an authentic piece of history in his hand, a solid but blemished piece used and fired in the war, was something he couldn't believe he had acquired.

His was a 1912 production, made one year after the original release of the platform, and he wanted nothing more than to find an original, manufactured in 1911. The checkered wood grips, the worn yet rugged blue finish, the grip safety—all of it made him wonder what its history truly was. Not to mention, he was eager to see who was going to be on the receiving end of it next. There was something profound and captivating about using such a relic to end the life of someone in the present day. It sent a satisfying twinge down the center of his back.

His thumb hit the slide release, and the sound of metal gliding against metal to chamber the round was pure music to his ears. The rest of his collection was hidden strategically throughout the house, but for some reason, today, this one was coming with him.

He placed the .45 at the six-o'clock position at the small of his back and inside the Kydex holster. He needed to make one quick stop before heading to the university.

He enjoyed picking out flowers for the wife, as he was somewhat of a traditionalist. Roses apparently weren't her thing, so he figured he would try something different.

Damien slid into the cab of his blacked-out Jeep Wrangler and headed toward a popular flower shop on Royal Street. They consistently had the best selection of fresh flowers—and women.

As he walked down the aisles of bouquets and potted lilies, he realized he was the only guy in the entire store. He liked that. After the third twenty-something-year-old passed him, he knew he had to find something quickly to cover up the fact that he was a kid in a candy store. He grabbed the first bouquet of white and yellow daisies he could find and paced to the register, ending up, of course, behind a thirty-year-old mom, the kind he wanted to follow home from soccer practice.

From there, he drove to the university, where he parked in a secluded spot near the back loading dock, making sure not to draw attention to himself. He slid through the back door and walked up the bright staircase that spiraled to the third floor. From what he'd gathered online, he needed to find SC318.

As he knocked and waited, he realized that his timing was imperfect. The next best thing was to locate the main office.

"Can I help you find something?" he heard from behind as he began walking away from the door.

As he turned, he noticed an older gentleman dressed in jeans and a white button-down dress shirt. It appeared to be a faculty member.

"Oh, no, I was looking for Sofia, but it appears I missed her," Damien said politely.

The gentleman stuck out his hand. "Byron Landry, good to meet ya. Yeah, she's usually at lunch about now. Should I let her know you came by?"

"That's okay. I'll stop by the office, but I appreciate the help."

As he made his way back down the stairs, he dragged the bouquet of flowers across the railings, petals falling to their demise. He was already screwing up.

Entering the biology department's main office, he approached the woman at the front desk.

"Hi, I was stopping by to see Sofia, but I think she's out at lunch. Would you mind if I left these here with you?" he asked.

The lady behind the desk knew good and well that Sofia was married and that this was, in fact, not Asher.

"Sure, I'll be sure she gets them," the woman responded as she swiveled in her chair to place the flowers behind her on the metal filing cabinet. "And who should I say these are—" As she spun around to face her desk again, he was gone.

The last thing Damien needed was to get others involved. He walked back out to the loading dock and waited. He couldn't leave without knowing she had received the message, but he needed to know soon. After all, he had dinner plans.

Chapter 18

Two hours later, Sofia returned from a prolonged lunch with colleagues and entered the main office to check her mail. She always found time to run by the office and say hi to the staff.

"Hey, girls," she said as she strolled past the front desk to the mail room down the back hallway. Each professor and faculty member had their own mailbox in the smallest of claustrophobic rooms, conveniently located near the back of the office, which meant passing the staff both on the way to collect your mail and leaving. The white daisies stood out like a sore thumb among the yellow and brown postal envelopes.

She picked up the bouquet and smelled several of the individual flowers. It instantly transported her back to her first date with Asher. He knew how much she loved flowers and, more than anything, being surprised.

Sofia walked back to the front of the office and began to open the door.

"Oh, great. You got the flowers," the lady said from behind the desk. "I meant to tell you someone stopped by earlier, but you were out for lunch."

"Yeah, I decided to grab lunch with the lab group. It's been a while since we've gotten together to go over the grant. Did you tell Ash I was out?"

"Actually, Asher wasn't here."

Sofia's face contorted, her eyebrows warping in unison with her frown. "Well, who are these from?" she asked, holding up the daisies with bewilderment.

"Sorry, I have no idea. I was gonna ask, but he walked out of the office before I could finish. He was rather noticeable, though—tall, clean-cut, tattoos. You know him?"

Sofia paused for a moment, surprised. "Maybe," she said. "Let me get back to you on that."

Slowly, she pushed open the office door and walked toward the stairs with the bouquet pressed against her nose. Her smile was ever so slight, and her nostrils flared as she remembered the attractive man at Kenney Seafood.

Before entering her office, she grabbed a flask from the lab.

"These will look just fine on the desk," she mumbled to herself as she filled the Erlenmeyer flask with tap water and cut the base of the bouquet. "No need to bring these home," she reassured herself.

Her office was quaint—a small corner desk, plus a coffee pot and microwave across the room on an old, wooden stand she'd inherited from the previous occupant. A shag rug and pictures of her work off the Pacific coast made the room feel like home when her only option was, in fact, to work from the university.

She placed the daisies on the corner of her desk, to the side of her monitor. As she opened the computer file for the NSF grant, her mind shot back to an image of the man. It was the tattoos that drove her particularly mad, along with the clean-cut beard and forthcoming demeanor.

Sofia plucked a lone stem and flower from the vase as she leaned back in her office chair. She grabbed the end of her knee-high skirt and raised it just below her waist. Then she laid her foot over the top of her knee as she brought the flower across the inside of her leg and up to where her thighs met.

She didn't wear panties for a reason.

The way he carried himself turned her on. She felt each petal run across her pussy and up to her clit ring. She drew the flower up and down until she became even more wet than she already was. Her eyes closed, and she leaned her head back.

It didn't take long for her to become fully satisfied. After, she remained frozen in the chair, revisiting his smile as she'd left the store.

A few minutes later, Sofia exited the building and walked to her car in the faculty parking lot. Damien was certain to park near the back of the loading dock, out of eyesight but with clear visibility of the parking lot. As she approached her car, he was disappointed to see that she wasn't carrying the bouquet.

"What in the world do I need to do, here?" he mumbled under his breath as he shook his head. "Maybe she needs a bit more direction."

Her car pulled out of the parking lot, and Damien sat at the loading dock, wondering whether she was ready, and if *he* was ready. He figured he would give it one more shot, but perhaps a more direct approach was necessary.

He pulled the pistol from behind his back, hit the magazine release, and checked that it was full.

"Perhaps she needs . . . a bit of encouragement."

Chapter 19

Ulises and Rosalie parked in a nearby garage and walked across Magazine Street to The American Sector. It was barely after sunset, and the city was humming with the urgent passing of taxis and buses.

Ulises thought Rosalie was stunning in the new dress she had purchased, a simple red gown with a single slit riding up to her left thigh. Her black stilettos and rose-gold necklace added a touch of sophistication to an otherwise ordinary evening.

She had been waiting in anticipation to dine at the popular restaurant, which had been booked solid for the last three months; planning dinner, a night out in advance, was something her husband was never willing to do. Getting a reservation within any reasonable amount of time was simply not an option. Luckily for the couple, they had recently acquired a reservation for two, a ticket that could be honored by the eatery on a day's notice.

As they approached the building, Ulises held open the door for Rosalie.

"Good evening," the hostess greeted them once they were inside. "Is there a name for the reservation?"

"We called ahead. We have a ticket reservation," Ulises said, handing her the paper.

"Perfect. If you'll follow me."

She guided them to a window-side table, and within

seconds, a waiter greeted them. "Is there anything I can get y'all to drink?" he asked.

"Pinot Noir for me, please," Rosalie said.

"Same." Ulises nodded.

"Excellent. I'll have those right out."

The restaurant and bar had a nostalgic but new feel to it, with brick and metal making up the greater part of the building, embellished with wood accents and battlefield memorabilia. Faint lighting and entrees served in battlefield tins added a touch of undercover activity to the experience.

The couple dined in the restaurant for a good hour and a half, enjoying the shrimp and grits and cast iron steak they had heard so much about. The entrees were everything they had hoped for, and more—servings arranged in an elegant manner, brought together with a simple yet baffling satisfaction of the palate.

They spent a moment over dessert taking in their fortunate situation, then paid their tab and decided to head out around eight thirty. As they made their way back across Magazine Street, the skies began to open, and Rosalie's once dry and seamless dress began to darken with the soft mist of the night's rain.

As they walked around the parking arm and up the ramp, Ulises opened the door for her, and she stole a brief peck on the lips. Then he made his way around to the driver's side and slid into the SUV, knowing he needed to get Rosalie back to the law firm so she could drive home from there. Her husband was all too nosy if she arrived home any later than usual. Ulises felt she was finally coming around.

All he heard was a brief whimper as she felt the belt wrap around her throat, pinning her neck to the metal bars that held up the headrest. As he turned his head to the back seat, his forehead was met with the cold barrel of a .45.

"Go ahead," Damien said with a grin, his face hidden in the darkness of the garage. "It only gets tighter."

At this point, Damien had the slack of the belt wrapped around his right hand, with his knee against the back of the seat. He pushed and pulled a touch more, tightening the belt another notch around her neck.

"Who the *fuck* are you?" Ulises screamed, pushing his head into the pistol.

"Oh, no one," Damien said, his calm voice an utter contrast to the hysteria.

Ulises inched forward toward Damien but didn't make it far. His cerebrum was dripping from the shattered windshield before he ever got close to the back seat.

Damien somehow managed to tighten the belt one more notch as he pulled with both hands. He could see, in the vanity mirror, the drool beginning to drip from the corner of Rosalie's mouth as her eyes welded shut. She kicked the dashboard in a last-ditch effort to loosen the grip.

He slid the metal prong through the bottom hole of the strap, and the strap through the loop, before leaning over the center console.

"Only confirming your reservation," Damien said as he licked the teardrop from Rosalie's cheek.

Chapter 20

At dawn the next day, Asher was woken early from a dead sleep. His first alarm usually went off around seven thirty, followed by four to five additional alarms, but Agnes had called him in bed not a moment past seven.

"Yeah, it's Ash," he answered, voice and movements sluggish, trying to process what remnants remained of the night's dreams.

"Hey, it's Agnes. You got a minute?"

If there was one thing he loathed more than the difficulty of falling asleep, it was being woken up early. He rolled over to the side of the queen bed, threw his legs over the edge, and rested his elbow on his knee with the phone hardly touching his ear.

"Sure, I'm rather bored," he said sarcastically.

The bedroom was a clear division of Asher's and Sofia's personalities. His side was simplistic, with nothing more than a small, wooden nightstand and dresser. A single black-and-white picture of him and his mother hung next to the headboard. An alarm clock and space for his watch lay on the barren nightstand, which harbored his pistol.

Sofia's side of the room, on the other hand, including the bathroom, was decorated with everything from abstract art to family photos.

It was fitting, the division of a single room between the two of them, though her nights were currently spent on the couch.

"I've got some new info on Mariana and Antoine," Agnes said eagerly. "It wasn't him."

"What do you mean it wasn't him?" Asher said, standing up and wobbling to the bathroom. "She was clearly strangled by someone and/or something, yeah?"

"Yes, but Antoine doesn't have any marks on his hands from whatever necklace she was wearing. There's clear marks on her neck from a necklace being used to strangle her, but his hands are clean. It wasn't him, Asher."

He leaned over the bathroom vanity, staring at himself in the mirror as he let the phone fall below his ear, trying to think of any solution or response to the unfortunate news. His head dropped, and his other hand rubbed his forehead as if some magical genie would appear to provide an answer.

"All right," he said reluctantly. "I'm gonna have to meet up with Cassandra and figure this thing out before we get any more bad news. Let me know if anything else comes up that we can bring to Pierre. We can use anything and everything at this point."

"Sure thing, but I'm afraid the bad news has already reached Pierre. He's got something else you should probably take a look at."

"You've gotta be shitting me. What the hell is it now?"

"Well, I'm not gonna spoil the surprise, but I will say the two of you have some catching up to do. And I'll tell ya one thing—you might wanna make it a point to get up to the station sooner rather than later. Boss is in one of his rare moods."

Asher stood up, arched his back, and leaned against the wall.

"Yeah, I'll make it a point to get up there today. Thanks for the heads-up." He hung up the phone and stared blankly at the floor. He knew if he couldn't make any headway on the murder-suicide, adding even more to his plate would put him over the edge.

As he began making his way back into the bedroom, the walls slowly shifted, and his ears rang to the point that he braced himself against the door and collapsed to one knee. His breathing became shallow, and the chest pain set in.

If I can only make it to the kitchen for some water, I'll be fine, he thought. *Get up. You're fine.*

He threw on an old pair of navy-blue cargo shorts and was on his way into the kitchen when he heard a quiet knock at the door. The chest pain shot from his chest up through his left armpit and into his neck. The ringing turned to an underwater deafness, pulsating from ear to ear as he paused between the living room and kitchen, the day's stress poised at the bottom of his stomach, rendering his appetite nonexistent.

"You're fine," he repeated. "It's only symptoms. *You're fine*," he mumbled under his breath as he made his way to the living room.

As he passed the couch, he grabbed one of the large, square throw pillows and tossed it onto Sofia's face. "You might wanna think about getting up. You're already late," he said.

As he opened the door, decades' worth of resentment flooded his being from head to toe. There, meeting his blank stare, was his father.

Chapter 21

"Is there something I can help you with?" Asher said with a stern look, glaring at Mauricio.

"Hey, son. Do you have a minute?" his father said in a nervous tone after a moment's hesitation. "I know this is rather unexpec—"

"Let me stop you right there." Asher had moved over the threshold and onto the front porch, closing the door behind. He folded his arms and leaned against the wall of the wooden porch, looking at the man in disbelief.

They watched each other in deafening silence for a good twenty seconds.

"You know, you can't show up on your son's doorstep after more than two decades of hiatus and spark up a conversation out of thin air. What are you doing?"

Mauricio started to speak, then paused, then forced the words out. "Like I was saying, Asher, I'm sure this is unexpected. And I get that. But I thought maybe it's been long enough. Maybe it's time to talk."

Asher shifted against the wall, unfolding his arms and shoving his hands into his pockets as he gazed into the morning sunrise. He looked at the man once again, then strolled over to the porch swing. He sat down, crossing his legs and clasping his hands in his lap. Looking back out across the houses, he took in how they were highlighted by the auburn rays jumping from one fence to the next, skipping the still-darkened green of the manicured lawns.

"Why?" he asked. "All these years without a single word, and now you expect me to take time away from my wife and career to give you yet another chance? You *had* a chance. You know, you had a son."

"I *have* a son," Mauricio corrected without breaking his gaze. "The truth of the matter is, we never really talked about what happened, and I don't wanna leave it undone. I don't wanna ignore it."

"Yeah, well, life goes on. My life went on. *Our* lives went on," Asher said, pointing back and forth between himself and their home. He began to rock in the swing, looking out into the front yard while shaking his head.

"So, what? That's it? You're never gonna talk to me again? We're simply gonna leave it at that?"

Asher nodded and swung faster. The tension and frustration in his folded hands caused his knuckles to bleed a lack of color. "Yeah, maybe that's best."

Sofia eased open the porch screen and leaned against the inside of the doorway. "Oh, I didn't know we had company. Should I put on a pot of coffee?"

Asher dove in before Mauricio could get a word out. "No, I think we're about done. Why don't I meet you inside in a minute." He gestured her back into the house.

She smiled and turned around, gently closing the door behind her.

"Five minutes. Give me five minutes, and if you don't wanna see me again, you won't," Mauricio pleaded. "Is that really so much to ask?"

Asher laughed. "So much to ask? Nah, but neither is being there for your teenage son when his mother dies. But, you know, things happen in life. Tragedies happen, and no matter what happens years down the road, sometimes we can't undo what we see and what we hear. Is it so much to ask that you leave be what you've already put me through?"

Asher's palms began to sweat, and his body trembled in a way he hoped only he could notice.

"Well, I guess there's no changing your mind then, is there," Mauricio said, sounding somber now.

"My mind has been made up for years. If there's anyone who can understand what I've gone through, it's my mother."

"*Could* understand," he corrected Asher. "Past tense."

Asher stopped swinging. His hands were no longer folded but flat on his lap.

He braced them against his thighs as he stood, malice crossing his face in a sharp grimace as he advanced two steps toward his father.

"Get the fuck off my porch."

Mauricio looked into his son's eyes and hesitated.

Sofia opened the door yet again. "I threw on a pot in the kitchen," she said, unaware of the tension cutting across the humidity of the early morning air.

Asher simply raised his hand with his index finger in the air, signaling for Sofia to wait. Mauricio looked to her, then back to Asher, as if awaiting an explanation.

"*Now,*" Asher expounded.

Mauricio nodded and smiled, shooting a quick glance at Sofia before turning his back and walking, at a painfully slow pace, down the three porch steps. As he reached the bottom stair, he turned around and grabbed a cigarette from his shirt pocket with one hand and a lighter from his jeans with the other. He lit the cigarette and continued to nod while staring at Asher.

Taking a long drag, the man looked around the yard, then back to his son, pointing the Camel directly at him. "Perhaps you need me now more than ever."

Chapter 22

Asher needed to speak with someone about his father's surprise visit. In the past, he had wanted a meaningful relationship with Mauricio, but after so many years of abandonment, he was no longer sure. He wasn't in the best place with Sofia, so he figured he would stop by to see Xavier on his way to the office.

He uncovered the Vette, gave her a quick wipe down with the ole microfiber rag, then slid into the driver's seat, which rested a meager foot off the ground. The kill switch was located inside the center console, beneath the unused ashtray. He popped out the tin, flipped the toggle, and listened to the side exhaust growl as he backed out from the carport.

The interior of the vehicle was black, and about as mediocre as the maroon exterior with its black stinger hood. But the smell, oh the sweet smell, transported him to the '60s—leather, gasoline, and raw horsepower, far from the little-blue-bottle wannabe "muscle" cars of today. The car wasn't close to pristine, but it was a beast.

Xavier was one of the few people Asher could rely on to have a meaningful conversation with regarding difficult topics, without fear of judgment. Maybe such a relationship with Cassandra was visible over the distant horizon, but he wasn't yet sure.

His friend lived alone in a simple, drab home off Tchoupitoulas Street halfway between Rouses Market and Tipitina's. As he pulled into the driveway behind Xavier's Camaro, he was quickly reminded of the trash talk that was about to ensue.

"Well *damn*, son," Xavier called out while looking Asher's car up and down as he emerged from under the hood of the black-and-white Camaro. "You better put that thing on a leash before somebody gets hurt. Although, we both know she can't run with the '69 over here."

Asher smiled broadly as he slipped out from behind the fifteen-inch mahogany steering wheel. "Yeah, yeah, we'll see about that." He laughed as he met Xavier with a handshake and a pat on the back.

"What's up?" Xavier asked. "I thought you'd be headed in to see Pierre right about now. I hear he's got some exciting news for ya."

"Damn, does everyone know about my cases before I do? I'm on my way but figured I'd stop by to let you see what you're up against." He gestured to the Vette. "Besides, I wanted to get your thoughts on something."

"Shoot," Xavier said, leaning back against the car.

"Well, long story short, my dad showed up at our house this morning. And I'm not really sure what to do about it."

"What do you mean 'what to do about it?' You haven't seen your dad in years."

"Yeah, that's the problem. *You* remember. He left right after my mom died, and I haven't heard a word from him since. On one hand, I forgot about him a long time ago. On the other, I'm a bit curious about why he left in the first place and what happened with my mom."

"Huh." Xavier nodded. The two of them sat, drooling over the cars, each pretty sure the other was admiring their own while worried about what would really happen if they decided to cut 'em loose. In all the years they'd worked on each other's cars—dropping a brand new, blown 383 into Asher's Vette and painting Xavier's only last year—they'd never put them against one another.

"Damn, I see you powder-coated the side exhaust, huh," Xavier said with admiration while pointing to the Vette.

"Cut the shit, dude." Asher laughed again, popping him in the chest with the back of his hand. "What the hell should I do?"

Xavier smiled and wiped his greasy hands on a white shop rag, which smelled of high-octane and 10W30. He only wished he could bottle the smell and make it his number-one cologne on a daily basis. He and Asher had been gearheads since high school. They'd bought their cars senior year and had been hot-rodding them ever since. It was one of the many things that brought them together on a regular basis outside of work.

"Well, you know how I think." Xavier shrugged.

Asher looked at him with a raised eyebrow. "Apparently not, fucker, or I wouldn't be here." His laugh was a bit more reserved this time.

The truth of the matter was that Xavier was one of the most loyal, down-to-earth friends Asher had ever had. One of the *only* friends he'd had. At the very least, he expected Xavier to say he should give his father a second chance, or perhaps let it be and move on. But what he didn't expect was what Xavier uttered next.

"I think you should be asking your wife, that's what I think."

He was surprised that Xavier wasn't giving him a straightforward answer, but perhaps his friend was right. Maybe

Sofia was the person he was supposed to confide in over such matters. After all, Mauricio had shown up to *their* home. It might do their relationship some good to talk about something other than their fights.

"And I think you need to keep your paws out of the cookie jar, if ya know what I'm sayin'," Xavier added as he popped Asher in the leg with the shop rag.

"Man, you better cut that shit out before I mess you up."

Xavier couldn't do anything but cut a smirk. Asher was handsome and fit, but his friend was absolutely huge.

Asher was the brains, Xavier the brawn.

"Alright, I'll talk to her," he said. "Now get your ass in that beat-up lemon and follow me in. Coffee's on you."

Chapter 23

Cassandra was on her way to grab coffee and beignets from Café Beignet. Dunkin' Donuts was closed due to renovations, and it was often out of the way, so the occasional French cruller for Asher wasn't an option. She knew he still needed his morning coffee, though, and anything she could do to brighten his day was a plus.

She parked her black Tahoe in the adjacent P405 Premium Parking lot next to the coffee house. She was in the mood for beignets, so she decided to change up the usual routine and do the touristy thing. Incoming clouds and a light, morning mist covered the city, making it difficult to see any farther than a block or two.

As she approached the large French windows on the first floor of the building, she could smell the powdered sugar and espresso pouring from the brightly lit shop buzzing with activity. She walked through the double doors as the automatic player piano was beginning a new jazz tune and grabbed a spot in line behind a family of four.

"Good morning," the gentleman greeted her from behind the antique cash register. "What can I get you?"

"Can I get a medium mocha, a large black coffee, and two orders of beignets, please?"

She received her number and coffees from the cashier, then

took a seat at the bar as she waited for her breakfast.

As she sat there, she considered what was going on between Asher and Sofia. For Sofia to pull her aside and ask about Asher's work the other morning was unusual and, quite frankly, inappropriate. Cassandra and Sofia had never gotten along well, but Sofia was crossing some sort of line, although she wasn't sure what it was.

She took a sip of her mocha and caught her reflection in the mirror behind the bar. Her long hair was up in a messy but stylish bun, and her black, flare-bottomed pants and white button-down shirt matched the checkered floor tile well. She liked to appear business casual but nice for work—and for Asher.

Cassandra's background was in forensic psychology. She'd obtained her degree from Tulane University but eventually became interested in the more hands-on, investigative side of things. After twelve years of running her own practice, she joined the homicide unit, where she was utilized in the interrogation and assessment of witnesses and suspects. Over the years, she'd pushed more and more for her direct involvement in the investigative process, which ultimately led her to working alongside Asher.

Although she knew it wasn't her place, she did try to help the man with his anxiety from time to time. At the end of the day, however, they felt such matters were best left to someone else if they were to maintain a healthy work relationship.

"Here ya go," said the waiter as he handed her the two bags of beignets.

"Thanks," she responded.

As she stood up from the barstool to leave, she found herself blocked by a man. He was standing just inches from her face, right in the middle of the only pathway to the door.

"Well, hey there," he said. "Leaving so soon? Is there any way I can buy you a coffee, a bite to eat perhaps?"

He looked her up and down, blatantly staring at her every curve, every interest. "At least let me help you get that," he added.

"Thanks, but I'm on my way out."

"Oh, come on. One coffee never hurt anyone."

"*Thanks*, but I really need to get to work. Maybe next time."

"I'll walk you out, then."

As she leaned over to grab her coffee from the bar, he put his hand on the small of her back and gestured to the door with his other, offering to walk her out while simultaneously overstepping his bounds. Without a moment's hesitation, she spun around, grabbing his wrist with one hand and driving his shoulder down onto the bar with her other. His face fell flat to the marble countertop with a slapping thud that rang throughout the shop.

The entire café stopped eating and stared directly at them.

"Touch me again, and I'll be the one walking *you* out, 'kay sweetie?" she said, her voice calm.

With his head still on the bar, he now had a clear line of sight to the pistol and badge on her hip. She let go of his arm, grabbed her coffees and beignets, and walked to the door. The café was dead silent other than the player piano.

The gentleman smiled, staring directly at her ass as she left. "I hate to see ya go, but . . ."

Chapter 24

As Cassandra exited the elevator, she saw Asher leaning against Xavier's desk. They were shuffling through photos from the Mariana-and-Antoine crime scene.

"The two of you are at it again, huh," she said, handing Asher his coffee.

"Sorry." He gestured with his cup. "Xavier already treated us."

"Oh, okay then. I see how it is." She winked at Xavier and grinned. "What y'all got goin' on?"

"Not much. Teachin' Asher a thing or two about abductive inference," Xavier said with a sarcastic tone.

"Uh-oh," Cassandra said, her hands raised. "Be careful with the big words around this one." She pointed to Asher. "You might wanna start with 'inference.'"

Asher nudged her in the ribs with his elbow, graciously pushing her away from the desk while cracking a smile of his own.

"Hey, three stooges!" Pierre yelled as he popped up behind Cassandra, causing her to spill a bit of coffee on her white shirt. "I need Curly and Moe in my office, now."

Asher and Xavier started briskly making their way to Pierre's office.

"Not you, numbnuts." Pierre nodded to Xavier. "I said Curly." He pointed to Cassandra.

Xavier saluted the boss, then turned around with his legs together like a soldier at attention and began walking back to his desk, keeping them straight as he stepped.

"That's what I thought, Hagrid," Pierre berated him from behind. Xavier shot him the bird over his shoulder without bothering to look back.

"No, thanks," the chief said as he turned back to his office.

Asher and Cassandra followed. She pulled the door closed behind her as Pierre plopped down into his oversized, leather reclining chair.

His office was chock full of thick, gray smoke from the cigar that was smoldering in the massive metal ashtray. His wooden desk was overflowing with papers no reasonable human could have made sense of, and his trashcan was vomiting fast-food wrappers onto the floor, forming a disarrayed pyramid of French fry cones and empty sauce packets.

Asher began to sit down in the chair at the foot of Pierre's desk.

"Don't bother getting comfortable," he said.

The detective's butt had barely touched the seat before he immediately stood back up.

"Look, y'all need to get on the ball," Pierre grunted. "It's been days, and all you two have is an unidentified weapon from the suicide. Do y'all have any idea why the hell this guy killed himself?"

"Actually," Cassandra began, "we don't think that's what happened at all."

Pierre stared at her with his eyebrows raised, waiting for an elaboration on that statement. "And?"

"Well, the position of his body suggests he was shot by someone else, and Agnes has some information on how she was strangled," Cassandra continued.

"And that's gonna help y'all crack this thing open?" Pierre asked as he took a brief drag from his torpedo, blowing the smoke into Asher's face.

"Not exactly," Asher chimed in, keeping his eyes closed against the assault. "We don't know where the pistol came from yet. The two weren't married, though. Apparently, they were having an affair."

"Great, so it's one big circle jerk at this point," Pierre mumbled to himself. "No offense, Curly."

He sighed, then continued. "Well, the good news is, I have some more info for the two of you. Two more bodies were found in a parking garage off Magazine Street. Unless y'all have something more important to screw around with, you can follow me up there. Some of the team is already there."

He smashed the cigar down into the ashtray, extinguishing the smolder. "Come on," he said, grabbing his black peacoat from the coat rack behind the door. "If y'all are in the mood for a double date, Sasquatch can come, too."

Chapter 25

Asher and Cassandra turned into the parking garage on Magazine Street, the Vette's exhaust bellowing between the cement walls and cracking back against the floor. Asher drove to the far corner of the second level, where he saw Pierre's old Cadillac parked next to Xavier.

A rod of lightning struck a nearby cruise liner, docked on the Mississippi, causing Cassandra to flinch as Asher flung open his driver's door. He met her around the passenger side and waited for her to crawl out of the low-riding seat.

The rain began flying in sheets, cutting straight across to the center of the garage, as if it had been waiting for their arrival. They walked over to the now heavily taped scene, lifting the yellow caution ribbons above their heads as they dipped under the line and greeted Pierre, who had arrived approximately five minutes prior.

"A little different from the first scene, yeah?" Asher said as he walked up to the driver's side of the Chevy Suburban.

Xavier was peering over Ulises's arms as far as he could to capture photographs of the car's interior. Before anyone could say a word, Asher noticed the obvious.

The victim's body was sitting upright in the driver's seat, his hands placed firmly at the ten- and two-o'clock positions of the steering wheel, a clean exit wound from his left temple. The bullet hole in the glass, however, was directly in front of Ulises's face, exiting the tinted windshield and striking the large, square pillar in front of the car.

"Yes and no," Xavier said. "Different location, same story."

Cassandra walked to the passenger side of the truck, where she could see Rosalie's neck strapped to the headrest with a brown leather belt. A small stream of dried blood flowed from the woman's ear down to her shoulder. Cassandra leaned over and peered curiously into the vehicle, her mouth covered with a black-and-white paisley handkerchief.

"What about the gun?" she asked Asher as he peered in from the driver's side.

"Looks like another 1911 from here. I can see the grip safety. Different make, though." Turning, he addressed Xavier. "You get an ID on the pistol yet?"

"No, but we can get it goin' right now," the other man said while flipping through pictures on the camera.

Xavier may have been big and awkward, but he was also efficient and detail oriented, much like Agnes. Asher felt lucky to be surrounded by such adamant workers, people who knew the value of hard work.

"I've already got the photos, but let me get my hands on it and we can get a closer look," Xavier said while grabbing an evidence bag and gloves from his case in the trunk of the Camaro. "One step at a time."

He walked around to the passenger side, where he would have better access, and leaned over Rosalie's body to grab the pistol, which was tucked barrel-down between the side of the driver's seat and the center console. Then he lifted the gun out from the tight space with his pinky inside the trigger guard, careful not to disturb the rest of the scene or touch the gun too heavily.

Xavier placed the pistol inside the clear evidence bag and walked it over to the front of his car, setting it delicately on the hood for Asher and Cassandra to see.

"You've got to be shitting me," Asher said without hesitation. "No fuckin' way."

"Who the hell uses that to kill someone, much less leaves it behind?" Cassandra said with her jaw all but touching the floor.

"Someone wanna fill me in?" Xavier asked in a confused tone.

He was great at his job, but he wasn't the gun nut Cassandra and Asher were. "Well?" he continued, perplexed by their nonresponsiveness.

"Xavier, do you have any idea what that is?" Asher said without looking away from the pistol.

"Um, clearly not," he said reluctantly. "It's old as hell, whatever it is."

The pistol was not only old, but minimal and heavily worn. The grips were dark, brown wood and checkered with a small pattern all the way through. The frame and slide were a dull black, containing decade upon decade of imperfections, and the trigger was solid, not skeletonized like the one from the previous homicide.

The rain became unrelenting, now reaching the scene and everyone involved. A wall of black was making its way into town, shadowed by a moving, gray band of water beneath the crawling mass.

"It's a Colt M1911," said Asher. "They're not exactly a throwaway piece, nor are they cheap, which makes it unfortunate that the serial number is gone on this one, too."

"A lot of them were used back in World War I, along with variations of the original model in countless other wars since then," said Cassandra.

"Okay, well, I'd love to let the two of you sit here and drool over this thing a little longer, but we need to get everything wrapped up," Xavier said. "It's really comin' down."

A second bolt of lightning inched closer to the parking garage, followed by a solid roll of thunder, which continued strong for eight seconds.

Asher felt the bottom of his stomach drop out from beneath him.

Pierre walked over to the three of them, his peacoat buttoned up with the collar popped. "I'm getting the hell out of here, but y'all need to figure this shit out," he said to Asher and Cassandra. "Any more bodies pop up, it's *your* heads on the chopping block."

The boss walked to his car, head down and shoulders up to shield his cigar from the assault of rain.

Asher immediately became lightheaded. The garage began to sway, and he broke out into a cold sweat. Before he could manage to excuse himself, he turned his back and retched over the railing that ran down the center of the building.

"Seriously?" Xavier yelled. "You're gonna fuck up my crime scene with that shit!"

Cassandra put up her hand, signaling that she'd take care of it. Asher crouched, both hands gripping the metal pipe. She put a hand on his shoulder.

"Shit, you all right?" she asked, concerned. "I thought *I* was the one who couldn't hold my own."

The rain continued to pelt the garage, washing away what contents of Asher's stomach were now on the yellow parking block. He sat on the cement floor with his back against the metal ropes beneath the rail.

"I got you," Cassandra whispered as she sat down with her arm around him, her hand on his leg. "We'll figure this out. We always do." Her head was now leaning against his.

"You promise?" he said. "I need your help. We can't fuck this up."

Now drenched in the evening rain, they sat on the garage floor, locked together, staring at the SUV and the daunting work before them.

All Cassandra knew in the moment, however, was that she finally had Asher in her arms.

Chapter 26

Damien had the day off work due to the rain, and he made sure to park at the same loading dock as before, earlier and with time to spare. He knew Sofia would return from lunch at any moment, and he wasn't going to miss her again.

At a quarter past one, Sofia's white Toyota Camry pulled into the faculty lot of the science building. Luckily, a space was available in front of the building, so she was able to make a dash to the breezeway, largely avoiding the downpour.

While running to the overhang, she covered her head with a Cell Biology textbook that had been sitting on her back floorboard for the past two years. *No one reads it anyway*, she thought. She flung open the door, shook the book off onto the black rug at the base of the stairwell, and made her way up to her lab on the third floor.

Once Damien saw Sofia make it to the front of the building, he opened the door of his Jeep and stepped out into the rain, allowing the water to pour over his jeans and plaid, maroon shirt, turning the bright blue of the denim to a darker, more somber tone. He casually removed his sunglasses and placed them into the front pocket of his shirt, where they became drenched, along with a can of Wintergreen Skoal.

"Let's try this again," he said aloud as he spit what was left of the dip into the storm drain.

He remembered where Sofia's office and lab were located on the third floor, so he decided to wait in the stairwell behind the double doors that led to the hallway; from there, he could see the lab entrance through the two narrow panes of glass. It wasn't long before she showed up carrying a plastic bag of what appeared to be leftovers, along with an oversized drink. He waited for the lab door to close before making his way down the hall.

The sign on the door read "Dr. Sofia Dupont, Marine Ecology Lab." He was surprised to see that Sofia had retained her maiden name after marrying Asher, but it wasn't uncommon. Many scientists in particular kept their last names after getting married so as to not dissociate their previous research from their professional identity. He leaned against the white-painted, cinderblock wall and rapped on the door four times. The narrow lab window was covered by black construction paper from the inside.

Sofia opened the door with her phone in hand, leaning her head backward in shock as she greeted Damien in a pleasant tone. "Oh, hello." She paused for a moment before it finally hit her. It was the guy from Kenney Seafood. "Can I help you?"

"Hi, I was just down the hall catching up with a friend of mine and recognized your picture on the bulletin board. Figured I'd stop by and say hey."

"Hey," she said as she opened the door and gestured for him to come in. "So, who's your friend?"

"Oh, Byron. Maybe he's more of an acquaintance than a friend, actually. It's funny the people you run into when you least expect it."

"True, true." She smiled. "Sorry, but I don't think I caught your name the other night. I was in a rush to get home and out of the crazy weather."

The lab was brilliantly lit and had two large, black workbenches at its center, holding a slew of light microscopes, parafilm rolls, and analytical balances. The space was immaculate. Not a single stool, a single marker, was out of place. A faint hum emanated from the fume hood, where her postdoc had been reluctantly working through lunch.

"Damien," he said without hesitation, reaching out his hand, accompanied by a grin. He needed to touch her, to get a feel for what was in store. "Sofia, I presume?"

"Yeah?" She smiled again.

"It was on the door." He pointed back. "It's a nice place you got here."

"Thanks. It's good to see you again."

He inched closer, now leaning his forearm and hip against the bench.

"Of course. It's good to see you, too."

She leaned against the table, her hands folded at her waist. Damien looked at the postdoc out of the corner of his eye, curious as to whether the man had any intention of butting in, interrupting their moment. Sofia followed his lead, checking her lab mate, then looking back at Damien to see what exactly he was going to offer up as his real reason for stopping by. Sofia shrugged and tightened the grip on her own two hands, acknowledging the awkward silence ringing throughout the lab.

"Okay, okay," Damien said with a devious smirk, rolling his eyes. "You got me. Maybe I wasn't 'stopping by.'" He gave the cliché air quotes. Then his finger made its way over to the sleeve of her blouse, rubbing the clear, working buttons at the cuff. "I wanted to see if maybe you were free sometime. Dinner, perhaps?"

The postdoc's neck snapped at the word dinner, now looking at the two of them from around the corner of the fume hood. Clearly, Sofia thought, her lab's subordinates didn't know how to mind their own business. "Dinner, huh?"

"Is that a problem? All I've been able to think about since we met is getting to taste that cooking of yours."

"I'm a bit burnt out on cooking, to be honest."

"Okay." He nodded while looking around the lab. "Your choice, then."

"I haven't been out to eat in months," she said while standing up, leaning back against the bench.

"Six thirty?"

His brown glasses were hanging from the front of his shirt, drawing her attention to his tanned, muscular chest.

"You're relentless, you know that?" she said with a raised brow.

"You have no idea."

She looked back to the fume hood, then to Damien, leaning her head toward the door. "Let's go for a walk."

Chapter 27

Asher's clothes were soaked from the day's work as he dropped himself down into the large, cushioned chair in front of Justin's fireplace. The warmth from the fire was a pleasant change of pace from what he had endured earlier in the day—all of it. The wind, the rain, the stress. He needed a break.

"Coffee?" Justin asked. "I made a fresh pot of French Market, Chicory."

"Absolutely," said Asher.

The therapist brought him a large, piping-hot cup adorned with a fleur-de-lis and an image of the Superdome. Justin was a Saints fan, but Asher had never been all that interested in sports. What mattered was that he needed a fresh cup of pick-me-up to bring himself back to square one and out of the sodden, humid day.

Justin, with his own cup of joe in hand, sat on the sofa across from Asher.

"So, where would you like to start today?" he asked.

Asher shrugged, still processing everything from the past few days, in addition to what he was now thinking after handling a second set of murders with Cassandra. There were a few things he needed to get off his chest, but he wasn't sure what exactly he should divulge.

"I'm not sure where to start, to be honest," Asher said.

"Okay, what about things between you and Sofia? Last time, we left off talking about what she thought, or didn't think, about your struggles with anxiety and how you felt Cassandra might fit into things. Any update on conversations between you and your wife?"

"Well, we got into it the other night, but I suppose that's nothing new. We ended up arguing over something stupid, yet again—groceries, I think. It never really went anywhere. We both just agreed things eventually have to change."

Asher wasn't lying, although he also wasn't providing the complete story, either. He had sensed something was off with Sofia, something he couldn't quite pin down, but he didn't feel the need to throw around accusations without evidence.

"So, what did y'all agree on? Do you think there's something that's gonna change moving forward?"

"I hope so. All I really want is to have a marriage where I'm not constantly questioned about my anxiety, where it isn't seen as a burden—and to control my anxiety, of course. I get that she's trying to help, but it often seems more like accusations and interrogation than help. I don't know."

Justin began writing on his yellow legal pad. Asher loathed it when therapists were more concerned with documenting a conversation than taking part in it, much like in his marriage. He often felt as if therapy more closely resembled a job interview than an open, honest, flowing conversation.

"She started to ask me something about Cassandra, too, but we were interrupted before we had a chance to talk about anything," he added. "That's something else I'm not too fond of, my wife being so concerned with my work relationships."

Justin stopped writing, placed his hand against his jaw, and turned his head to the side. His grin signaled to Asher that he was either in agreement, or he was about to take opposition to his comments.

"You ever stop to think maybe you're pushing her away when all she's trying to do is help?"

Here it came—the therapist's assumption that they know more about your experiences than you do. Asher detested such questions.

"Do I think I'm wrong for feeling a certain way about how my wife treats me? No."

"Well, I'm not trying to imply you're wrong, Asher. I'm simply asking whether or not you think maybe her problems don't necessarily have something to do with you. Maybe her problems are really about something else, and they just so happen to manifest themselves while you're around. Perhaps she isn't angry *at* you, but *around* you."

Asher got what Justin was suggesting and considered that there might be something to it, but he wasn't sold just yet.

"Maybe," he said. "I mean, I guess I never thought about it that way."

"So, maybe y'all need to sit down and have a conversation about what *she's* going through. Maybe if you can help her, you can help yourself."

Asher's hands began to grip the chair with force. He crossed his legs and stared into the corner of the room, making sure to ignore Justin's piercing gaze as the man awaited an answer. Yet again, he felt he was being accused. Interrogated.

He looked back to the therapist while bouncing his leg up and down, tapping his hand on the corner of the chair. Justin opened his palm and turned his head, signaling for a response. Asher leaned forward with his elbows on his knees, hands folded, looking at the centerpiece of assorted flowers on the ornate, glass coffee table.

"Would you consider it a problem for someone to anonymously send flowers to your wife?" Asher asked.

Chapter 28

"Sofia? Someone sent flowers to Sofia?" Justin asked, rather stunned, his eyes wide.

"Yeah, although she claims she has no clue who it was. It certainly wasn't for me."

"Any idea who it could've been?"

"Not really. All I know is you don't anonymously send flowers to someone unless there's a good reason for that person, or someone else, to not know who sent them. Besides, she's been acting weird lately."

Justin paused for a moment, then began writing more notes. Asher sensed that even the therapist was trying to work things through in his head. It was a strange occurrence to comment on, the anonymous delivery, without either brushing it aside or forming accusations.

"What would you classify as acting weird?" Justin asked.

"I don't know—coming home without saying a word to me, not coming to bed at night but preferring to sleep on the sofa, questions about my work partner, *anonymous flowers*."

Justin placed his pen and paper onto the table between them, then adjusted himself from side to side on the sofa, attempting to buy some time and become more comfortable for what he was about to say.

"Let's take a step back from Sofia for a moment and focus

a bit more on you, on your physical and psychological symptoms, yeah? We can always come back to her later. Remember, we can't always control what others think, or even what *we* think sometimes, but we *can* control how we respond to it."

"Fine. What do you wanna know?"

"Well, what about work? What about your relationship with Cassandra that you brought up during our last meeting? Are you having any physical symptoms or anxiety while at work?"

Asher folded his arms, crossed his legs, and once again stared into oblivion. He knew that looking someone directly in the eyes while speaking was more respectful; you could tell more about a person by doing so. But having to explain his anxiety was already uncomfortable as it was.

"Cassandra and I do seem to be getting a little closer to one another. I mean, we work great together, and she's always willing to help me when others aren't."

"When others aren't willing to do what, specifically?"

"Listen. Understand. Earlier today, for example, my anxiety got the better of me, and she was the only one who even acknowledged it and spoke to me about it. I guess I just appreciate her for that."

Justin frowned, giving him a skeptical and curious look. He picked up his pen and paper from the table. "And?"

"And, what?"

"And, what happened? Why do you feel you appreciate her? Do you appreciate her more than others?"

"Like I said, she was there for me today when no one else was. I had an anxiety attack at work, and she pulled me aside and talked to me. She didn't judge me. I don't know if I appreciate her more than anyone else. Although, I think we've gotten closer than we've ever been before."

Asher knew where Justin was going with this, but he wasn't comfortable coming out and saying it point-blank quite yet. He needed time, time to think through his marriage and the daily stress that enveloped his home.

"Well, like I've said before, one of the best ways to reduce your symptoms is to expose yourself to the underlying causes and triggers of your anxiety, not avoid them. For *you*, perhaps it's people."

"People aren't exactly my thing, Justin."

"Unfortunately, your *job* is people, no?"

"No. My job is enigmas—riddles that ignorant people aren't even aware they're telling me, questions asked by decedents. My *job* is problems. Although, my marriage seems to be a problem lately here, too."

Asher was now twirling his shoelace with his finger, his leg propped on his knee. He was beginning to realize that maybe his marriage, his personal life, wasn't as separate from his career as he had hoped. He couldn't help but fixate on the way Cassandra was able to console him, hold him in a way Sofia hadn't been able to do for so long.

"My job needs to remain my job, and my marriage needs to remain my personal life," he continued. "What I need is to figure out a way to talk to Sofia about things without her blowing up on me."

"Sounds like a logical plan to me. Let's make it our goal for next time. Talk to Sofia and see where y'all stand. Like I said, maybe she's dealing with things that don't really have anything to do with you, and that's okay."

Asher now nodded in time with his shoelace twirling, his eyes jutting back and forth between the corner of the room and the dancing fire, avoiding Justin's awkward stares.

"Sounds good," he responded.

"Oh, one more thing," the therapist added. "Maybe rethink the coffee, yeah? It tends not to mix well with anxiety. Caffeine can be a fickle bitch."

Chapter 29

The next morning, Asher arrived to work early before his meeting with Cassandra. They planned on reviewing the crime scene they'd scoured the previous evening in an effort to make headway on the origin of the murder weapons and see if they could squeeze any more leads out of the photos.

Asher opened his office door and dragged himself to his old metal desk, pulling the string on the lamp that sat in the corner—his eyes weren't much for the morning light. He thought he'd give Justin's suggestion a try, so he grabbed a bottle of water from the vending machine downstairs, bypassing the morning brew altogether.

His office resembled his home study, only somehow more simplistic, older. The frigid, white-tile floors were made warmer by a black rug under his office chair, and the walls were embellished with only a mounted white-tailed deer buck he'd shot as a teenager, along with a photograph of him and Sofia walking through the Quarter.

The rest of the building floor smelled of coffee grounds and nicotine, the scents slowly creeping their way under his door, infiltrating his newly minted, coffee-free zone. Sobriety wasn't looking too promising.

Before he was tempted any further to brew an illicit pot, he heard a rapid double tap on the door, and Cassandra walked into the room.

"Morning, been here long?" she asked, placing Asher's large, black cup of dark-roast compulsion on top of his desk calendar.

"You know, some days, I'm sure you are the anti-Christ."

"Well, good morning to you too, hun," she responded, her tone overly excited.

"Sorry, Doc has me tryin' out this no-gasoline-in-the-veins type of thing to see if I can *tame* myself. Day one and I'm ready to hang myself from an arabica tree with espresso-flavored dental floss," he said before taking a vertical swig from the clear water bottle.

His eyes scanned Cassandra from head to toe. She was dressed in tighter-than-tight blue jeans and a black V-neck that accentuated her C-cup breasts. A light shade of freckles lay scattered across her chest. Her pistol sat on her right hip next to her silver badge. Her hips were just right, a subtle curve flowing from her thighs up to her small waist, where her stomach was nearly visible, her shirt scarcely touching the top of her jeans above her belt.

He needed to remain seated a while longer.

"Well, I thought maybe you and I could spend some time catching up," she said, then reached behind her back and locked the door without breaking eye contact.

"Catch up? You mean, make progress on the latest case."

She walked around Asher's desk, moved his coffee to the side, and propped herself on top of the calendar, placing her thighs on either side of "date night" scheduled for next week. She lifted her leg over Asher's, placing him directly, although at a slight distance, between her legs.

"No, I mean, *catch up*," she said, leaning back on her hands, exposing the smooth, tanned skin between her navel and jeans.

"I see. Maybe I should take a second, then, to thank you for helping me out yesterday," he said in a more serious tone. "I really appreciate it."

"Of course. You know I'm always around if you need me." She smiled, leaning forward and pushing a tuft of hair behind his ear.

He wasn't sure why, but in that moment, Sofia's face jutted into his mind. Here he was, with a sensual woman sitting on his desk, practically asking for it, and all he could think about was his nagging wife.

His stomach began to tighten, and his vision narrowed, causing Cassandra's image to become only a small part of a tapering field of view.

"Besides, it's not your fault you're worried," she said. "It's simply something we can work on, as partners. All you need is someone to lean on, someone who doesn't question you."

It was as if Cassandra was explaining the precise reason he and Sofia were bitching at one another, and she didn't even know it. How was she so good at this but so bad for him at the same time?

The nausea was no longer sitting quietly in the background. The jabs of discomfort spread through his shoulders and over the top of his head. A single bead of sweat ran its way from his forehead down through his eyebrow and around the corner of his eye. He was being pulled, tugged in opposite directions between the life he felt obligated to live and the one he so desperately wanted.

"Thanks, I appreciate that," he said as he stood up, pointing to her blouse. "I like the shirt, by the way. It works."

Cassandra bit her lip with a grin, watching as he walked around the desk to unlock the door.

"Hey," she called with concern as he opened the door, and he looked back. "Like I said, I'm always here."

Chapter 30

The examiner's building was the one place Asher visited regularly that induced feelings of dread. It reminded him of where he was going to end up, inevitably and along with everyone else, whether or not he overcame his anxiety and mended his marriage. Visits to the morgue, in particular, injected an undue amount of stress and anticipation into his life.

As he walked through the door and into the room of frigid, metal boxes, Agnes was sitting on a stool, adjusting her day's notes with one hand while popping her pack of Marlboros on her leg with the other, packing the tobacco farther down into the paper tubes.

"I thought tobacco was bad for you," he said sarcastically.

"Ya know, I heard the same thing about being a self-righteous prick." She smiled. "How's the life? Or the wife? Or both?"

"Well, I'm here with you." He winked. "Miss me much?"

"Of course, love. I'm guessing you're here to talk about the second lucky couple?"

"You know me. How they lookin'?"

"Other than dead? Familiar. We have a middle-aged male with a gunshot wound to his right temple, and a female, roughly the same age, who was strangled. This time, we know with what.

Rather original if you ask me, although pretty damn twisted."

Agnes walked to mortuary cabinet A3, pulled the lever, and rolled out Rosalie's colorless corpse. Asher immediately noticed the difference between the ligature marks around her throat and those found on Mariana's body.

"Goddamn, how do you keep warm in this hellhole?" Asher said as he shrugged his shoulders upward and pulled his elbows to his side.

"Years of practice, sweetie. As you can see, the ligature marks on this one's throat are a bit wider and far more pronounced than the previous one. Not to mention, she still had the belt around her neck, pinning her to the headrest, when you found her."

"Any idea how hard it is to strangle someone with a belt?"

She turned around to adjacent cabinet A4 and rolled out Ulises's body, pointing to the medium-sized exit hole from his left temple.

"I'd be asking how hard it is to strangle one person while holding someone else at gunpoint."

"Good point."

Agnes reached into her pack of cigarettes, pulled one out, and lit it with a long red lighter, the kind you would use to light a barbeque pit.

"You don't ever worry about catching this place on fire with that thing?" he asked with large eyes. "Isn't it a bit dangerous, given where we're at?"

"Depends on what you mean by 'dangerous.'" Now it was her turn to wink.

The cold air from the open boxes was beginning to make Asher tremble. Icy air always set off his nerves. "So, is there anything that's different between the two sets of murders?" he asked.

"To be honest, not really. I mean, there was obviously a difference in strangulation, but other than that, they're pretty much identical. I'd say they were shot with the same caliber gun, but you already know that. What are you thinking is the link between the two?"

"So far, the guns. The fact that the murder weapons were left behind at both scenes doesn't fit, and it's blatantly obvious. Nobody does that, especially with the type and quality of pistols we're finding. It's definitely on purpose. Plus, the serial numbers are shaved off, which I suppose doesn't surprise me much."

Agnes took a brief drag, then another, then another. She was puffing like a coal-driven train at that point.

"Looks like you have your work cut out for you," she said.

"Yeah, you ain't lying. Keep me updated, will you? I gotta get back to lookin' at these pistols and see if I can put two and two together."

"As always. Tell your lady friend I said hi, would you."

Asher wasn't sure which lady friend she meant in that moment. "Sure thing. Be sure you don't burn the place down, yeah?"

Chapter 31

Asher seemed to have left for the day, so Cassandra figured she would try to make headway of her own with whether forensics had been able to obtain camera footage, or fingerprints, from the parking garage.

She made her way across the white, barren hall to meet with Xavier.

"Hey, good to see ya, girl. It's usually Asher comin' to bug me. How's it goin'?"

"Good. Tryin' to figure things out before Pierre jumps any further down our throats. You?"

"Same. Unfortunately, there isn't much to tell. We have some footage from the garage, but other than that, it's a no-go. Grab a seat," he said as he pulled out a chair for her in front of the large, flat-screen TV to the side of his desk. "I can show you what we have, but it doesn't show much detail."

Xavier turned on the TV and fast-forwarded through a couple hours of random cars entering and exiting the garage, along with drivers walking to and from the stairwell.

"Here we are," he said as he hit play. "It's about 8:35 p.m. when you see them walking from the stairs over to the Suburban. If we go back far enough, we can see them arrive in the garage right before seven."

He ran back the tape, then forward a bit more.

"And, in between, we see *this* guy." He stopped the recording at about 7:15. "Tall, black coat, sunglasses. But that's about all we've got."

"Huh, no luck enhancing it?"

"Nah, we tried. The footage is too choppy. We can make out the clothing a bit clearer, but no facial features."

"Damn. Well, it was worth a try. It's something."

"Yeah. You two make any headway on the pistols?"

"Not really. They're clearly tied together somehow—both 1911s, .45 caliber, serial numbers gone. We need to do some more digging, though, to see if we can trace them to any thefts."

She leaned back in the chair, crossing her hands at her waist and pursing her lips. "Huh, what about prints? Were y'all able to pick up anything from the cars or the guns themselves?"

"Well, not from the first scene, probably because it was in a hotel room where things could be wiped clean, and there really wasn't much to touch. But we did pull a partial from the back, driver's-side door from the second murders," he explained while sliding the paper over to Cassandra. "We don't have a match on it yet, but chances are we won't get anything from it. It doesn't look like enough."

They sat, staring at the piece of white paper with the partial black fingerprint covered by a thin slice of clear tape, both of them knowing things were not playing out as well as they needed them to.

"I'll keep working at things on this end," he said. "Let me know if y'all make any headway on the guns."

"Yep, will do." She stood up, pushing her chair under the desk.

"Hey," Xavier said as she walked away. "You and Asher

okay?"

She turned around with her forearm resting lightly on top of her pistol. "Why do you ask?"

"No reason. Sorry."

They locked eyes for a moment, neither saying a word. Then she spoke. "Did he say something to you?"

"Nah, I'm imagining things, I guess. Ignore me." He spun around in his chair with his back to her and began working at his computer. She stood for a moment longer, waiting for him to turn back around and elaborate on why he was suddenly shoving his nose in places it didn't belong. He didn't.

"We're great," she said almost inaudibly to his back. Surely, Xavier didn't think so.

Chapter 32

Cassandra needed a pick-me-up after her less-than-positive meeting with Xavier, so she decided to grab an evening coffee from PJ's. The simple act of getting a coffee allowed her to drain her mind and make room for important considerations, such as why in the hell Xavier was bustling around her and Asher's business.

Although merely a block away, PJ's was less crowded than Café Beignet at this time of day, and she needed to quickly return to the office to continue working on the origin of the two murder weapons, anything she could give to Pierre. Like most shops in that area of New Orleans, PJ's was a hole-in-the-wall, adorned with antique stonework surrounding small French doors at the entrance. The smell of almond biscotti and espresso curved around the building's edge and dispersed out onto the crosswalk, putting a delightful cap on an already beautiful, sunny evening.

After receiving her white chocolate mocha from the barista, Cassandra headed into the adjacent room of sofas, leather chairs, and brick walls to grab some napkins for the drive back to the office. As she turned, she was unfortunate to quite literally run into Sofia.

"Oh. Hello," Sofia said as her coffee splashed over the edge of her cup, creating a brown spatter on the pocket of Cassandra's jeans.

"Hi . . ."

"Shoot, let me get that for you," Sofia said as she handed Cassandra several napkins. The woman's wide eyes and anxious smile told Cassandra she was inevitably about to experience at least three or more minutes of small talk.

Fuck, she thought.

"Oh my gosh, I am *so sorry*! I was grabbing an espresso before I rush back to the university—rushing a bit too much, perhaps. I needed a break."

"Yeah, maybe."

"You have a minute?"

Hell, no, Cassandra thought. Aloud, she said, "Yeah, sure. What's up?"

Sofia sat at one of the two giant, brown leather chairs facing a glass coffee table, placing her purse next to her in the lounge and her coffee at the edge of the clear circle. "I wanted to talk to you about our run-in at the house the other morning. I really didn't get a chance to explain myself."

"No need, really. It's fine," Cassandra said as she wiped her jeans, the stain not budging.

"No, it isn't. Things between Asher and me have been a bit rocky lately, and I was hoping I could get something from you that could help. It was clearly a poor decision on my part."

Cassandra scrunched the corner of her mouth while giving a slow nod. "Yeah, maybe."

"Well, I apologize."

"Thanks. Look, I've really gotta get going. We're on a pretty strict timeline with this case we're working on, and I've gotta get back to the office. But I appreciate it."

Sofia nodded, though she felt somewhat disappointed that

she hadn't been able to get more than two seconds to apologize. "Okay, well if you need anything, don't hesitate to ask. Thanks for listening."

"Yep, no problem."

Cassandra stood up, grabbed her coffee from the table, and pulled the bottom of her shirt down in an effort to cover the new stain on her new jeans.

"Actually, there *is* something you can do for me," she said.

Sofia remained seated, sipping her coffee, anticipating any sense of remorse or regret Cassandra might have for her attitude.

"Actually, never mind," she continued. "I'll speak to Asher about it myself."

Sofia leaned her head back, frowning. "What do you need to ask me about that has to do with Asher? I thought we were keeping work separate from our personal lives?"

Cassandra smiled. "Exactly."

Chapter 33

Asher arrived home early, prior to Sofia, and decided to set himself up for an evening of relaxation. He opened all the windows in the kitchen and living room, poured himself a glass of Cabernet, and plunked himself down into the chaise lounge, listening to the light evening drizzle hitting the grass.

The ribs were still in the smoker where he'd put them that morning, and they'd be done in time for Sofia to arrive home. They hadn't spoken much since the other evening when the mysterious, anonymous flowers were delivered. This evening was the time to have a discussion about what was really going on.

About two hours later, Sofia arrived home from the university. The house smelled of garlic and herb ribs with a side of spicy Cajun mashed potatoes. The humid air had infiltrated the house and pushed aside the air-conditioning's work.

"Hey, babe," Sofia said, carrying multiple folders of paperwork as she walked through the kitchen door. "Something smells good."

"Thanks, ribs should be out any second now. How was work?"

She tossed the folders onto the kitchen table and went straight to the counter, grabbing the open bottle of Cabernet.

"You don't mind if I steal some, huh?"

"Help yourself."

Asher walked outside, under the carport, to take the ribs out of the smoker. Grayness billowed out of the steel box, and the satisfying smell of hickory hit him square in the face. "That's what I'm talkin' about. You smell that?"

"Looks like you've outdone yourself again."

"Well, let's go find out, shall we?"

They sat at the dining room table, slowly picking at the ribs while finishing off the pot of mashed potatoes. He loved the feel of providing a good, home-cooked meal for his wife.

"So, we never really got the chance to finish talking the other night. Between work and all that's been goin' on around here, we've both been exhausted," she said.

Asher continued to gnaw at the last bone, making sure not to let any of the hard-earned meat go to waste. "Sure, what's up?"

"You been able to talk to your dad some more? He seemed pretty intent on speaking with you the other morning. I don't know, y'all seemed intense out on the porch."

He paused his nibbling for a brief second, looking at Sofia from behind the half-eaten line of meat. "No. I don't really care to go chasing down ghosts only to satisfy someone else— especially someone who decided they didn't give a shit years ago. Would you?"

She settled back in her chair, one arm on the table, the other sipping her glass of wine, which was already nearly empty. "I guess it depends. If it was my father, maybe. I mean, don't you wonder why he left? Aren't you curious what really happened with your mother?"

"Sometimes. But if I really wanted to know, I'm sure there

are other ways for me to find out that don't involve bringing him back around."

She frowned, her eyes filled with sympathy for what Asher had felt all those years. "Well, if you wanna talk about it or anything, I'm here."

He continued chewing. "Yeah, everyone is 'always here.'"

Sofia tilted her head. "What's *that* supposed to mean?"

"Nothing. Sorry. I'm just beat. Today was rough."

"Okay," she said as she walked to the counter and grabbed another bottle of Cabernet from the black wine rack next to the toaster oven. "How *have* things been at work?"

"Aside from working a case that seems to be goin' nowhere, it's been great. Pierre's constantly on our backs about coming up with leads for these homicides we're working, and, honestly, things have been at a standstill. We're goin' down every which road we can and . . . we got nothing." He ran his hand flat across the table.

"Sorry," she said with her back turned, pouring her wine. "That sucks. There is one thing in particular I've been wanting to ask you about, though."

Asher was now done, an empty plate and glass before him. "Okay . . ."

"I ran into Cassandra at PJ's today."

"Okay. And?"

"She's been acting really weird around me lately. I tried talking to her the other morning when she came over, which was awkward, and she didn't have two seconds to talk with me today at the coffee shop."

Asher looked outside, his tongue working in his mouth to remove the shards of pork now wedged between his teeth. He shrugged. "And you want me to do what? I'm not sure what the obsession is between the two of you lately, but it doesn't need to involve me. I don't know what you want me to do, Sofia. Force her to talk to you? This isn't high school. I'm not gonna be y'all's go-between."

She slammed her wine glass down onto the counter. "What do I want you to *do*? She's *your* partner, Asher. You'd think I would be able to talk to her without getting an attitude all the time."

"Why do you need to be talking to her to begin with? I don't go to the university and start chatting up all *your* colleagues, do I?"

"That's not the point, and you know it."

He walked over to the counter, throwing his plate down into the sink, silverware bouncing up and hitting the fixture. "Please, tell me the point. Get to the point. What's really your problem with Cassandra? Is that it? She has an 'attitude' with you?" He elaborated with air quotes.

"You know what, never mind. Forget it."

"No, you wanted to start this conversation, let's do it. What's your problem with her?"

"That's it. She has an attitude with me every time I'm around her, and the two of you seem to be getting a bit too close for comfort. *That's* it."

Asher huffed and began walking to the door. "So that's what this is really about then, me and her."

Sofia shrugged. "Yeah."

"And what do you think there is to talk about, exactly?"

"You tell me. I can't talk to you about anything lately without you blowing up on me."

"That's because I'm getting hit from all angles, Sofia! Everyone has something to say about my relationships.

Everyone!"

Sofia cocked her head sideways. "What do you mean 'everyone?' What other relationships is *everyone* talking about?"

"That isn't something you need to be concerned with."

"Fuck you," she said as she walked past him and out to her car, slamming the kitchen door behind her.

Chapter 34

The following day, the office was nearly still, not much sound or activity anywhere. Asher was looking forward to an uneventful day reviewing the security footage Xavier had sent the previous evening, in addition to digging further into any firearm thefts.

As he closed the door upon entering, he noticed that the light had been left on in the mailroom. One thing the building did not have was a detail-oriented janitorial staff.

Going into the mailroom, he found that his personal box contained a lone envelope protruding from the opening.

No other boxes contained mail.

He grabbed the envelope, turning it from back to front. "Detective Huxley," the piece read—no return address written. He didn't receive much mail, especially mail personalized to him. The majority of office letters to all members of the team were broad solicitations that never saw the light of day.

He walked to his office, turning on his desk lamp before sitting at the edge of the table. Then he opened the envelope with a long, metal opener, and his stomach hit the floor.

My Dearest Asher,

It is a pleasure to finally be working with you. That is, to understand the adulterous mind. You are now acquainted with my love of the game. Best of luck in your current, and future, endeavors.

Yours truly,
The Spouse

P.S. Tell your father I said hello.

Asher collapsed into his chair, the letter falling onto his desk calendar. *Fuck me*, he thought as he dragged his hand down the front of his face, rounding out the top of his neck. He glared into the corner of the room, staring blankly at the empty white space. "This *isn't* happening," he said aloud.

The sound of the office door closing rang throughout the empty floor. *Please be Cass. Please be Cass. Please be—*

"It's good to see *someone* is working," Pierre said as he stormed past Asher's office.

Asher slid the letter down onto his lap, making sure not to let Pierre see the mail. "Yeah, I don't know where everyone is at. Slow day, I guess."

"I assume I'll be getting an update on this shit storm sometime soon." The man's voice slowly faded away as he spoke.

Asher's phone rang.

"Where the hell are you?" he asked Cassandra upon picking up. "There's something we need to talk about."

"Asher, I've got other things I need to take care of right now. I was—"

"Look, I need you to listen," he said in a stern whisper as he stood up and closed his office door. "We just got a letter, or *I* got a letter, that you need to take a look at. Where are you?"

"Well, that's what I was trying to tell you. I'm in the parking lot by Café Beignet. I was eating lunch at the Napoleon House, and someone broke into my car."

"*What?* What the hell? How?"

"I don't know what in the world this is all about, or who this is, but I ain't fuckin' around anymore. How quickly can you get down here?"

Asher grabbed his leather jacket off the chair in front of his desk and hit the light. "Yeah, stay put. I'm on my way. You call anyone else yet?"

She was pacing back and forth between her car and the toll booth. "No, figured I'd get you down here first before I phone it in."

"I can stop by the station on my way and grab someone to process everything," he said as he walked down the hallway and through the double doors. "Oh, and Cass . . ."

"Yeah?"

"Don't touch anything."

Chapter 35

As he stepped out of the Vette and onto the blacktop, Asher could see the small shards of broken glass gleaming in shades of aqua and white beneath the driver's door of Cassandra's SUV. She was leaning against the cement wall in front of the Tahoe, shaded from the day's blistering sun, staring at the square hole where the tinted window had once been.

"You shitting me?" he said as he walked to the truck.

"Yeah, I only wish I was here when they busted it."

Dustin, one of the senior patrolmen on the NOPD, was a step behind Asher. "I wish I could say I'm surprised," he said. "Anything missing? You have any firearms in the car?"

She pushed off the wall and shook Dustin's hand. "Nope, had mine on me, and nothing else is missing. Wasn't a whole lot to take. All I can see is they opened the glovebox and center console, neither of which had anything in them."

"Smart on your part. It drives me nuts when people leave their guns in the car. What you carry?"

"A Springfield 9mm, XD-M," she said.

"Nice. Springfield's a great brand."

Dustin removed a black case from the exceedingly large trunk of the patrol car. He set the case on the hood, opened it, and slipped on a pair of blue latex gloves. "How long was it parked here? Was it here overnight?"

"No, not long. Maybe two, two and a half hours ago. I wasn't far away. I was eating lunch at the Napoleon House just up the block." She pointed past PJ's.

"Gotcha," Dustin said as he placed a cigarette in the corner of his mouth, lighting it with a reusable lighter. "You didn't touch anything, right?" he asked, multiple beads of sweat running down the side of his face.

"Nope." Cassandra looked to Asher.

"Good. I'll check the open glovebox and center console. We can usually pull some prints off the door itself, but we won't be able to dust inside the car."

"Usually? This happen often?" she asked, making her way back to the shaded wall.

"All the time. It's usually kids, believe it or not. They jump from lot to lot around town, typically at night, targeting trucks and SUVs. They tend to know those are the cars with people carrying pistols. That's what they're really lookin' for."

"Huh, that's crazy."

"Yeah, I've processed cars with cash and drugs inside— none of it touched. All they want is guns, pistols mostly."

"Y'all ever catch 'em?"

"Oh, yeah. All the time. It usually isn't one or two cars either, but several that get broken into in the same lot. At least one will usually give us prints."

Asher walked to the cement wall and joined Cassandra in the shade. "Not quite the same here, though, is it? No other cars were broken into, and uh, I'm not sure if you can tell, but it's the middle of the day."

Dustin was slowly turning the fingerprint brush in his right hand while taking a drag from the cigarette in his left. The black powder lined the edge of the driver's door from the top down to the base of the window. "True. This is a little different from the break-ins that we usually process." Dustin leaned in closer to the car door, attempting to spot any prints that might have been made visible by the powder. "There we go. Two nice ones."

He grabbed a line of clear tape from the kit and pressed it firmly against the powder on the edge of door. "We don't know if these prints will be from you or them, but this is where we usually see 'em." He pulled the tape off the door and pressed it down onto a piece of white paper for safekeeping. "The sad part about all this is that we catch 'em, they spend the night in jail, Mommy bails 'em out, and then they're back on the street the next day. They don't learn if you keep giving 'em access to the cookie jar."

Dustin sighed. "What you gonna do about the window? You taking it home to get it fixed later, or you gonna have someone come out to the lot and do it?"

"I'll probably call someone and have it done here," said Cassandra. "Not really in the mood to be driving around with shards of glass flying in my face."

The patrolman chuckled. "I hear that. We won't know anything for a while. We've gotta run the prints through our system and do some digging, but we'll give you a call if something turns up."

"Thanks, man," Asher said, shaking Dustin's hand as well.

The sun was now in full force, beating down onto the blacktop as if they were standing in a frying pan. Asher and Cassandra were both drenched with sweat and ready to get the hell out of Dodge.

"Why don't we sit in the car for a bit where we have some AC, and you can make a call to get the window replaced? I think

I have an idea for how we can turn your day around." Asher smirked, the corner of his mouth turned upward.

"I don't know. That creepy grin of yours makes me nervous when you have these 'ideas.'"

"Just get in the car," he joked, and opened the door for her. "Besides, I think you need to blow off some steam, and I know just the place."

Chapter 36

The indoor shooting range was faintly lit and chilled, lined with rough, cement floors and red-brick walls. The scent of gunpowder and various metals permeated the building as individual rounds struck the bullet traps downrange.

Upon entering a private suite, Asher and Cassandra placed a couple of boxes of target rounds on the padded, rubber table and unholstered their pistols.

"Go ahead," he said. "You're up first."

She flipped the toggle switch, turning on the range light, before pushing the other switch down, which brought the empty target holder to the bench.

After situating the target, she hit the magazine release on her Springfield and filled it with only seven rounds, then slid it back into the magwell and racked the slide. She felt the cartridge shift from inside the magazine to inside the chamber. "Best of seven?" she asked. "It's only fair, given your limitations." She batted a twinkling eye.

Asher's Rock Island held only seven rounds, given it was a larger .45 caliber in comparison to Cassandra's 9mm, which held an impressive twenty.

"Go for it." He gleamed back.

The target was a green silhouette, slightly smaller than an

actual person and cut off at the waist. A little white circle at center mass had scores of five to one radiating from its core.

Each shot landed between the three- and five-point scores, all considered highly effective for the purposes of self-defense. The slide remained back, the magazine empty, as Cassandra placed her pistol down onto the mat. "Looks like you have some competition," she said as she returned the target to the bench.

Asher snickered. "Whatever you say."

The sound of neighboring shots was muffled by earplugs; it was as if the gunshots were being released underwater, yet the smell was that of a stale, terrestrial landscape.

He replaced her target with a fresh, holeless piece of paper and hit the switch, sending the silhouette downrange. It stopped at precisely the same distance as Cassandra's, lit by one of the individual recessed lights in the ceiling.

Asher loaded his magazine to the brim and chambered a round, lifting the pistol to eyesight with only his right arm. He sent all seven rounds downrange in a mere five seconds. The final hot and empty casing was released from the ejection port and hit Cassandra on the arm. "Goddamn, Ash! The least you could do is control your brass." She laughed as she said it, though.

"What was that? I'm an *ass*?" He leaned in sarcastically, as if he couldn't hear.

Asher placed the empty pistol back onto the rubber mat and hit the toggle switch, pulling the target back toward them. Cassandra raised a lone eyebrow when she saw only five holes at center mass in the five-point range. "Looks like two of your shots got away from you," she said brashly. "You know, using *two* hands helps prevent you from pulling your shots, showoff."

"Nope. Believe it or not, I was always taught to shoot with

both eyes open," he responded as his fingers pointed out the two additional holes now present where the eyes of the silhouette should have been.

"Now you *are* an ass." She shoved his shoulder and grinned.

"If you can't get it done in seven, you're gonna need more than a pistol anyways. Those little things you call bullets are cute," he said as he leaned against the wall, pointing to her 9mm.

"Yeah, yeah. Holster your ego there, hot shot."

"You wanna give it a go?" he asked, pointing to the .45 on the mat.

"Nah, I'm good. After shooting enough over the years, I've learned not to touch anything other than Springfield. No offense."

"None taken."

She stepped back up to the bench, placing the individual rounds into the magazine of her pistol. "Thanks for taking me here. You really do know what settles me down."

"Well, maybe I know you a bit more than you think."

Their smiles somehow beamed under poor lighting.

"Oh yeah, you were sayin' something on the phone about a letter?"

"Yeah, this fucker sent me a personal letter this morning. Looks like murdering four people isn't enough. He wants to screw with us."

"Seriously? What did it say?"

"Not much. Looks like showboating to me, enticing us. We can take a look at it later, once we're back at the office."

"You sure?" she asked, placing the magazine into the pistol, pulling back the slide.

"*This* is what's important right now." He pointed to the target.

Why the hell would I wanna be in the office when I can be here with you? he thought.

Chapter 37

As they pulled into the parking lot, Asher and Cassandra could see the technician completing the installation of a new driver's window on her Tahoe. Just in time. The blazing sun was beginning to die down, now mellow on the edge of a teal horizon, and they were both ready to return to work after the brief hiatus meant to salvage their sanity.

"Thank goodness," Cassandra said as she stepped out of the car. "I was hoping it would be ready to go. Y'all clearly don't disappoint."

"Yep. She's done," the technician responded. "Just need your signature, and we're all set."

Cassandra signed the electronic form, shook the tech's hand, and checked out her new window. "Have a good one," the man said as he started his van and sped off.

"Well, I still need to get it tinted, but at least I'll be shielded from the wind on my way home. Thanks for keeping me preoccupied." She turned to Asher.

"Of course. No problem at all. Besides, we need to spend some more time at the range. If you're gonna keep shooting that cute little nine, we need to get you all the practice we can."

Cassandra stuck out her tongue, leaning back against the driver's door.

The sun was beginning to wilt, and the thin, ginger rays made their way across the rooftops, striking the top half of the SUV along with their eyes. Cassandra raised her hand to shield her view from the light. "You know, I think I'm gonna head out and call it an early evening. I know we have a lot of work to do, especially with the letter and all, but our evening doesn't have to end early."

"Yeah?"

"You can join me if you'd like. Pierre isn't gonna kill us any more than he already will once he finds out about the letter, whether it's today or tomorrow."

Asher turned, looking out into the city, the light striking the bridge of his nose and accentuating his five-o'clock shadow. "I'd love to, but he already has me on a short leash. You understand, yeah?"

She grinned and nodded, understanding but also disappointed. "Yeah, I gotcha. Maybe next time."

He leaned in and opened the driver's door for her. "See you tomorrow morning?"

Climbing in, she started the engine. "Breakfast?"

"Absolutely," he said with a broad smile.

Chapter 38

It was late in the evening, but Asher returned to the office, knowing he needed to make headway on the letter and have something for Pierre in the morning. After stepping out of the elevator, he walked through the double doors and into the once-again tranquil space. Nearly everyone had gone home, but he did notice someone sitting in the lobby, waiting. His breathing became labored and his stomach plunged when he saw his father stand and begin walking toward him.

Asher stopped and rolled back his shoulders. "What are you doing here?"

Mauricio stood still, placing his hands in his pockets, knowing his son was about to raise concern with him, yet again, for showing up unannounced. "I told you. I need to speak with you. You didn't give me much of a chance the other morning, and I think you owe me at least—"

"I *owe* you? I owe you what, exactly?"

The man took his hands out of his pockets and folded his arms, leaning against the wall. "You owe me *time*, time that we lost."

Asher felt his nerves shivering, shooting from his shoulders down through his hands.

"Time *we* lost? No, time that you forfeited. You left, not me.

I have work to do. I assume you can show yourself out."

Asher began walking down the hallway to his office, leaving Mauricio standing in the lobby.

"Asher, please."

He turned around, placing his briefcase on the floor, and walked back to his father. "You know, I was in a great deal of pain when you decided to up and walk away. I lost my mother, and all of a sudden, you were nowhere to be found. I don't owe you shit."

Mauricio nodded. "Maybe, but it doesn't mean I'm not here now."

Asher gave him a cold, thin grin. "Maybe now is a bit too late."

"So, you have no desire to know how I'm doing, why I'm here?"

Asher picked up his briefcase and pulled the keys from his pocket, placing the office key into the doorknob as they clanged and clacked. "Damn it, this place needs to replace these piece-of-shit locks," he said, kicking the bottom of the door.

His father smirked. "Or, maybe patience is the key. Gimme that."

Mauricio grabbed the keys from Asher's hand, removed the jammed one from the doorknob, and slowly reinserted it into the keyhole. The knob turned with ease as he pushed open the panel, gesturing for Asher to enter. "Sometimes, we make things difficult for ourselves."

Turning around, Mauricio began walking down the hallway.

"So, that's it?" Asher said. "All of that, and you just walk away."

"You said it yourself. You don't have the time. I only hope it's not too late once you find it."

Then his father walked out the double doors, with not another word said.

Asher tossed his briefcase onto the desk, slamming the door behind himself. He sat in the chair at the front of his desk with his face in his hands, leaning forward. His body went cold, then flashed hot. The nausea was setting in, and he could hear the ringing becoming more and more pronounced, bouncing from left to right.

He stood and tried to walk it off, but doing so only made him more lightheaded.

A knock came at the door. Xavier. They were supposed to meet to discuss the letter.

No. I can't, Asher thought. *Not now.*

Remaining as slow and quiet as possible, he locked the door. All that was present to catch his backward fall was the cinderblock wall. He slowly eased his body down onto the floor, inch by inch, fumbling for his phone to call Sofia.

"I just can't."

One empty ring, followed by another. And another. No answer. Surely, calling a second time would make her pick up the phone.

Another string of hollow rings sealed the fact that he was alone.

His muscles began to tense, trembling in union. The heat was now more than he could bear, and his face was drenched with a continuous downpour of sweat. Nothing was coming together, and he had everything to lose.

The phone rang.

Chapter 39

It was Sofia.

"Hey, babe. How's work?" she asked.

"I've been better." Asher's voice trembled. "I think I'm gonna be getting home a bit late, so don't wait up."

A moment of silence rang out over the line.

"Everything okay?"

"Yeah, I'm just behind on some work with Xavier, and we need to get up to speed. I'll be home as soon as I can, though."

He was now lying flat on the floor, one forearm over his forehead, the other hand holding the phone tight to his ear, eyes closed. He felt as if he could vomit at any moment. He needed to hold it together.

"Okay, well I'm on my way home now. Should I get you something for dinner?"

"No, no. I'm okay. I'll figure it out."

Another dead silence told him that she was skeptical, but all he needed in this moment was to be alone, without the flood of concern from those around him.

"Okay. I guess I'll see you later tonight, then."

"Alright. Sounds good."

He was surprised when he heard the textbook click of the other end hanging up without any additional goodbye. He didn't need it. Or at least, he didn't suspect he did.

This wasn't the first time he had found himself in this position, literally needing to pick himself up off the floor. On countless occasions, he was trapped in his own home with no one in sight. That was usually when it hit—when he was alone, whether mentally, physically, or both. Asher was notorious for getting into his own mind, and he knew it.

The pins and needles were now making their way from his fingertips up through his shoulders and down to his legs. Each individual prick sent a shockwave throughout his body. The world was overwhelming his being, consuming him, and all he could do was wait it out.

Or, he could act.

His breathing was shallow, and his chest squeezed with gut-wrenching pain. The room slowly began to spin. Another knock at the door.

He *never* canceled on Xavier, much less stood him up. Asher was torn between answering the door, knowing the next few hours of work with Xavier would be pure torture, or staying put, drowning in his own self-pity.

He remained still. Silent.

Just think of the box, and everything will be fine.

A while back, Justin had suggested the strategy of thinking about an empty, black box to ease the symptoms of an anxiety, or panic, attack. The thought was: if you can picture an empty, black box and nothing else, the things causing your anxiety, the negative, circular thoughts flooding your mind, cannot exist because your box is empty. This was one of the few practical approaches to managing anxiety Asher used and regularly favored.

It was easy to start. A simple, square box, empty and filled with nothing but air. But soon, the box would become inundated with thoughts, one at a time. An image of Sofia and their arguments would pop in at the top left corner, a counter-image of Cassandra at the bottom right. Then he would clear out the box, start from scratch. But the image of bodies and strangled victims would jump into the empty square, filling it to the brim.

He actively pushed the thoughts away, turning the box upside down and shaking it vigorously.

The problem with the empty box was the same problem that arose when one was told not to think about something, about anything—all you could do then was think about it. Likewise, all Asher could really picture, usually, was a box filled with the thoughts that were supposed to evade him.

But on occasion, it did work.

An hour passed. Then two.

He needed to get home to his wife. The last thing he wanted to do was not show up, leaving her at home alone only to wonder where he was, what had happened.

He grabbed his jacket from the chair, bunched it up like a pillow, and placed it under his head on the frosty tile floor. The automatic lights were now off in the hallway, his office dark. Not a single sound could be heard throughout the office floor.

A third hour had come and gone.

His phone, now at two percent battery, was on the floor next to him. The red light blinked, one strobe. A second strobe. A third. Fourth.

Time had lost its meaning, and the phone would soon die. As did his ability to drag himself up and out of the door.

Chapter 40

The Museum of Death was slower than usual, and Isabelle and Chance had been able to sneak away from work for a midday rendezvous. As they entered the building, a cold, bitter stench washed over them—a perfect setting for having finished a meal only ten minutes prior. There was no line to enter, and the couple quickly received their tickets.

"Two please," Chance said to the tall, gangly man behind the counter.

The gentleman punched a single hole in each card through the left eye of the skull pictured on the ticket stubs, "ADMIT ONE" stamped at the bottom. "Here you are. We only have three rules," he said. "No photos, no touching the exhibits, and no food or drink. Restrooms are behind the theater in the back."

The entry point to the museum was a quaint, off-white curtain hanging to the right of the cash register.

Behind it, the room was vibrantly lit. The exhibits were divided into sections that flowed subtly, one into the next. It was a large room with memorabilia on the walls, relics in glass showcases, and divider walls down the center of the room, splitting the showings into different themes—serial killers and their letters to law enforcement, genocide, car crash victims, death masks of the rich and famous.

All of it sent a twinge down Damien's spine as he observed from behind an upright coffin tucked away in the corner of the room.

The couple was admiring the Hillside Stranglers' memorabilia and associated artifacts. Chance wasn't much for thinking about death, nor relishing the atrocities people had committed in the past. Isabelle, on the other hand, had somewhat of an admiration for the creativity and relentless revenge of certain killers.

"It's crazy how they placed the bodies in plain sight for everyone to see," she said. "Right there on the hillside. Ballsy, huh?"

"You mean, *sick*," he responded. "I don't know how you look at pictures of that shit."

She smiled with deep dimples. "It's interesting. I like it."

Yeah, you do, Damien thought.

The couple moved to the center of the room, hand in hand, for a closer look at the John Dillinger death mask and newspaper clippings of the manhunt. Dillinger, a bank robber and murderer, had been shot in the back of the head by federal agents in 1934. The bullet had exited beneath his right eye and could be seen as a small hole in the death mask.

"You know, many people saw Dillinger as a modern-day Robin Hood," Isabelle said. "He was pretty smart to evade the cops for all those years, no?"

Chance's face was pale, sickly. "He was in prison for like, nine years. What do you mean he was smart?"

"I don't know. Seems like he was able to escape on more than one occasion and live the life he wanted from time to time. What's wrong with that?"

Chance looked at her with disgust. "Where did they say the bathrooms were again? I gotta take a piss."

She knew the look. He needed to puke. "Behind the theater." She pointed.

Isabelle continued to admire the Dillinger section, leaning in to see the death mask up close. She loved the ability to be mere inches from such a figure's face nearly a century later. *He may have been a murderer, but damn was he gutsy—strong-willed*, she thought.

"Crazy, isn't it, how you can almost see his body as it was the day it happened?" Damien said, approaching and leaning his head in close to Isabelle's shoulder. "They say the crowd went nuts, when he was shot. People were trying to get as close to his body as possible so they could dip a handkerchief or newspaper in his blood to take home."

Her eyes gleamed. "I can't say I wouldn't have been one of those people. You a fan?"

They both stood up straight, no longer leaning over to peer at the mask.

"Who? Dillinger?" He gave a half-baked snicker. "Nah, he was a bit too mediocre for my taste."

"*Mediocre?* What the hell does that mean? He was a badass. He robbed from the rich, gave to the poor. He did whatever the fuck he pleased."

Damien's mouth contorted, his face bunched, eyes squinting. "Maybe. But he did get caught, and he did seem to enjoy the attention."

Isabelle folded her arms and leaned against the wall with a grin that stretched from ear to ear. She was enjoying the conversation, eating it up.

"Okay, then. Give me one name. Name *one person* on your

list who surpasses your 'mediocrity' test," she said.

"Okay," said Damien.

His body was now thriving with excitement. He'd never gotten the chance to have a decent conversation with many people about his admiration of what society had deemed serial killers, murderers, criminals. Most of them were no different than everyone else on the street, aside from the fact that they had the nerve, the balls, to seek revenge against those who had wronged them. The majority of society stood by and let their peers walk all over them, whether it be for a prestigious career, marriage, or money.

Finally, someone who gets it, Damien thought.

"Kemper," he said with a grin.

"The Co-ed Killer?" she asked with surprise. "Are you *shitting* me? Ed Kemper did nothing more than prey on some naïve women, and he's been in jail for decades. Surely you can do better than that."

You bet I can, Damien thought.

"No," he said. "Ed Kemper was sick and tired of being belittled by his mother, so he actually *did* something about it. He decapitated her and had sex with her corpse. She wouldn't shut up, so he put her vocal cords in the garbage disposal."

Isabelle knew Damien had a point, and he was making it clear. "But Kemper got caught."

"Kemper turned himself in. He wasn't caught."

"Really? You think that makes him better, more admirable than Dillinger?"

"He was done. He had nothing else to accomplish and didn't wanna be bothered with it any longer. The son of a bitch not only took the revenge he deserved, he requested death by torture as his penalty."

"Yeah, I guess you're right," she said. "He really didn't give a fuck."

"You mean, other than his mother's neck."

part two

FATHER

Chapter 41

As Asher walked into the office the following morning, Cassandra and Xavier were already seated at Xavier's desk, hard at work. Asher had had a rough night with virtually no sleep, so he was dragging himself into work a few minutes later than usual.

"Well, well," Xavier said. "It's about time you join us. Bit of a rough night?"

Asher was in the same pants and shoes he'd been wearing the prior evening, only now with a fresh button-down shirt, accentuated with some cologne. He flung himself into a chair in front of Xavier's desk, dropping his briefcase onto the floor beside him.

"You could say that. Although, a night with no sleep isn't much of a night at all."

"You didn't *sleep?*" Cassandra asked.

"Nah, who really needs that stuff anyways," Asher said sardonically. "Caffeine is the only necessary component to a productive day. Speaking of . . ." He grabbed his water bottle from inside his briefcase and took a giant swig. "I can't have any."

"Well, you're already familiar with *this.*" Xavier slid the letter across the table. "What do you make of it?"

He took another drink of water. As much as he didn't care

to admit it, the water in place of coffee was starting to make him feel better—aside from the no-sleep issue, ironically. "No clue. In my opinion, it's just another narcissistic asshole looking to screw with us or, at the very least, misdirect our attention elsewhere. Most serial killers are high in narcissism, no?" He looked to Cassandra.

"Yeah, most of them are. However, we shouldn't rule out what the letter is trying to say. What does your dad have to do with all of this? That's a rather large point to gloss over, is it not?"

Asher adjusted himself in the chair while running his hand across his bloodshot eyes. The last thing he wanted to do was drag his father into his work life when he apparently couldn't keep the man out of his personal life.

"I suppose so," Asher said. "But 'tell your father I said hello' is a meaningless statement. What am I supposed to do with that?"

"Ask your dad," Xavier said.

Asher laughed, his eyes darting out into space. He shook his head and bit the corner of his lip. "What could my dad possibly have to do with these murders? You suggesting he's involved with this somehow?"

Cassandra leaned back in her chair. "I'm not saying that either way. All I'm saying is that whoever this is, they know you personally, and your dad is referenced in the letter. Can't you see that? Not to mention, he suddenly pops back up in your life, and you think that's just a big coincidence?"

"Let's not get ahead of ourselves here," said Xavier. "It's one thing for some psychopathic killer to be stalking Asher and know who his dad is, but it's another thing altogether to say his dad is responsible for these murders. Let's take a step back."

"Thank you," Asher said, emphasizing each word while staring a hole through Cassandra. "Either of you have anything productive to say about the letter, other than that my father is responsible? Anything we can look into while I'm working on my family matters?"

Asher was clearly frustrated. He was sleep deprived, on edge, and becoming overly bitter—a bad combination. But Xavier and Cassandra knew this was his bread and butter. The sarcasm helped Asher think through things, and they were accustomed to his passive aggressiveness at times like these.

Cassandra was looking down at the floor, running back through the letter in her mind. "The letter did mention something about 'the adulterous mind,'" she said. "Maybe the killer is trying to say something about motive."

Xavier raised an eyebrow. "That's possible. I mean, we now know that both couples were dating one another but married to other people. So yeah, there's probably something to that. I can take a deeper dive into the victims' backgrounds and see if relatives or friends know of anyone who may seem a bit sketchy."

"You sure?" Cassandra asked. "Asher and I can take the lead on that if you want. It isn't exactly Crime Scene 101."

"Yeah, I'm sure. We don't really have anything else to go on from the scenes themselves at the moment, so it'll keep me busy."

Asher nodded. "Thanks, man. I appreciate it. This will give us some time to take another look at the guns and see if we can make a connection there. We're nearly done going through the firearm theft records, so we should know something soon about where they came from. All of this is moving slow enough as it is, so it'll be good to have an extra set of hands."

Asher could hear the clatter of heavy boots making their way over behind him. Xavier sat up straight, eyes wide. "Heads up." He gestured with a nod.

"In my office, numbnuts. Now," Pierre said as he walked past the desk.

"Great," Asher sighed. "I can't wait to hear the good news."

Chapter 42

"Sit your ass down," Pierre said as he walked around behind his desk and took a seat in his overly large leather chair. "We have some shit we need to get straight."

Asher sat down and folded his arms, a frustrated scowl on his face. "What can I help you with, *Boss?*"

Pierre blew a derisive huff from his mouth and threw his feet up onto the desk. "Shut the hell up. You're screwing this thing bigger than anything you've fucked up in the past, and let me tell you something. You don't figure out who's behind this shit, you *and* your little sidekick are both done."

Asher smirked.

"Something funny? Something you wanna get off your chest? Because I have all day. I don't have a damn thing to do, other than sit around and babysit this entire floor."

Asher shook his head. "No, nothing's funny. But you sit here and act like we're not making any headway on this. That's all we do. That's all we've *been* doing."

The chief stood up and walked around to the front of his desk, sitting on the edge of the table in front of Asher.

"Okay, tell me, then. What exactly is it that y'all have been doing, because I don't see it. All I see is one set of bodies popping up after another, and all you have to show for it are connections everyone else is making."

"Well, we know the couples weren't married. They were all dating one another but married to someone else. I'd say that's a rather large development that's important, don't you?"

"Yeah, I do. And that was all Xavier. Try again."

Asher felt as if he'd been punched in the gut.

"Okay, the pistols."

"What about them?"

"They're both high-end 1911s with the serial numbers shaved down. Surely that isn't a mishap. There's gotta be something there."

"And that something is what?"

Asher shrugged. "I'll let you know as soon as we have something."

Pierre began pacing back and forth from the door to his desk, his face in a grimace. "Oh, that's real nice. You'll let me know? You have dick, Asher. What else is there?"

"We have a print, a partial, pulled from one of the doors at the second scene."

"And?"

"Nothing yet, but it looks promising."

"Promising? Are you shitting me? My wife looks promising every night, but that doesn't mean I'm getting any ass today, now does it."

Asher raised both hands, palms up, while shrugging yet again. "One can hope."

"Shut the fuck up. If you don't start making some headway on this thing soon, I ain't shitting you, you can pack your bags and walk. You got me? Is there anything else you wanna give me? Anything else you wanna explain while you're here? Because I'm two seconds away from pulling your ass off this case."

Asher took a deep breath, letting it out over eight slow seconds while crossing his hands on his lap. "Well, there is one more thing."

"Great, what the hell is it?"

"A letter."

"A letter? A letter from *whom*?"

"We're not sure yet, but my best educated guess would be the killer," he said carelessly.

"Are you fucking kidding me? A goddamn letter, *from the killer*, and you're sitting here feeding me garbage about a fucking partial print? You know, sometimes I wonder why I put you on this team in the first place."

"We only just received it, and we aren't even sure what it means at this point, which is why I hadn't brought it up until now."

"Where is it? Where is the damn letter?"

"Let me grab it," Asher said.

He walked out to Xavier's desk.

"All done?" Xavier asked.

"Nope, I just need to borrow this." Asher snatched the letter from the other man's hands, then turned back to the chief's office.

"Here," Asher said a moment later as he handed the letter to Pierre, who was now back on the corner of his desk, teetering on the edge of a nervous breakdown.

Pierre read the letter with a stern face, his chin poised on one hand with his elbow resting on his gut. He tossed the letter onto his desk and stared at Asher. "And what do you think the letter means? Please tell me you're at least able to make sense of something that's being handed to you on a silver platter."

"'The adulterous mind' is an obvious reference to the

couples who are cheating on their spouses, but beyond that, we don't really have much to go on."

"Really? You don't have much to go on? The damn thing is addressed *to you*, numbnuts. And it mentions your father."

"Honestly, that's most likely just the narcissist coming out in whoever wrote it. Most serial killers are narcissists, so it doesn't necessarily have to mean anything."

"Look at me," Pierre said, and when Asher did, he almost had to stare away, the man's gaze was so harsh. "Figure this shit out. The next time I see you, I want leads, not guesses. You got me?"

The chief stood up and made his way back around his desk, where he sat down in his chair.

"Sounds like a plan."

"Now get the fuck out."

Asher walked out of Pierre's office and headed back to his friend's desk.

"Well, what was that all about?" Xavier asked.

He sat down and took a significant guzzle of water from his new bottle. "Let's just say we're on a timeline."

Chapter 43

It was the end of the day, and Asher needed to leave early for his appointment with Justin. He figured he would pass by Cassandra's office on the way out to see what time she would be in the following day.

"Hey, girl. You heading out yet?" he asked.

"Yeah, I'm about done. I'll walk with you."

They made their way into the lobby, riding the elevator down to the first floor. Upon stepping out onto the wide-open, marble floor, they saw that the driveway in front of the building was lined with white and black news vans. Unfortunately, there was only a single way out—through the media frenzy.

"Please tell me that ain't for us," she said. "How in the world does our work get out so quickly?"

"Oh come on, Cass. It's the news. They know *everything*," he said with loaded sarcasm.

"Looks like it's time for the dark sunglasses."

"You mean, like the cops in Texas?" He slid his own aviators over his dry, heavy eyes.

Asher opened the lobby door for Cassandra, and she stepped across the threshold and out onto the drive. She was immediately flanked by reporters as she attempted to cross the cement path and into the parking lot.

"Excuse me!" one reporter shouted. "What can you tell us

about the recent murder-suicide cases? Doesn't the department find it odd that two of these cases have occurred so close together?"

Cassandra stopped, glancing back at Asher before looking into the cameras and flashing lights. "We don't really have anything to report at this time, thanks," she said curtly.

"As of now, it's nothing more than an unfortunate coincidence," Asher added. "If we uncover any additional information, you all will be the first to know." He was lying through his teeth, of course.

The truth was they had little to go on as of yet, and Asher knew little more than the media knew. The last thing the department needed was for reporters to find out a competent serial killer was corresponding directly with the lead detective of the New Orleans Homicide Unit. That would be virtually a one-way ticket out the door for Asher.

He and Cassandra split ways, heading to their respective cars, but the media followed Asher, letting her off the hook. "So, you mean to tell me that two couples were killed in the same manner a few days apart, and we're expected to believe this is all one big coincidence?" another reporter continued.

"Quite frankly, it isn't my job to keep you comfortable at night," Asher snapped back. "Sleep tight."

Chapter 44

sher walked up the steps to Justin's home and rang the doorbell. "Evening, Asher. How's it going?" Justin said as he opened the door. "Have a seat. Can I get you anything? Some water or tea?"

Asher took a seat on the sofa, exhausted from the stressful day that had preceded their meeting. "Water would be perfect," he said with a somber tone.

"So what's up? It's been a few days. You look beat," the therapist said as he handed him the clear bottle and took a seat in the recliner. "I think, last time, we left off talking about Sofia and the mysterious flowers. Any headway on that front?"

The office was quiet today—no fire, no whistling of the wind hitting the corners of the home, only conversation between the two of them. No smell of coffee, only the absent fragrance of water.

"No, not really. We talked the other night, but it ended pretty bad. We just started arguing and yelling at each other. It wasn't a long conversation."

"Huh," Justin huffed as he clicked his pen and began writing. "What started the argument?"

"Same ole shit. She mentioned something about Cassandra, and I was expected to play umpire between her and my work colleagues. Nothing I really care to be involved with."

"What exactly did she say about Cassandra? You remember?"

"She ran into her at a coffee shop, I think, and she said something about Cassandra acting weird toward her, not wanting to give her the time of day. Personally, I don't think it's my place, or responsibility, to be in the middle of the two of them. I don't see why she has to be talking to my coworkers anyways. I guess my thought is, why is that even necessary?"

Justin nodded. "Yeah, I suppose that's a fair point. Maybe she's wanting to show that she can be cordial with the people you work with."

Asher looked around the room. "Maybe. But I think what it really comes down to is the fact that I have a female partner, and she doesn't like it."

"She said that?"

"Not in so many words, no."

The therapist continued to write.

"What are you writing in that thing anyways?"

He smiled. "Oh, nothing. Just my shopping list for this week's groceries. The wife goes crazy if I don't have it ready for her by morning."

Asher chuckled. "Nice."

"Okay," Justin said, "so what else is new? You and Sofia talk about anything other than Cassandra? Anything else been getting between the two of you lately?"

"I wouldn't say it's something that's been getting between us, but my dad randomly showed up at my house, and work, over the last few days."

Justin stopped writing. "Just out of the blue? He showed up without giving you a heads-up first?"

"Yeah, that's what *I* said, right? No phone call, nothing. Just showed up on my doorstep one morning, then at my office yesterday."

Justin made his way over to the table and grabbed a coffee cup. "You don't mind, do you?" He signaled to Asher as he began pouring himself a fresh cup. "Sorry, but I need a warm cup for this. You've got me intrigued now."

"Glad I can be of service."

"So, any idea what made him show up all of a sudden?"

"Nope. I find it rather strange, though, that he's so adamant about talking to me. He continues to insist that we need to talk. There's also some bizarre stuff at work that makes his sudden arrival even more suspect, but I can't really get into that."

Justin took a large sip from his cream-and-Splenda coffee, then placed the cup down onto the table between them. He clicked his pen back into action and made a brief note.

"So, are you gonna speak with him?"

"No need. He made it very clear when he left that he no longer cared, and I stopped caring the moment he walked out. There's nothing to talk about."

The therapist nodded. "Well, remember what we talked about before. Exposure helps. Keeping all of that bottled up without talking to anyone about it, other than me, might do more harm than good. If it's communication with people that's difficult, more of that may actually help."

"Perhaps." Asher felt there was nothing more to say. There wasn't anything Justin could explain to change the way he felt about what his father had done. Working things out with Sofia and Cassandra was one thing, but willfully dragging that man back into his life was another beast altogether.

He feared the letter was going to do it for him, though.

"All I know is I have a lot on my plate right now between

working on things with Sofia and being pressed so hard at work. I think if I can figure out these cases I'm working right now, things should fall into place at home. The stress at work alone makes having any sort of personal life hard right now."

"That's an interesting notion. So, what's stopping you from accomplishing that?"

Asher turned his head to the window and noticed that the wind was beginning to pick up, and a slight drizzle had begun.

"For starters, my wife is interfering with my work, but having a partner means everything to me."

"Okay, if your wife is everything to you, then don't you think it's prudent to make sure that you set some boundaries with Cassandra."

Asher smiled and snickered under his breath.

"By partner, I meant Cassandra."

Chapter 45

The concert had ended, and Chance was backstage with Isabelle, winding down after a packed show with his band at the House of Blues on Decatur. The drummer was the only person left at the afterparty, but his ride was waiting out back of the building.

The backstage dressing room was filled with the sooty haze of cigarette smoke and the ambiance of a college frat party—empty beer bottles, overflowing ashtrays, and mediocre lighting. Guitar cases, amplifiers, and a practice electronic drum set were sprinkled across the room.

"Alright, I'll see you later, man," Chance said to his drummer as he closed the door and turned to Isabelle. "I don't know about you, but I cannot go home like this. I need a shower. I feel disgusting."

"Why don't you go ahead and hop in, and I'll be right behind you," she said while pushing herself up onto her tiptoes to give him a peck on the lips. "I gotta shoot a text to someone first."

"I'll see you in there."

The dressing room had a small, run-down bathroom with a walk-in shower that was far from pleasant. The floors were made of cold, honey-colored tile, and the smell of bleach poured out from the shower doors as Chance stepped inside. He turned the single shower dial to hot, but all that came out was an ice-cold, numbing spray.

"Son of a *bitch*!" he screamed.

"You okay?" Isabelle shouted.

"Yeah, I'm good. This water is freezing, though."

She giggled and shook her head. "Someone's just gotta have a shower before we leave," she mumbled under her breath.

She was sitting on an old barstool, texting her husband: *Hey, I'll be getting in a little late, but I'll be home tonight. Don't wait up!*

If she was lucky, she wouldn't be coming home at all, but that would be up to Chance. His wife was out of town with girlfriends for a few days, so they could always crash at his place.

She placed her phone on the arm of the nearby couch and pulled her blouse up over her head. She loved showers with him, the feel of his soft skin and naked body pressed against hers. Somehow, they always managed to squeeze in a quick rinse together before parting ways.

Before she could grab the clasp on her bra, she felt the cold, metal strings tighten around her throat at the exact moment the stool was kicked out from beneath her. Her body fell to the floor, but Damien was quick to kneel on her back, pinning her face-down.

His hands pulled in opposite directions, tightening the steel cords until Isabelle couldn't breathe. Her neck was pulled backward so sharply, the strings began to cut into her throat, a steady stream of reddish purple running between her breasts and pooling beneath her stomach.

What little breath was able to escape her lips formed in blood-shaped bubbles that slowly popped at the corner of her blueish lips. A brief, single moan flowed from her mouth as her arms flailed in an attempt to grasp his gloved hands, but the thinner of the two strings was an inch deep into her larynx, a pulsing stream of red mist painting Damien's jeans.

Her legs kicked one last time as her head fell limp to her chest, both strings now embedded deep into her esophagus. Damien loosened his grip, and her body dropped to the floor, her neck folded at its center. He wiped his hand across the sweat dripping down his cheek. A thin streak of cherry smeared across his beard.

Damien made his way to the bathroom and opened the door without hesitation.

"There you are. I thought you forgot about me," Chance said as he pulled back the curtain, only to be met with the pistol shoved against his forehead.

Damien looked down between the man's legs and frowned with pity. "Damn. Looks like I did her a favor," he said as he squeezed the trigger, sending Chance's head backward into the wall.

Chapter 46

It was 9 a.m., and Asher had slept in well past his usual morning alarm. The previous day's drama with Pierre had sent his anxiety into overdrive, and he needed a late morning to recoup. Walking into the kitchen, he started a fresh pot of decaf, something he'd never thought he would have to endure—precious coffee without the caffeine. He wasn't even sure what the point was, but he needed it.

Sofia was gone, and he had the house to himself for the morning. He planned on taking his time. He was beginning to cherish being home alone—the quiet, the lack of distraction, the absence of tension. An unfortunate but clear truth was that it was all around better for him to begin his day without Sofia. There was enough tension at home in the evenings, and he didn't need it twice a day, at least not until he could figure out how to deal with the drama between her and Cassandra. The morning was still.

Until a knock at the back door echoed throughout the kitchen. No one ever came to the back door, especially at this time of day.

What the hell. Can I ever get a peaceful morning? he thought. *I'm checking out who this is before I open the damn door, I know that.*

He walked to the kitchen sink and leaned his head between the window curtains. "What the fuck?" he said aloud.

Mauricio knocked again, this time harder. "Come on, Asher. I know you're in there. Your car is out front."

Asher slowly backed away from the window as if retreating from a drooling rottweiler flashing its yellow canines. He sat on the sofa and waited, motionless. His heart began to race, thumping harder and harder until he felt the pulse deep in his throat.

"Come on, man. Open the damn door. This is ridiculous. Asher, open the door."

He reclined slowly, placing a pillow under his head, not sure if he was in for the long haul or only a moment longer.

The coffee pot beeped.

"Oh, that's nice. You have the time to make coffee but can't open the door for your old man. Real nice, Asher."

Asher closed his eyes and crossed his hands over his chest.

"Okay. I guess I got the message. I'll leave you be, then. Enjoy yourself while it lasts, son. Don't say your father never tried to help you. All I can say is, I hope you know what you're doing."

A shot of adrenaline coursed through Asher's veins, shooting from his chest down through his feet. He jumped up and ran to the front window of the house. He could see Mauricio pacing down the driveway to his car. The man stopped at the car door, grabbing the handle, and looked back over his shoulder to the home. It was as if he needed one last picture of his son's house to stick into his mind.

Asher ducked back and out of view.

He heard the car door slam and the engine start.

Immediately, he ran into the bedroom, grabbed his car keys and gun, and jumped into the Vette. He shoved the pistol grip into reverse and slammed the gas, sliding the front end of the car out into the street, narrowly missing the mailbox. Then he threw the transmission into gear and forced his foot to the floor, the side exhaust howling throughout the neighborhood as it echoed from one house to another.

He might not have wanted to answer the door and speak with his father, but that didn't mean he didn't want to know what Mauricio was up to.

Chapter 47

Asher put his tailing skills to use. He made sure not to lose sight of Mauricio's car while also not getting close enough to be seen. This was exceedingly difficult, as his vehicle was far from subtle. There weren't exactly C2 Corvettes driving around New Orleans by the dozens, not to mention how the loud rumble of the car's exhaust advised anyone and everyone of its approaching presence.

He was able to keep a safe distance and was surprised to see Mauricio pull into Tulane Medical Center. Keeping an eye on him once he parked proved more difficult than doing so while driving. Bad weather was rolling in, and Asher knew he needed to see where his father was parking and entering the building if he stood any chance of locating him upon leaving.

Luckily, Mauricio didn't drive into the parking garage but rather parked near the main entrance of Tulane Cancer Center. Mauricio walked briskly into the building with his umbrella and a file folder in hand. Asher wasn't sure what to think. Was he there for a friend? A relative Asher wasn't in touch with? Surely he wasn't *that* sick, if at all. He looked healthy to Asher—better than he could remember from his younger years, even.

Nearly two hours passed, and so did the rain.

Mauricio exited from the same entrance he walked through before and made his way back to his car.

His visit here is only a small piece of the puzzle, Asher thought. *I need more information.*

He waited until Mauricio was driving out of the parking lot to start his car, then resumed following him at a distance.

As they came to a four-way stoplight, Mauricio glanced back in his rearview mirror and could see the Vette about eight cars back, Asher sitting in the driver's seat with his aviators on, his arm resting on the door with an open window. Mauricio wasn't naïve. He wasn't oblivious to the habits of his son. After all, he was the one who'd tracked down Asher to provide him with the information, not the other way around.

He wanted to see if his son had the nerve to do something about it. Did he have the audacity to continue following him and figure it out for himself?

Mauricio sped through the next light as it turned yellow, then made a sharp turn down a side street.

Asher remained close behind.

"Well, that's an interesting turn of events," Asher mumbled to himself as he eased into the parking lot of a local bar. He parked the Vette at the corner of the gravel lot behind a green dumpster, well out of sight.

Inside, Mauricio sat at an open stool, a clean, white napkin in front of him.

"Hello," the woman said from behind the bar. "What can I get you?"

"Beer will do the trick."

Mauricio had been at it for nearly a year, and today drove the final nail into his effort to beat it. At the very least, he was going to leave on his own terms, remembering his times with close friends and doing what put him at ease.

The bar was empty. It was the appropriate metaphor for the

last years of his life—drowning his solitude in guilty pleasures, waiting for closing time. Luckily for him, he had the better part of a day left, and he would be sure to use every last drop of time remaining. Besides, he wasn't truly alone. He had the company of a mediocre barkeep who was willing to feed him small doses of liquid poison until he was pushed out the door and forced to face his last days.

Nearly six hours later, Asher watched his father stumble out the front door, a young, thin woman closing the door behind him. For a split second, Asher contemplated intervening.

Bitter heads prevailed.

He was surprised, however, to see that his father did not climb into his car, but instead, grabbed some paperwork from the passenger seat and began walking down the shoulder of the road and through the gate of a nearby apartment complex. At least his conscience was put at ease knowing he wouldn't have to watch his father drive drunk.

It was getting late, and if he wanted to avoid another argument with Sofia, Asher needed to get home at approximately the same time he normally would if working from the office. He called it a day.

At least he had something. Now all he needed to do was visit the hospital and bar himself.

Chapter 48

eanwhile, in the building, Mauricio opened the front door of his apartment and stumbled into the kitchen. He grabbed a cold water from the fridge, downed half the bottle, and walked to the bar top. There, he stood in silence for a moment, staring at the folder containing the chemotherapy schedule before sliding it off the counter and into the trashcan.

Mauricio stumbled into the bathroom, fumbling for the light switch and tripping over the rug at the foot of the vanity. He pulled back the clear curtain and started the shower before removing his clothes. He wasn't sure why he was bothering to shower. The alcohol had done its job, and he was numb, no longer focused on the inevitable, which was his primary goal of the evening.

A shower would steady his mind and ruin that.

After sitting on the edge of the tub and thinking about it for a minute, he turned off the water and heaved into the toilet. What breakfast was left in his body from earlier that morning was no more, and the once brightly colored mat at his feet was now faded with a brownish-green hodgepodge of meals.

The vivid lights pushed him into a daze, and the room was spinning out of control. The sink jumped into the doorway, and the door slid across the room and into the adjacent wall. He managed to stand and make his way to the light switch, flicking it off before he walked to a modest desk at the foot of his bed. After grabbing the edge of the table for balance, he sat down in the office chair.

He knew the end was near. He knew—as a matter of fact—that nothing was left for him, and he was okay with that. But in this moment, one small task remained that he needed to complete.

He reached into the desk drawer and pulled out a clean, white piece of printer paper, along with a black pen. He heaved yet again, but nothing remained.

Dear Son, the letter began. His hands shook so violently he wasn't sure Asher would be able to read the writing, but the message was too great to forfeit.

Mauricio wrote for a good twenty minutes as beads of sweat formed on his forehead and poured down the side of his face, pelting the paper until it was a mix of black ink and wrinkled moisture.

He was signing off and leaving his son with one last piece of advice, whether he wanted it or not. It was unfortunate, however, that it had to be delivered in this manner and not in person. Although, he understood why Asher had responded the way he had in recent days.

He folded the paper twice and placed it inside an envelope. Then he licked the opening and set it against a black-and-white photograph framed at the corner of the table. The picture was a childhood photo of Asher sitting on his father's lap at his fourth birthday party. Mauricio wasn't sure what was to become of the letter, but at least he'd written it. He had done his part.

If his son did his job, all would fall into place.

He climbed into bed and pulled the string on the bedside

lamp, plunging the room into pitch blackness. He had always wondered what it would be like to fall asleep and never wake up. The ironic truth about any such death, perhaps, was that no one could ever know.

He closed his eyes one last time. He pictured baby Asher on his lap, bouncing him on his knee, tickling him until his birthday-cake smile could no longer handle it. Little Asher loved it when his dad picked him up and threw him over his should like a sack of potatoes. "Delivery! One order of rotten little baby, comin' up."

He took in a large breath of nighttime air, his child's face clear as day, before his chest fell. The room was now doubly dark.

Chapter 49

Dinner had ended, and Asher was in his home office, fiddling around with a new song he was learning, trying to subconsciously figure out what his father was up to. The sheet music was open on the ottoman, his guitar perched atop his thigh. He made his way through the beginning of "Blue on Black" by Kenny Wayne Shepherd, his favorite blues guitarist.

Taking a swig of decaf, he adjusted the volume on the amplifier. For Asher, playing guitar was one of the activities that shed all anxiety and concern flowing through his body, while simultaneously aiding his attempt to understand what problems he couldn't solve. It was his walk in the park, so to speak.

Mid-riff, his phone lit up on the end table. Pierre's name flashed across the screen as it vibrated.

"Hello," Asher answered, placing the guitar next to him on the sofa as if it were his acquaintance.

"Where the hell are you?" the chief answered. "We got problems."

"I'm at home, why?"

"Because your worst nightmare just came true. We have a third couple found in a dressing room, House of Blues."

"Jesus Christ," Asher said. "Same guy?"

"By the looks of it, yeah. Xavier and a few others are down

there now starting to process everything, but you need to get your ass here tomorrow to see what else you can squeeze out of it. Or earlier, if you can."

"Yeah, I'll be there tomorrow."

"Didn't I tell you this shit would happen? Where are you at with that damn letter? You make any headway on it yet?"

Asher paused, knowing that not only had he not made any headway with the letter, but his father was also still pressing him and acting more strangely by the day.

"No, I haven't. Although, I can meet up with my dad if I absolutely have to. I really don't care to, but we have nothing else to go on right now."

"I told you to do that from the beginning, dickhead. This is your last chance. Talk to him and figure this shit out."

Pierre hung up the phone without warning.

"Hey, I thought I heard you talking to someone. Everything okay?" Sofia said as she walked into the room.

"Yeah, everything's fine. It's just the chief."

"He doesn't usually call you at home this late. Something goin' on?"

He looked at Sofia with a sideways glance. Not only did Pierre never call him so late, but his wife never cared about who was on the phone, much less what Asher was talking about.

"Yeah. I might need to start working on a resume, *that's* what."

Asher tossed the guitar pick onto the sofa beside him and leaned back, drawing a deep breath while considering his options. Something had to change. A common denominator needed to show up across the murders. There were too many consistencies for it all to be random killings with no message.

"A resume? What are you talking about?"

"I'm out of a job if I don't figure this thing out. He's already pulled me aside and threatened me once. I have a feeling I won't be around much longer if I don't wrap this."

Sofia leaned against the wall and bowed her head. "What are you gonna do?"

"The one thing I swore to myself I never would do, I suppose—talk to my dad. It's all too big of a coincidence to think he isn't involved somehow. He just randomly shows up in the middle of an investigation saying he hopes I know what I'm doing, and now he's mentioned in an anonymous letter we get from someone? No, it's all too much. I'll find him tomorrow and figure this whole thing out, as much as I don't care to."

"Well, if you need me, I'll be in the kitchen," Sofia said blankly, and walked out of the room.

"Sure."

Asher picked up his phone and began dialing Cassandra's number while pacing around the room, walking from the door to his desk, back to the sofa, then to the door again. The phone began to ring.

"Hey, you got a minute?" Asher asked.

"Yeah, what's up?"

"I just got off the phone with Pierre. Things are getting more fucked up by the minute."

"What do you mean? What is it?"

"We have another set of bodies. Xavier is already at the scene, but I plan on making an appearance tomorrow. Pick me up in the morning?"

"Of course. I'll be there first thing."

"Thanks, Cass. I'll see you soon."

"Have a good night."

"Goodnight."

Chapter 50

Cassandra rang the doorbell, breakfast in hand, and waited for Asher to answer. The morning was beautiful. A light fog lingered throughout the city streets, and sunlight shot between the homes in bands of orange and gold. She could hear movement inside. As usual, she was hoping Asher would answer and not Sofia.

He opened the door, shirtless and clearly not fully awake. "Oh, hey. Come in. Just give me a minute."

Cassandra could see Sofia lying on the sofa, her eyes barely open, still covered from her lonesome night in the living room. Before Asher could close the door, Cassandra gestured to the back of the house. "Can we talk in private?"

"Let's head out back. I don't wanna *disturb* anyone," he mumbled derisively under his breath.

Sofia sat up on the couch, still wrapped in covers. She stared at them with a penetrating gaze and propped her feet up onto the coffee table. "No need—it's time for me to wake up, apparently."

Asher and Cassandra made their way to the sunroom anyway. He snatched his cup of decaf off the counter while passing the kitchen. "Can I get you anything?" he asked in midstride.

"Nope. I'm all set." She gestured with her coffee.

They walked onto the sunlit porch. Asher could tell something was off. Cassandra immediately sat in the hammock. "Your French cruller is in the box."

"I figured, thanks. So, what's up? You look exhausted."

Cassandra paused and began to rock back and forth in the suspended lounge. "I really don't know how to say this, so I'll just come out with it. Your father passed away last night, Asher. I was notified this morning on my way over."

He placed his coffee on the table and sat back in the chair, frozen in that position.

"We don't have a cause of death yet, but they're thinking he was terminally ill. Pierre was gonna call you, but he thought maybe it was best you hear it from me."

Asher nodded. "Yeah. Of course."

"Sorry. I know what y'all were goin' through. I'm sure it couldn't have been worse timing."

"To tell you the truth, I followed him yesterday," Asher said with his head down, fiddling with his hands.

"You *followed* him? Why?"

"Because he's mentioned in the letter we got, and Pierre insisted I reach out to him. As much as I didn't wanna admit it, maybe he does have something to do with all of this. Don't you think it's a mighty big coincidence he shows up when all of this goes down? Although, I'd be lying if I said I understood any of it."

Cassandra had a confused look on her face, her eyebrows bent and her mouth twisted to one side. "I suppose. However, that begs the question: why come running to you?"

"Exactly. I have no idea."

"Well, I'm sorry to spoil your day. If you'd like, I can go with you to see Agnes. I'm sure you're wanting to talk with her to see if she knows anything else. Like I said, she's thinking natural causes, but with all that's goin' on, you never know."

"Thanks, but I'll probably head over there myself. If you don't mind, we can still meet up afterward to check out this third scene at the House of Blues. I know it's probably the last thing I should be doing, given the news, but I'm sure Pierre isn't gonna let up anytime soon unless we have something to give him. You okay with meeting me over there later?"

"Of course. I'm always good with meeting up," she said while shooting a wink and accompanying smile in his direction. "There anything else I can get you for now? You good?"

"Yeah, I'll make it. It's a tough pill to swallow, but I'm glad it came from you."

Cassandra made her way over to Asher, standing before him with arms wide open, inviting a hug that—particularly now—he much needed. He embraced the offer and held her, feeling better about the news that had been thrust onto him only moments prior.

Of course, of all moments, Sofia chose now to round the corner and enter the sunroom through the screen door. "Can I help you?" she snarked at Cassandra.

"No, but thank you. Your husband, on the other hand, may be in need of some assistance. I'll be out front, okay?" She turned to Asher, running her hand down the front of his chest.

Then she strolled past Sofia, brushing her shoulder ever so slightly.

"Excuse me?" Sofia said.

Cassandra continued walking into the house and out the front door.

"Really, Asher? What the *hell*? You two getting comfortable enough?"

"Sorry, is there a problem?" he spat back.

"Yeah, your girlfriend can't keep her hands off my husband. We do have a problem."

"Well, it doesn't really seem like that's a concern of yours anyways, now does it, with you sleeping on the sofa and all."

Sofia's mouth dropped to the floor. "Maybe I should just find somewhere else to sleep altogether."

Asher shrugged. "That's your call, not mine," he said as he opened the porch door. "Oh, by the way, my dad died last night. I would've told you sooner, but my girlfriend was too busy making you look bad. Sorry."

Chapter 51

gnes had finished her examination of Mauricio's body when Asher arrived. She greeted him with an affable hug and could immediately tell that although he wasn't close to his father—from what she had heard—the man's passing was putting an undo amount of stress on the already overwhelmed investigator.

"Hey, hun," she said while embracing him in a full-on bear hug. "How you holdin' up?"

"I'm hangin' in there. You?"

"Oh, you know me. I'm at it every day, all day. Sorry to hear about everything that's goin' on. First the difficulty with all these cases, and now your father. I can only imagine."

She pulled out a chair for him in front of her desk. "Have a seat, love."

"Thanks. You know, I have no idea why you continue to be so nice to me. Not many people in my drama of a world have the type of tolerance for me that you do."

"You could say it's to entertain my own curiosity, but I like to think it's simply because you're likable." She smiled.

"I'll take it."

"I assume you're here to get an update on his passing, yeah?"

"Yep. Cassandra was telling me that you already suspect it

was natural causes, an illness possibly, but other than that, I'm not sure what to think. I knew he was visiting a hospital regularly, but I'm not sure for what or whom."

Agnes nodded in agreement. "Yeah, he was actually being seen at Tulane Medical for stage 4 lung cancer. He was following an aggressive treatment of chemo, but the cancer was too far along. From what I see in his records, it had already spread from both lungs to his lymph nodes."

"Any idea if you can tell how long he's had it?"

"Not really. Lung cancer is pretty rough, so it likely moved quickly. I'm sorry."

He stood up and began wandering around the room, walking from the desk to the exam table, checking out the microscopes the lab used to examine tissue samples.

"Can I ask you something a bit strange? I promise I'm not crazy."

She placed both hands behind her head while rocking in the chair.

"Shoot. In this profession, I promise you there isn't anything you're gonna shock me with."

Asher giggled. "Hold that thought."

"You okay? Do we need to sit down and have a heart-to-heart about this?"

He held up his index finger. "Like I said, hold that thought."

"Go for it."

"Can you go over my father's file and examination again, only this time seeing if there are any similarities between his death and the recent murders?"

She stopped rocking. "Seriously? I mean, I can. But what in the world are you thinking? We know his cause of death, Asher."

"I don't know what I'm thinking. That's the problem. We

received a letter from what appears to be the killer responsible for the murders, and it mentions me by name, along with reference to my father."

"Shut the fuck up. What?"

"Yeah, exactly. I have no idea how he could be connected to all of this, but if he's mentioned in the damn letter, there has to be some link."

"Yeah, sure. I'll do it. Although, it's gonna be a bit hard to ignore the cancer and look for something else entirely. It's pretty clear-cut how the victims died too, but sure. I'll take a look."

"Thanks, Agnes. I appreciate it. Like I said, I'm not sure it makes sense, but I'll take absolutely anything and everything I can get right now."

"No kidding. I'm surprised Pierre hasn't hung you out to dry at this point. I have two more bodies over there. That makes six." She pointed to a row of freezer boxes. "But I'm sure the chief already brought you up to speed on that."

"Not the details, but yeah, I know. I'm actually heading over to the scene when I leave here, but I'll be back tomorrow to talk again if you think you'll be done with the exams by then."

"It'll be a close one, but I'll be done. You just focus on the scene like you do best, and I'll take care of things here. You know I got you."

"Yeah, I know. You always do."

"We both know by now these aren't murder-suicides, but I can't really do much for you beyond the examinations and providing a *cause* of death. I need you to be on top of this for us to have a clear-cut *manner* of death as well. It's fairly safe to say homicide at this point, but you need to catch this fucker."

He began to walk out, but Agnes stopped him as he pushed open the lab door.

"Oh, by the way," she added.

"Yeah?"

"The methods this sicko is using to strangle the female decedents are getting worse. Be sure your stomach is up for it tomorrow."

Chapter 52

As Asher walked into the dressing room, the stench of dried blood and brain matter didn't merely smell bad. It struck him in the face and invaded his throat and sinuses to the point that he gagged and backpedaled, pulling his shirt up to cover his nose and mouth. He took a moment to collect himself at the doorway, but even from there, he could see the dehydrated pool of blood at the center of the floor.

He entered the room again, this time with a clear effort to keep himself from vomiting. Still, he could taste the rot. *Come on, stomach, don't fail me now.*

He made his way to where Isabelle's body had been found, her head barely attached to her chest by a thin strip of flesh and muscle that remained at the back of her neck. Her body was now in Agnes's hands, but he could picture where she'd once rested in the outline of bodily fluid on the hardwood floors that butted up against the tile of the bathroom.

Agnes was right. The killer was becoming more callous.

With the first murder, no object of strangulation was found. The second time, not only was a belt left at the scene, but it was used to strap and choke the victim against the headrest. Here, of all things, guitar strings were pulled so forcefully against her throat they cut three quarters of the way through the poor girl's neck.

This is insane, Asher thought. *Who the hell does this?*

"I can see you're already enjoying yourself," Cassandra said as she walked into the room.

"Sure, either that or I'm about to lose my lunch."

"You're making a habit out of that, huh."

She crouched next to Asher, staring at the mess in which the girl's body had once lain. "You find any similarities yet? They seem to all be pretty different to me."

Asher nodded. "I agree. I hate to oversimplify things, but I'd say the similarity is strangulation; that's the point. The question is why the two different causes of death between individuals. Why not just shoot them both and be done with it?"

"Good question. Agnes say anything about necrophilia? Maybe the point is for him to have power over the female victims, then humiliate the bodies."

"She hasn't mentioned it. She would have brought it up if there were any signs of it, though. Besides, that would've been rather difficult with the last victims in the parking garage."

"True. Where was the male found?"

Asher looked toward the bathroom, which was open. He could see a fan of blood spatter against the shower wall, adorned with individual runs of brain matter dripping down and onto the rim of the tub.

When he entered the room, as shockingly vile as the remnants were, the first thing that stood out was how neatly the pistol was placed on the edge of the bathtub, as if it were completing a balancing act for everyone to see.

"Well, I suppose he wasn't in the right frame of mind to place it here so conveniently after he shot himself point-blank," Cassandra said sarcastically.

"I would have to say . . . no." Asher stood in awe. "It's amazing what such a small piece of lead can do to a human head."

Cassandra walked back to the doorway and looked at the center of the dressing room, then glanced back to the bathtub. "What are the chances we're dealing with two killers?"

"*Two?* What makes you think that?"

"Well, how hard would it be for one person to keep two people at bay while strangling one of them? Don't you think that would be a near-impossible feat in and of itself?"

"No, not really. Look at BTK. He tied up and strangled an entire family while holding them at gunpoint, all by himself. He wasn't exactly a young gun either."

"Not to mention, the two bodies were found in completely separate spaces. Wouldn't you run out of the shower the second you hear your girlfriend screaming for her life?"

"He had a gun. Maybe he held the girl at gunpoint, strangled her before she had a chance to cry out, then moved on to the boyfriend. You'd be surprised how many victims go along with their captor before they realize it's too late. Hell, according to Kemper, some of his victims were smiling and laughing while he put duct tape over their mouths in the back of his car."

"According to Kemper? What is this? You're starting to sound about as reliable as the psychiatrists who set the nutjob free after he killed his grandparents."

"Is there a reason Xavier didn't collect the pistol yet?"

"He said we would probably wanna see it as is. If we think that's the key, he doesn't wanna disturb it until we have a chance to get down here."

"Smart man."

The pistol was another 1911, chambered in .45 ACP. The

black slide butting up against the brushed-aluminum frame with wooden grips made the gun pop, some might have said with an air of class. The skeletonized trigger and hammer screamed 1911, beautifully complemented by the smooth grip safety. "Kimber" was engraved into the matte finish of the slide.

"Here we go again, yet another one," he said.

"An Ed Brown, an authentic Colt M1911, and now a Kimber. What is he trying to say? 'Fuck you, I've got money?'"

"No, no, no. It means more than that. It's a message. We just haven't figured out the code yet."

"If we don't figure it out soon, it's gonna be *us* splattered across some random bathroom."

"Sure. And Pierre will take pleasure in doing it himself."

Chapter 53

Asher was always struck by how quickly funerals took place after someone had passed away. It was only forty-eight hours since he had met with Agnes to discuss his father's death, and it was already the morning of Mauricio's burial.

"You about ready?" Sofia asked. "We should probably get goin' if we're gonna get there early."

"Yeah, just let me grab my glasses."

As they made their way to the cemetery, Asher had a feeling he couldn't pinpoint. He was both indifferent toward and saddened by his father's death, and his wife was the same. Her feelings about the current state of their marriage clearly did not match what she felt toward his loss—simultaneous resentment and empathy.

As they drove down the paved road of the cemetery, the skies began to open, dropping a light sheet of rain that moved steadily across the grounds. Sofia parked the car alongside the main road, adjacent to the burial site.

Provided Asher was the closest living relative of his father, he was in charge of Mauricio's service, or lack thereof, along with his burial. He decided a burial ceremony alone was appropriate and chose to skip a service altogether. As important as the responsibility was, he couldn't stand to imagine what it would be like to hold a service no one would attend.

"Anyone else on their way?" Sofia asked.

"I'm not sure. Xavier said he would stop by, but other than that, I haven't heard from anyone."

Five chairs were placed to each side of the coffin underneath a large, black tent, which rested not far from a southern live oak. Rain misted the chairs and casket. The couple took a seat and soon thereafter could see Xavier's car pull behind their own.

"Looks like he decided to make it after all," Asher said.

"Did you expect anything less?"

"No, not really."

Xavier was well dressed in a suit for the occasion. Typically, he wore athletic jeans and a V-neck, or other modest attire. He made his way under the canopy, carrying his umbrella and a bouquet of flowers, which he put to rest on top of the coffin.

"Hey, guys," he said. "You mind if I take a seat here?"

"Of course, hun," Sofia said. "It's good to see you."

"Always good to see you too, sweetie," Xavier said as he hugged her.

"Hey, man. Sorry for your loss," he added, shaking Asher's hand.

"Thanks. I appreciate it."

The rain became unrelenting as they sat in silence, paying their respects to Mauricio, with Xavier supporting his friend and colleague.

"Would any of you like to say a few words?" the director asked. "It looks like it may be the three of you."

As suspected, Asher and his guests were the only attendees, but he was okay with that. He wasn't sure what he would say to anyone else who would have arrived—he was long out of touch with his family on his father's side.

"No, I think we're good," Asher said. "Thank you, though. We'll probably be a moment longer, but I appreciate it."

The three of them sat for a good hour, largely in silence and barely out of reach from the falling rain, which began to let up after a brief moment. They all understood that not much needed to be said, given the circumstances.

From a distance, Cassandra could see the three of them sitting side by side under the awning. She sat in her car, which was parked around the bend in the road. Her hope was that Sofia wouldn't accompany her husband, that she could be there for Asher the way a genuine partner needed. But her hope, simply, was not enough.

Cassandra backed her car down the road and into a lone parking space. For a moment, she contemplated just showing up. She could show Asher that although his wife was merely acting, Cassandra was the more magnanimous woman. On the other hand, Sofia was digging her own grave being the person she was when she was with Asher.

She threw the SUV into drive and slowly crept to the cemetery exit. She could see Asher and his wife, arm in arm, in the rearview mirror, confirming she had made the right decision.

Chapter 54

As Sofia and Asher entered their home, a clear reversal of emotions was openly evident. Asher tossed his keys onto the counter as Sofia hung her purse on the back of the kitchen chair.

"That was nice, no? It was small, but I think that's all that was really needed," she said.

"Sure, I guess so." He poured himself a glass of sweet tea and leaned back against the counter. "So, you got home awfully late last night. Where were you? I didn't see you until this morning."

She opened the kitchen cabinet and grabbed the coffee canister. "You want some?" She gestured.

"Considering I can't have regular coffee, I'd say no."

Placing a filter into the coffee pot, she packed it with grounds. Then she filled the eight-cup pot to the brim and dumped the water into the black brewer.

"So, no answer?"

"When you're wanting to keep track of every move I make and question what I'm doing all day long, yeah, I'm gonna ignore you. You don't see me questioning what *you're* doing home early all the time with that 'coworker' of yours."

"I'm not questioning what you're doing all day long. I'm

asking where you were all night last night. I went to bed pretty late, and you weren't home. But you were here this morning. I'm just wondering where . . ."

Sofia walked out of the kitchen and toward the sunroom, opening the porch door and taking a seat in the hammock. Asher wasn't far behind.

"So that's the point we're at?" he said firmly. "We just take off all night to do whatever we want and don't need to share where we're going or what we're doing?"

"You're a big boy. What? Do you need me to check in and make sure you have dinner? Is there something you need from me?"

Asher laughed and shook his head. "Nope. Not at all. You go ahead and relax for the rest of the day. I'll be sure not to disturb you."

He turned around and walked back into the house, slamming the screen door as hard as he could, the wood splintering vertically along the edge of the frame and breaking from the hinges. He rarely became physically angry and was generally one to keep his emotions bottled up, not only so no one else had to deal with his feelings but also because he felt an advantage, an edge over others in such situations.

"Are you *serious*, Asher? That's real nice. Go ahead and break the front door too while you're at it!" she yelled.

He tried, but he was only able to shut the front with enough force to knock a picture off the wall as he left.

"What time will you be home?" Sofia screamed across the house, her voice echoing around the brick corners and out to the street. "Do I need to have dinner ready, big boy?"

Chapter 55

Asher slammed the door of the Vette, shoved the key into the ignition, and dropped the shifter into gear. As he lit up the tires, he couldn't help but think how he would rather be anywhere but his own home.

Maybe Xavier is home. It's still somewhat early. He'll know what to do.

As he pulled into the drive a few minutes later, Asher could see that Xavier's car was there. Lucky, considering the man was a workaholic. He might've even gone into work after the funeral.

"Hey, man. Long time no see," Xavier said as he stepped outside. "Everything all right? I was just about to head down to the office."

"Yeah, just another day at the loony bin, that's all. You got a minute?"

"Sure, come in. I don't have any decaf, but I have some leftover shrimp po-boy from lunch if you're hungry."

"Hell yeah. You know I'm always up for some shrimp *anything.*"

Asher took a seat at the bar and tossed his sunglasses onto the counter, leaning back and rubbing his weary eyes. Xavier made his way to the fridge and grabbed the leftovers.

The inside of Xavier's home looked as if it had been cut straight from a '70s magazine—wood-panel walls, orange countertops, and linoleum and shag carpet floors. All of it screamed "single man with not a care in the world."

"So, what's up? Sofia raisin' hell again?" he asked as he tossed the food into the microwave and hit the minute button.

"Yep. I don't know what to do, man. I feel like I can't say a damn thing to her anymore without her blowing up."

"You try talking to her about whatever it is?"

"Yeah, her problem is really with Cassandra, I think. I mean, we've talked about my stress and anxiety issues, which she seems to be more okay with lately, but every time she gets like this she ends up bringing up Cassandra. I don't get it."

"What do you mean she's doing better with your stress and stuff?"

"I just don't like her wanting to talk about my anxiety issues all the time, and I'm stressed to the max with work and Pierre right now, which makes it even worse. She's been getting all bent out of shape because I never wanna talk about it, and I have a short fuse when it comes to that shit."

"Gotcha. Well, you say anything to Cassandra?"

"*Cassandra?* What am I gonna say to her? 'My wife doesn't like you, so don't bother coming to my house anymore.' I can't do that to her, man. Besides, she hasn't done anything wrong. I work with her. I can't tell her to stay away."

"Okay, okay. I got you."

The microwave beeped. Xavier slid the paper-wrapped sandwich in front of Asher. The spice of fried shrimp and French bread permeated the room, and the faint sound of sizzling meat could be heard creeping out from beneath the brown paper.

He took a giant bite of the po-boy and sighed.

"Good?" Xavier asked.

"Oh, yeah. You know how I like it."

They laughed wildly, Asher nearly spitting out his food.

"You're ridiculous, man," Xavier said with a smile. "Feel better?"

"Much," he mumbled, mouth full and eyes closed.

Xavier always knew how to recharge Asher, no matter the trouble. The dim, golden light and the smell of Southern hospitality brought him back to square one.

"So, any other advice?" Asher asked.

"Well, the only other thing I got is to confront Sofia about it face-to-face. Squash it then and there, and don't let it back in. Alternatively, you could talk to Cassandra, but that's clearly off the table."

"I tried talking to Sofia, and all I get from her is that Cassandra is being unreasonable and rude to her, which I don't really think needs to be brought up at all, considering my wife doesn't need to be hanging out with my colleagues."

"I can see that, but just for the sake of it, give it a try. Sit her down and tell her how it is. She doesn't need to be butting into your work life. You stay out of hers, she can stay out of yours. I don't see anything harsh about that. Work is work."

Asher huffed. "Yeah, we'll see how that goes. Maybe I'll phrase it a bit differently."

Xavier chuckled and threw the dish towel into his face.

"What is it with you assaulting me with rags?" he said, trying to be serious but failing miserably.

"I don't know. There's just something about your face." Xavier snickered.

"Okay, I'll give it a shot. But I'll tell you now, I don't think she's gonna go for it. Me defending Cassandra isn't gonna end well."

"You're not defending her," Xavier said sternly. "You're drawing a giant chasm between your wife and your work life."

"Yeah, I'm sure Sofia will see it that way. Let's get out of here before I clean out the rest of your fridge."

Chapter 56

Once Asher had stormed out of the house, Sofia needed to blow off some steam and speak to someone. She didn't want to be home any more than he did. She grabbed her phone and car keys, leaving only a brief moment behind Asher, though first making sure he wasn't going to return.

As she drove to Damien's home, she was replaying the conversation with Asher in her head—how did it start? Was she in the wrong? Did he have a point? He seemed to have started nearly every argument they'd had recently. She didn't believe she was overreacting to Cassandra. If anything, she thought Asher was underreacting. Regardless of whether Cassandra was his work colleague, she didn't need to be treating his wife this way.

Fuck her and the broom she rode in on. Besides, I have someone who is, in fact, interested in me now—someone who doesn't pine in their own bullshit twenty-four seven.

After pulling out of the neighborhood, she immediately phoned Damien to make sure she could stop by. They had met only twice in public, but she thoroughly enjoyed being alone with him. He didn't want to talk about work or Asher. He simply wanted to be, to exist with her.

He picked up on the second ring. "Hello?"

"Hey, it's Sofia. How's it going?"

"Good, good. And you?"

"Eh, I've been better. Where are you?"

"I'm at work. What are you up to?"

"Driving. I was actually calling to see if you wanted to get together. I have an unexpected break in my schedule and thought we could grab a bite to eat or hang out at your place, depending."

"Yeah, for sure. I'm actually at work right now, but I can leave in a few. Let me pack up my things and close shop, and I can meet you at my place in, say, thirty minutes? I can text you the address."

"Sounds great. See ya soon."

"See ya."

As she left the Garden District and passed the Pontchartrain Expressway, she felt a sense of warmth, a sense of excitement, coursing through her veins. If Asher didn't want to fight for their relationship and stand up for his wife, then she was under no obligation to take that burden upon herself.

As she turned down Damien's street, she could see his Jeep in the driveway. She parked on the side of the road adjacent to an empty lot and walked the half block to his house. He didn't live far from his job in the Quarter, which she loved, since they were always close to the music and liveliness of the city if they ever wanted to go out as opposed to staying in.

She walked up the driveway and around to the back door, which was secluded and surrounded by a beautiful garden— okra, tomato, and bell pepper plants decorated the walkway, dotted about in the midst of several birdbaths and wooden benches. The taut, evening air invited more butterflies and cardinals than the eye could count.

She knocked, and Damien was quick to answer.

"Hey, girl. Come in."

"Thanks," she said while holding a hug several seconds too long.

Damien's home was warm and inviting. Much like the exterior, the inside of his home was decorated with a variety of plants, and art from the French Quarter adorned the walls. The hardwood floors stretched throughout the entirety of the home and were complemented by high-vaulted ceilings and exposed, wooden trusses. The smell of pine filled the room.

"You're not at work today?" he asked.

"Yeah, I should probably go in a little later, but I figured it wouldn't hurt to stop by for a bit. What about you? You were able to leave work okay? I know you've gotta take advantage of opportunities while you can, with the weather and all."

"Yeah, I pretty much make my own schedule, so it's no problem. What's buggin' ya? Sounded on the phone like you're having a rough day."

"You could say that. Just the same ole crap at home—dealing with the husband's drama. Nothing new. I'd hate to spend all our time talking about that, though."

Damien smiled. "I agree. Hopefully, we won't have to worry about that much longer."

Chapter 57

It was getting late, and Asher needed to see Agnes to get information on the bodies from the most recent murders before too much time lapsed. As he pulled into the parking lot, he noticed Cassandra's Tahoe.

He walked into the frigid room to find the two of them already looking at Isabelle's naked corpse. The woman was laid out on a steel table that was slightly angled, a lip running around its outermost edge. A drain hole sat at the lower end near the feet, which led the eyes down to a set of locking wheels at its base. Isabelle's body had already been examined, an incision made down the center of her sternum, which had been sewn up and contained a bag with the various organs Agnes had weighed and sampled.

"There he is," Agnes said. "I wasn't sure you'd make it to the party."

"Oh, you know I can't miss this. How's the exam going, or has it already gone?"

"It went well. Just bringing Cassandra up to speed."

"Anything new from what we've seen with the others?"

Agnes reached into the pocket of her lab coat and pulled out a lone cigarette. For some reason, it was her go-to reaction anytime Asher showed up to talk autopsy. "Unfortunately, no. Like I said yesterday, the only thing I noticed is whoever's doing this is getting more ballsy. First, he used a piece of jewelry, likely something that the decedent was already wearing, to strangle the first girl. The second was strangled using a belt, and this one, fucking *guitar strings*. I can't even begin to fathom what motivates someone to do this."

Asher shook his head and folded his arms. "Well, I half expected things to start getting worse before they get better. What about my father? Were you able to look at everything as a whole? You see any connections between him and the three sets of murders?"

"Sorry, but no."

"What are you looking for with your father?" Cassandra asked.

"I just wanna know if she sees any connections between the different murders and his death. Like I said before, I find it ironic that he showed up out of nowhere, he's mentioned in the letter we got, and all of a sudden he's dead. I had my doubts, but I don't buy that none of it's connected."

Agnes lit her cigarette and pointed to Isabelle's head. "Although there's no connection with your father, there is something interesting—something that worries me."

Cassandra's eyebrows shot upward. "That sounds promising."

"Petechial hemorrhages."

"Come again?" she asked.

"Sometimes they're small, but you can usually see them if you look closely," Agnes explained while handing her a small magnifying glass. "They can be as small as a pinprick, but they're in the white part of the eye. It's essentially broken blood vessels that form from an increase in blood pressure when blood flow is cut off to the heart."

Cassandra grabbed the magnifying glass and looked closely. "I don't see anything."

"Exactly," Agnes said. "She doesn't have any, but the other two women did."

"Okay, so what does that mean?" Asher asked.

"Well, he may or may not have meant to strangle her, but regardless, the strings cut so easily and deeply through her neck that the only thing keeping her head attached to her body is her spine and the small strip of splenius muscle dorsal to her vertebra."

"Goddamn," Cassandra said.

"Yeah, I'd say we need to worry," Asher added. "He's clearly not letting up anytime soon."

"I'd say he's getting pissed, more angry in his killing. Either that, or he's getting sloppy," Agnes said.

Cassandra shrugged. "Or he's just getting warmed up."

"Well, that's pretty much all I have for you. Cassandra said something about a print y'all pulled from one of the scenes. You have a match yet?" Agnes asked Asher.

"No, it turned out to be a dead end. It was only a partial. One more thing I need to tell Pierre about that he's gonna have a field day with."

"Good luck with that."

Agnes leaned over to her desk and flicked her cigarette into the ashtray, an ember floating up into the air, disappearing as the light slowly faded from a burning orange to a dim nothingness.

"Aren't you worried that one day you'll burn this place down smoking those in here?" Cassandra asked. "I wouldn't think this is the safest place to be doing that, no?"

Agnes snorted. "Spend time with your partner much?"

Chapter 58

It was nearing dusk, and Asher and Cassandra were leaving the examiner's building, walking to their cars after being debriefed by Agnes. The three of them shared a sense of hopelessness, as the only new information arising from Agnes's exams was the fact that the killer was becoming more brutal, and Asher's father was somehow—reason unknown—connected to the murders.

The air was packed with a dense humidity that could be felt in the lungs, a thick vapor that was hot and counter to the inside of the building. As they entered the parking lot, the air of desperation was expounded by a sense of nervousness and anticipation.

"I have some personal business to tend to and catching up to do tomorrow, now that the burial is over with. I probably won't be in the office, which I know is poor timing, but we need to stay on top of things, especially looking into any recent thefts for 1911s. Keep me posted if anything comes up, yeah?"

"Of course." Cassandra smiled as she nudged Asher with her elbow. "I got you."

As she looked up to see her car sitting at the center of the parking lot, she noticed something that cut straight through her and touched on her deepest fears of uncertainty. She stopped dead in her tracks, her gaze focused on the SUV.

"What? What's wrong?" Asher asked.

"Do you see that?" She pointed to her car.

"What?"

"*That*," she said, raising her arm even farther.

"Your gas tank door? What about it? You must have accidentally left it open when you filled up."

Cassandra shook her head and took a step back.

"What?"

"The last time I got gas was two days ago, Ash."

He shrugged, feeling that she was overreacting. People accidentally did it all the time.

"Look, I'm sure it's fine. You want me to close it for you?"

"*No.* I don't think it's a good idea to go anywhere near it."

He cocked his head to the side and threw a slanted glance her way. "Are you serious right now? It's a gas tank door, Cass, not a brick of TNT."

"You have no idea what someone could have put in there or done to it. First my window is busted out, and now this?"

It was late, and the parking lot was all but empty. A car sat in the back corner of the lot, which butted up against another building, not too far from Cassandra's Tahoe. The vehicle's headlights were on, but no one was visible through the tinted windows, which were made darker by a lack of streetlamps.

"You see that?" Cassandra asked. "That car has been sitting there since we came out."

"Yeah, other people work around here. What the hell are you freaking out over?"

At that moment, the car began to creep toward them, but it turned toward the parking lot exit just before reaching them. It continued to inch away until it could no longer be seen from the front of the building.

"See, it's gone. Let's get you home," Asher said as he grabbed the keys from her hand and began walking to the Tahoe.

"Seriously, Ash? You're just gonna start the damn thing?"

"What do you expect to do, leave your car parked here indefinitely because the damn door is open on your gas tank? Stay here if you want. I'll start it."

As he approached the car, he could see that the gas cap itself was closed, and it was only the door that was open—a mistake virtually everyone made at least once in their lifetime. He twisted the cap to double-check that it was secure, then closed the door. He also pulled the driver's doorhandle to make sure it was still locked, which it was, before unlocking it with the remote. Hitting the button, he climbed into the SUV, leaving the door open for Cassandra to see.

"See, I'm still alive. Even my sense of humor is intact."

"Yeah, yeah. Just start the damn thing."

He slid the key into the ignition and turned it once, activating the headlights and dashboard. He turned it once more, and the engine started without fail. Asher popped his head out the door and looked to her with a gleaming set of I-told-you-so eyes.

"Happy? No need to ring the crime scene unit just yet. Although, I'll wait to see if you make it home."

"Jackass," she snarled, giving his shoulder a fairly hard punch.

She climbed into the driver's seat and closed the door before rolling down the window. "Thanks. You know how I get while working these cases. It's as if I'm never careful enough."

"Yeah, I know. Just remember, in order to get to you, they have to deal with me, too."

She knew how cliché and over the top that sounded, but all

she cared about was that he would feel the compassion.

"Have a good night," he said.

"You know, the night doesn't have to end."

He shook his head, though he gave her a small wink as he did. "Sleep tight."

Chapter 59

The next morning, Asher slept in and awoke to Sofia getting into the shower. His only plans for the day were to collect Mauricio's belongings from his home now that Xavier and the rest of the unit were done with their search and documentation of the apartment. That was one aspect of his job he appreciated—his weren't the only set of eyes on a crime scene.

He made his way into the kitchen and started a pot of decaf while preparing his usual bacon sandwich. He wasn't lucky enough to get a personal coffee and doughnut delivery from Cassandra *every* morning, although he appreciated it more than words could express when he did.

After returning from the bedroom, he placed his pistol on the dining room table and made a fresh cup of coffee to complement the sandwich. The smell of smoked bacon and coffee grounds filled the room. Every now and then, he dabbled in the dark arts of flavored creamer and sugar, and this was one of those occasions. A splash of butter pecan and a pinch of raw sugar livened up what was sure to be an otherwise dismal day.

As he enjoyed the combined effects of crunchy bacon and sweet notes of pecan, he stared at his .45 at the opposite end of the table. He could recall the exact day, the exact moment, his father had gifted him the sidearm as a teenager. Much of his family and acquaintances didn't understand, and even judged him for, owning a firearm at such a young age. However, the majority of those individuals were not raised in a household with a father who taught his children to respect and properly handle such weapons. He was grateful that he'd had the opportunity to take part in hunting, competitive shooting, and other such outdoor activities in his younger years.

It was his sixteenth birthday, and Asher had always been intrigued by the sport of competitive shooting. Lucky for him, his father was already involved in the NRA's Bianchi Cup shooting competition, so he had a solid foundation from which to learn. Mauricio gifted Asher a beautiful, brand new Rock Island 1911, chambered in .45 ACP. Ever since then, Asher had not only shot the pistol regularly in competition but also carried the sidearm while on duty with the New Orleans Homicide Unit.

Upon finishing his sandwich, he washed his hands and grabbed the cleaning kit from a lower cabinet in the living room. He hit the magazine release and pulled back the slide, ejecting the round from the chamber while thumbing the slide stop upward. His father also taught him how to care for the material possessions he had earned in life, and that included cleaning his firearms.

The vibrant smell of bore cleaner and oil lubricant took over, vanquishing the lingering scent of bacon. The parkerized finish of the pistol now gleamed with a slight shimmer, and the wooden grips became enriched in their grain and texture. He returned the magazine to its well and chambered a single round, placing the pistol back into its leather holster on the table. He threw on his sports coat and made a coffee to go.

Heading back into the bedroom, he could hear that Sofia was still in the shower, so he opened the bathroom door to let her know he was leaving.

"Hey, I'm heading to Mauricio's place to gather what I can to bring back home. Xavier and the boys are done, so I should be in and out pretty quick."

She didn't answer.

"Hey, you hear me? I'll be back later."

Still, no answer.

Asher pulled back the corner of the curtain, only for Sofia to grab him by the wrist and pull him into the shower fully clothed, coat and all.

"What the hell, are you serious?"

"Shut the *fuck* up," she said as she yanked him to her. "I don't need you to talk right now."

Asher spun her around and unzipped his pants. Her attitude was a welcome distraction.

Chapter 60

As Asher approached Mauricio's apartment, yellow-and-black crime scene tape barricaded the crème-colored front door. He unlocked the deadbolt, ducking beneath the tape, and entered the apartment, immediately struck by the putrid smell of the room, undoubtedly a consequence of his father's passing—which surprised him, considering the body had been found rather quickly.

The apartment was overly simplistic, both in its design and its décor. The white walls were nearly empty, and the furniture consisted of nothing more than a couch, coffee table, bed, end table, and desk. The barren landscape of the home hinted at the fact that Mauricio hadn't lived there long. Even the cabinets contained little to no food.

As he entered the bedroom, he saw his father's life as it had been seconds before his death—vomit on the bathroom floor, a pen and paper on the desk at the foot of the bed, shoes in the doorway, and an empty bed where his father's body had once lain. He could tell, as Xavier had explained, that there wasn't much of a scene to investigate. No pills, no alcohol, and no sign of a struggle. This information, along with a diagnosis of cancer, made it more difficult for Asher to do his job as a homicide investigator. He didn't have much to go on, other than his wretched gut feeling.

Perhaps there really was nothing.

Given the lack of items, he knew it would be easy to collect Mauricio's personal effects, which included only some clothing, his desk, and a rugged leather trunk hidden within the closet.

As he opened the chest, he saw a binder, two pistols, and a modest collection of jewelry.

Xavier apparently didn't think this was relevant. That's too bad.

Asher sat on the floor and removed the binder from the trunk. As he flipped through it, he realized it was more of a photo album than anything else. The first few pages contained old, black-and-white photos of his parents and himself at birthday parties, holidays, and family functions, mixed with a few color images dating back to right before his mother had passed away.

As he looked closely, he noticed several pictures of his father's shooting competitions, in addition to Mauricio standing next to the old Chevelle he had restored before Asher was born. Classic cars were another interest he and his father had shared. The shooting photos consisted of competitions at both local and national leagues, including the NRA.

What in the world?

He removed two photos from the clear sleeve of the album and brought them to the lamp. He pulled the string and placed the photos near the lightbulb, squinting his eyes to assure himself of what he was seeing. Sure enough, he couldn't believe it.

This time, he spoke aloud. "You've gotta be kidding me."

He could see his father posing in the two photos at what appeared to be different shooting competitions several years apart. In the first photo, which appeared older, Mauricio was holding a polished Ed Brown Classic Custom. In the second photo, it was a two-tone Kimber.

Asher pulled out his phone and opened the photos of the pistols used in the homicides.

"Well, fuck me." He laid each picture next to his phone.

The guns were identical.

He flipped through the rest of the album to see if he was missing anything, anything at all—other photos with different pistols, someone else with the same 1911s, anything. But these were the only two photos of his father with his competition pistols.

His attention moved to the two guns in the trunk. He picked up a Smith & Wesson 1911 and a Sig Sauer 1911, both beautiful firearms, although drastically different in style. The Smith & Wesson had a natural, stainless steel finish with wooden grips and a serrated slide, and the Sig Sauer was stainless steel with a brown, thin-coat finish and polymer grips. The two firearms couldn't have been any more different, although they were designed from the same platform.

"Someone was obsessed with a certain pistol," he mumbled under his breath. "I should've known."

He placed the items back into the trunk and carried it out to his car. The rest could wait.

Outside, he sat in the car with the door open and immediately phoned Cassandra.

"Hey, I thought you were taking the day off," she said. "Everything okay?"

"Yeah, everything's fine. Can you meet me at my place in about twenty? There's something I need to show you."

A dead silence was all that came over the phone.

"You there?"

"Yeah, I'm here. Is Sofia gonna be okay with that?"

"What are you talking about?"

"Me coming over again with her not around. Is she okay with that?"

"Cass, I couldn't give any less of a shit about whether or not she's at the house. Can you meet me? Please."

"I'm on my way."

Chapter 61

As Cassandra pulled into the driveway, she saw Asher's car beneath the carport. She knocked on the door, and he answered abruptly.

"Hey, thanks for coming on such short notice."

"No problem. You home alone?"

Asher paused and looked at her with a jaded expression. "Yes, *Cass*, I'm home alone. Although, it isn't Christmas, and I haven't missed my flight. So, I think I'll be okay."

"Sorry, I'm just asking." She threw her hands up as if she were being held at gunpoint. "You and I both know how this is gonna end once your wife shows up."

He refused to make his partner walk on eggshells in his own home because of his wife's insecurities.

"Coffee?" he asked with a smile.

"Are you offering decaf or the serious stuff?" She chuckled.

"Both, although I know how much of an addict you are, so I'll make some high-octane syrup. I'm good with tea, myself. Why don't you grab a seat and get acquainted with some pictures of Mauricio. They're right there on the table." He pointed. "Check out the pistols."

Cassandra pulled out a chair and made herself at home. "These are some small pictures. How can you even see what he's holding? Can you really make out what these are?"

"Seriously, you need to get some glasses. It's clear as day," he said, coming to lean over her shoulder, one hand on the table and the other on the back of the chair. "Look," he added while tossing his phone on the table. "Scroll through the first photos of the Ed Brown and the third set of pictures with the Kimber. I'm telling you, they're an exact match. Small cup, big cup? Cream? Sugar?"

"French vanilla and sugar, please," she said without breaking her gaze. "Hey, I've been meaning to ask you . . ."

"Yeah?"

"How is it that you're good with tea but can't handle coffee anymore? Isn't that a bit of a contradiction?"

"No, it's weird. Tea doesn't set me off the way coffee does. I'm not sure what it is, but yeah, if you don't want me showing up to work like a three-year-old on cough syrup, it's best I stick with decaf and tea."

"Whatever you say, crazy," she said, twirling her finger next to her head.

"Hey, *you're* the one with the insane partner."

"Oh, there's no need to remind me. I'm lucky enough to be triggered by your presence every single day."

He set her coffee down on the table and pulled out a chair for himself. "So, what do you think? You see it?"

Cassandra squinted as she glared at the photos, bouncing back and forth between the phone and Mauricio's pictures.

"Maybe a little, but you're gonna have some convincing to do if you show this to Pierre. He isn't gonna close this thing out based on two random pictures that are decades old in addition to your hunch."

He giggled as he took a swig of ice-cold, sweet tea. "Well, it's a bit more than just some pictures and my hunch. Like I said before, we've got the letter, which mentions Mauricio, the fact that he started showing up in the middle of all this, and now the pictures. That's a mighty big coincidence, no? I mean, shit, it's my *father*. You think I'd throw my own dad under the bus on a hunch?"

Cassandra didn't miss a beat. "You know as well as I do that you weren't close enough with him for that to be a factor."

"Well, I think we should show this to Pierre. Besides, we'll know soon enough if it really was him, won't we?"

"What are you talking about?"

"The murders. They'll stop."

She looked at him with a heavy doubt. "That's awfully reckless, no? Just wait and see if anyone else dies? Are you kidding me?"

He leaned in close and grabbed the pictures from her hands. "You know something I don't?"

Sofia burst through the kitchen door then, carrying an oversized load of groceries in both hands, huffing and puffing after the laborious walk from the car. She dropped them onto the countertop along with her purse.

"Oh, hey. You're home early," Asher said, jumping up to help.

"Not really. I left work an hour ago so I could stop by the store first. I didn't know we were having company," she said, staring at Cassandra.

"You need some help? Is there anything left in the car?" he asked.

Cassandra remained seated at the dining room table with her legs crossed. She took a sip from her coffee cup, the cup with "Hubby's #1 Biologist" written in large, green letters across the side.

Asher stood between them, waiting for either to say a word. *Please, don't kill her*, he thought. Although, he wasn't quite sure which one he was addressing.

"Comfortable?" Sofia asked.

"*Always*," Cassandra responded instantly.

"Okay, you know what . . ." his wife snarled.

Cassandra stood up and handed Asher his phone. "I'm gonna get going. I'll see you tomorrow. Thanks for the coffee."

Sofia stood in the center of the kitchen with her arms folded, staring daggers at Cassandra as she walked out the front door.

"Are you shitting me, Asher? *Really*?"

"Um, no. But I do have an appointment with my therapist," he said with a blank face. "Don't wait up."

Chapter 62

As Asher sat on the sofa, Justin could see a look of exhaustion and angst smeared across his face. Asher's eyes were tired, but his legs couldn't stop moving, bouncing up and down.

"You look a bit on edge," Justin said. "Can I get you anything?"

"No, I'm good."

Justin took a seat in the recliner and picked up his glasses from the end table.

"So, how's life treating you? How are things with your father?"

Asher immediately stood and began walking around the room, looking into the fireplace as if he might have found something he was missing.

"Eh, I've been better," he said as he picked up the fire poker and moved the logs around. "You don't mind, do you?"

"Not at all. It is a bit chilly in here."

Justin crossed his legs and gave Asher a moment to process things, hoping he would begin to explain matters on his own. He was incorrectly optimistic.

"So, how can they be better? Were you not able to reach out to your father and sort things out?"

Asher was silent for a prolonged moment.

"My father's dead," he said without stopping his prodding of the glowing logs.

Justin repositioned himself in the chair, attempting to find any position that would make the conversation more natural, more comfortable.

"I'm sorry?"

"He's dead. He passed away at his apartment a few days ago."

"I'm sorry to hear that, Asher. That must be adding to the stress and anxiety you're feeling already between work and your home life, no? Are you sure you don't wanna sit down, talk face-to-face perhaps?"

Asher just sat next to the fire on the brick ledge and stared deep into the flames, the iron poker still in hand, smoking from the heat it now carried. He turned to his therapist with a blank expression. "I'm comfortable where I am."

"Okay. How are you handling your father's passing? The last time we spoke, you seemed to be rather distant from him, and appeared to be struggling with his sudden reemergence in your life. Has that changed at all?"

"It doesn't really matter at this point. All that matters is whether I can put two and two together and solve these murders we're working on. We think he was involved somehow, but I can't really divulge any more than that right now."

Justin took a moment to write on his notepad. After looking up at Asher for a second, he continued to take notes.

"And you somehow think that's gonna make things better?"

"You don't need to patronize me," Asher said with a smirk and a shake of his head.

Justin leaned back, clicking his pen and placing it on his notes before setting it aside. "I don't mean to do anything of the sort, Asher. Really. I'm just wondering how you think that's gonna help you personally."

He continued prodding the logs, playing with them for the mere sake of having something to do other than aiding the fire.

"Well, I think it'll help me professionally to solve the cases, which would take a bit of stress off my personal life. I've already been threatened to be let go if I don't figure it out, and that takes away from my home life and marriage. Aside from that, it would tell me the real reason he came back after all these years."

"Sure, I get that."

"Like I said before, it's hard to put time and effort into my personal life when the stress from work spills over. It consumes everything."

Justin nodded in agreement. "So, you've been coming to me for a while now, and although it always helps for people to talk about things, I think it would help even more if I could directly support you in some way, don't you think?"

Asher stood up but remained fixated on the fire. "You tell me."

"Well, I'd say so. If it's closure you're looking for, you think that solving these murders you're talking about, at work, will help you get that?"

"Maybe not completely, but probably, yeah."

"Then good. That's a step forward. Is there anything else to do with your father that would help you get closure, or do you think solving the murders alone will do that?"

Asher took a moment to himself, a moment to process and think about his past both with and without his father. He hadn't spoken to Mauricio in so long, he wasn't sure it was worth dredging up the past any more than he had to.

"I don't know."

"Well, you've mentioned that your father left not long after your mother passed away, yeah?"

Asher nodded without a word.

"Is there anything from that point in time you still don't have closure with," Justin continued, "or do you think it all stems from him being gone in recent years?"

"A bit of both, I suppose. I mean, I was a teenager when my mother passed away. To be honest, it all happened so quickly—him leaving and all—that I don't even really know what happened to her. He told me that she was killed, which is what inspired me to eventually become an investigator, but I never really could ask how, or why. I never thought I could handle it."

Asher broke his gaze and looked to Justin. "What are you getting at, exactly?"

"Sometimes, we think that our current anxieties and struggles are due to what's goin' on in the present, but often they can be from something that happened well into our past. I'm just wondering if that may be the case for you."

Asher shrugged, not sure if he agreed or disagreed with what the therapist was proposing. "And how am I supposed to figure that out?"

"We could talk about it, goin' further and further back, or alternatively, you could determine that for yourself."

"By doing what, precisely?"

"Well, you're an investigator, no? Of all people, you should have access to how your mother *really* died."

Chapter 63

The following morning, Asher arrived in the office to see Xavier and Cassandra hard at work.

Xavier had been unsuccessful at finding a match for the partial print recovered from the second set of murders, so he was attempting to track down any additional footage that might exist from the cameras at the hotel where the first murders took place, as well as the backstage cameras at the House of Blues. The parking garage footage from the second homicides was too blurry to be of use.

Cassandra, meanwhile, was wrapping up her search of the state's database on firearm thefts. Much like the partial fingerprint, this line of inquiry was a dead end.

Asher passed by Xavier and knocked on his desk before signaling his way down the hall. "Hey, let's go." He passed Cassandra's desk and asked her to join them as well. "Come with."

They followed Asher down the hallway to his office without saying a word. Upon entering, they remained standing, confused as to what Asher was anxious to divulge after being gone for only one day. All Cassandra knew was that he had a gut feeling about the photographs he had shown her the day prior. Asher took a seat in his chair and turned on his desktop.

"What's up?" Xavier asked.

"We need to investigate my mother's death."

They looked at Asher with stunned confusion. "What are you talking about?" Cassandra asked. "Your mother died decades ago. You always said it was a homicide."

"Yeah," Xavier added. "Two seconds ago you're suggesting your father has something to do with these cases, and now you think your dead mother is involved?"

"No, I know for a *fact* my father was involved, I just don't know exactly how yet. I also don't know the *cause* of my mother's death. Sure, it was apparently a homicide, but I need to know who and how. We have a manner of death with no cause. Unfortunately, that was a conversation my father and I never had."

Cassandra looked confused. "And you haven't done this yet because . . ."

"Because I didn't have a reason to. She was gone, my father left, and that was the end."

Both of them stared at Asher as if he was having a mental break, as if he was losing it.

"Okay, so what do you need us for?" Xavier asked.

"I need unbiased opinions as to whether the two of you think all of this could have been the workings of my father. I have no idea what the case file says because I've never looked at it."

"What are you waiting for?" Cassandra asked.

"Feel free." Asher gestured to the chairs in his office, implying they might be a while.

After a good twenty minutes, he had accessed the file and was continuing to read, not saying a word, keeping Xavier and Cassandra in unnecessary suspense.

"You care to share?" Xavier asked.

"Sure, go ahead." Asher turned his computer monitor to the front of the desk to face them. Then he sat with his legs crossed, waiting for them to arrive at the same conclusion he had.

"So, that's it? She was strangled, and no suspect was identified?" Xavier said.

"I think that's a strong coincidence, don't you?" Asher said. "First, my father shows up out of nowhere, then the pictures from his apartment show pistols that perfectly match the first and third guns from the homicides, and now this shows my mother was strangled when the female victims are being strangled in *our* homicide cases. Come on, really?"

Cassandra and Xavier looked at each other with apprehension.

"Not only that," Asher added, "but look at the last entry in the report."

They continued to browse the file, speed-reading with wide eyes and pale faces.

"You see that? There was a second victim, a male," Asher said.

"A male who was apparently shot," Cassandra said.

"Not only shot, but shot *himself*."

"Sure, but we know the males in our homicides aren't actually shooting themselves, Asher," Xavier said. "They're *being* shot. We're working double homicides, not murder-suicides."

"You aren't serious," Cassandra said. "There's no way Pierre's gonna go for this as evidence. This is all circumstantial at best."

Xavier nodded. "Yeah, man. I wouldn't recommend it."

"Then what *would* you recommend?"

They both remained silent, and that was more than enough to bolster Asher's point. "Exactly."

"I thought you brought us in here to give you our objective opinion?" Xavier asked sternly.

"Did I say that? Oops. At least now I can say 'we' made a discovery when I bring this to Pierre."

Chapter 64

Asher knocked on the chief's office door, the blinds pulled down over the window, covering the yellow-lit room.

"Come in."

Asher walked into the office and closed the heavy, wooden door behind himself. Without explaining anything, he handed Pierre a manila file folder that contained the photos found in Mauricio's apartment, photos of the two identical 1911s from the first and third crime scenes, a printout of the case report on his mother's murder, and the letter received from the killer days prior.

"What's this?" Pierre asked. "I hope this isn't another damn request for better snack machines in the lounge, because I swear to god, if you complain one more time about—"

"I think we need to close the three double homicide cases."

Pierre tossed the folder onto the desk and adjusted himself in his chair with his head against his fist, spewing sarcasm at an unbelievable rate. "You feeling okay, numbnuts? You need a minute to collect your thoughts? You aren't replacing coffee with chocolate, huh? Trust me, that'll fuck you up worse than the joe."

Asher sat down in front of Pierre's desk. "What? No. Look at the file."

The man leaned forward and opened the folder, flipping through the photographs and case reports. "I don't get it. What the hell am I looking at?"

"It's what we need in order to confidently close these homicides. I told you about the letter we received, right? The letter that mentions my father. Well, as you already know, he's since passed away. When I collected his belongings, the two photos you see in front of you show him with the exact same pistols that were used in the first and third sets of murders."

"Exact same? You mean same models?"

"I don't think so. I think they *are* the 1911s. In addition to that, and him being mentioned in the letter, we did some digging into my mother's death as well."

"We?"

"Yes—myself, Xavier, and Cassandra. I never looked into it before, but we found that my mother's homicide was . . . well, she was strangled. In addition to that, a man was also shot at the scene. His death was ruled a suicide."

Pierre rocked back and forth in his chair, staring at the pictures in front of him. "And you want me to close these cases based on your hunch?"

"Respectfully, I don't consider it a hunch."

"No? Then explain to me why the letter we received says 'Tell your father I said hello.' Why would your father refer to himself in the third person?"

"Easy. Serial killers often do whatever they can to throw us off their tracks. I mean, look at Zodiac. Sure, they were able to decode some of the cyphers he sent them in the mail, but they never did figure out whether his misspelling of words was on accident, nor what the thirteen symbols of one cypher said, which supposedly identifies the killer. It was just a jumbled mess, according to officials."

"So, all of this work, all of this time investigating these cases, and you just wanna pin this on your father."

Asher didn't waver either way.

"I just wanna solve the cases, and this is where the evidence points."

"Circumstantial evidence."

Asher remained silent.

"You're putting me in a real bind, you realize that? What do Xavier and Cassandra have to say about this?"

"Nothing more informative than what I've already told you."

Pierre stood and walked over to the minibar in the corner of the office behind Asher, where he poured himself a whiskey on the rocks. As he leaned against the wall, he took a long, drawn-out sip from the frosted glass and began to explain to Asher exactly what would happen if things went south.

"Let me be perfectly clear on this," he said, standing there behind him. "One, if this backfires and more bodies turn up, your ass is *gone*, clean and clear."

He took another sip and closed his eyes, savoring the smooth, smoky taste. Asher's stomach began to stir, his palms soaked in sweat. He felt his heart beginning to race as it moved the fabric of his shirt above his chest.

"Second, no one—and I mean *no one*—knows that you were the lead on this case. Understood? *I* put it together, and *I* made the call. The last thing we need is a media shit storm about how our lead investigator has it out for his own father."

"Understood," Asher mumbled, shaken.

Pierre walked around in front of him and placed his drink onto the desk. "I hope you realize how fucked up this is, the position you've put me in. You bring me circumstantial evidence with nothing else to go on . . ."

The chief sat and folded his hands in his lap, a dead glare cutting through Asher. "At least there's one positive thing that will come from all of this if you fucked up."

Asher turned his head, trying his best not to gag.

"I'll have your personal judgment to blame," he continued, "and I won't have to deal with your ass anymore."

Chapter 65

Asher decided to take the rest of the day off work, and he stopped by Kenney Seafood to pick up fish for dinner. Perhaps fried redfish and fresh, homemade French fries would put Sofia in a more appealing mood to smooth things over.

He arrived to an empty home with plenty of time to spare before she would leave the university. After filleting the redfish and cutting thick, skin-on fries, he warmed a couple of pans with hot vegetable oil. Then he dipped each fillet into the pale, golden egg wash and coated it with his favorite, Louisiana Fish Fry. As he placed the meat into the pan, the scent of home—fried seafood, warmth, and comfort—filled the room.

On time, Sofia arrived home and greeted him with a simple, "Hey, how's it going?" as she made her way into the living room. She turned on the TV and reclined on the couch without another word.

"Hey, I thought we could have a nice, sit-down dinner tonight. What do you think? I'm making some fish and French fries."

"Sure, I just need a minute to unwind."

"Okay, it won't be much longer."

He let the conversation be and continued to prepare the food, considering all the while exactly what he needed to discuss with her, precisely what he needed to get off his chest. *Everything pretty much boils down to her issues with Cassandra, and me needing space.*

The lure of fresh seafood and Cajun fries was apparently strong enough that he didn't need to announce he was done cooking. Sofia walked into the kitchen, poured a glass of tea from the fridge, and removed a couple plates from the cabinet for the two of them.

"Looks like you're wrapping up," she said as she stripped a large fillet of fish from the oil-soaked paper towels covering the ceramic plate, along with an oversized helping of fries.

"Yeah, just about. Looks like you're hungry. You want some cocktail sauce?"

"Sure."

He grabbed a glass bowl from the cabinet. A few spoons full of horseradish, ketchup, some lemon, and a touch of Tabasco was all that was needed to top off the crusted, fried fish. He added three spoons of the sauce to a glass saucer and placed it in front of Sofia as he joined her at the dining room table.

The perfect crunch coating the fish, mixed with the sweet spice of cocktail sauce, put a joyous touch on what Asher believed was going to be a tense conversation. He savored the moment and delighted in the comfort of Southernly cooking as he hesitated to utter what he had been thinking since the day prior.

"So, I've been meaning to talk to you about yesterday," he started. "I know we've had this conversation a million times before, but—"

"Then why are you bringing it up again?"

He was struck by her sternness, considering the way she had acted in front of Cassandra the previous day. Although, given her disdain for the woman, he wasn't overly shocked.

"I'm bringing it up again because she's my partner, Sofia."

"No, she's your *work wife*, Asher. Don't you get that? How do you think that makes me feel?"

He paused to consider whether he should take the comment seriously. "My work wife? And you think that's actually a thing?"

"It's not my opinion whether it's a thing. It's more so a fact."

"And what do you propose I do, exactly? Refuse to work with her because y'all don't get along?"

"That's not what I'm saying at all. I'm simply suggesting that maybe there should be a line between working together and hanging out in our home, alone with her."

He stopped to take a bite of the crisp fish, centering his thoughts before he responded. A swig of ice-cold tea washed down the satisfying flavor.

"So, you think that men shouldn't hang out with their female colleagues other than when they're in the office? I mean, I just—I just can't get my head around this. What do you think we're doing when we're 'home alone?'"

"That's not really for me to speculate, Asher. It's the principle of the matter. I don't like it, and I shouldn't have to explain myself any further."

He was becoming weary of the argument—the claim he had to endure all too often. *That's exactly what you're doing. Speculating. I shouldn't have to defend being cordial with my colleagues.*

"And if she continues to come over?" he asked.

She put down her fork and looked him dead in the eyes, licking the last bite off of her lips and brushing the hair from her eyes. "Then I'll take that to mean I can do as I please."

"Do what you *please*? Oh, you think *that's* how this is gonna play out?" He laughed, struggling to control his contempt for the conversation. He took one last bite of food and downed the remainder of his tea, a perfectly good dinner gone to waste, just as he had predicted. It was as if he could precisely foresee the way she would provoke him, and he no longer cared to be taunted and dredged through the mud.

Standing, Asher walked to the counter, dropping his plate and silverware into the sink. The clatter startled her, causing her to jump in her seat. "I'll tell you what," he said calmly. "You do what you gotta do."

"What the fuck does that mean? I get to sleep in the bed tonight?"

"You can throw a damn rave for all I care," he said. Then he walked into his office and quietly closed the door.

Chapter 66

The following morning brought horrible weather. Violent rain pelted the windshield as Cassandra pulled into Asher's driveway. The skies mirrored a black screen as the streetlamps flickered in single pinpoints lining the roadway, only outshone briefly by flashes of lightning running across a solid sky. She debated waiting it out versus making a mad dash for the door without an umbrella.

I'll have time to dry off over breakfast, she thought, and headed out.

Asher answered the door after only a few seconds. "Anyone hungry?" she asked.

"I'll take that off your hands," he responded, grabbing the coffee and crumpled bag from her hands. "Let's go out back. Not everyone is awake yet."

"Are you ready? Do you just wanna head out now?"

"Nonsense. I wanna enjoy my breakfast."

The rain hitting the clear and green glass of the sunroom created a relaxing ambiance over breakfast. Asher took a generous bite of his French cruller and washed it down with his piping-hot, black coffee. His eyes were drawn to Cassandra's breasts, which were made more luscious by her dripping shirt.

"You need a towel? Looks like the rain got the better of you," he said while wiping the glaze from his mouth.

"Yeah, if you have one handy," she said, rocking back and forth in the hammock.

He ran inside and returned with a white hand towel from the kitchen. "Here ya go. Looks like you have a bit of something on your collar, too," he pointed out. "That's a mighty colorful stain you got there."

She looked down, careful not to spill her mocha onto her white blouse. "Huh, probably just some lipstick from this morning. I tend to be a bit clumsy when getting ready. Thanks." She gestured with the towel.

"As always, thanks for the breakfast. It's only once in a blue moon I get catered to around here."

"I can see that." She smiled. "It's my pleasure."

Cassandra rolled her way out of the hammock and tiptoed to Asher, pulling out the chair next to him while peeping her head around the corner and into the house. "So, tell me. Are things getting any better with Sofia? I mean, it seems like she's been on edge lately."

"You don't need to worry about her. She's been at my throat for a while now, but I don't think there's anything you need to do to assuage her worries."

She put a hand on Asher's leg and leaned her head against her hand. "It's not *her* worries that I'm concerned about."

"I appreciate that. It's nice to have someone who's worried about *you* every once in a while."

"Of course. Isn't that what a partner is for?"

"What do you say we get out of here? If we stay any longer, we'll be on trial."

Cassandra grinned. "I have a feeling we're *always* under the microscope."

Chapter 67

As Asher and Cassandra stepped off the elevator, they were greeted by Xavier, who darted over to them the moment they caught his eye.

"Hey, Ash. Can we talk for a second?" he asked.

"I'll be in my office if you need me," said Cassandra.

Asher walked to Xavier's desk and took a seat. It was early enough in the morning that the cold air from the AC was audible as the machine pushed it through the ceiling vents, turning an already bleak building into a desolate icebox.

"What y'all been up to this morning?" Xavier asked as he threw on his windbreaker and rubbed his hands together, pulling his arms in tight.

"Not much, just coming from my place after having breakfast. What you been working on? You're here a bit earlier than usual."

Xavier paused, giving Asher a questioning look. "Cut the shit, dude. Why is it the two of you show up here almost every morning together? Don't you have your own damn cars? I told you to stay out of the candy, my boy."

"And I told you to keep your comments in your own damn department." Asher chuckled. "I might as well put on a broken record at this point—*we're partners*. It's bad enough I have to get it from my wife, but now you?"

"Okay, okay. I'll let it be. Just don't—"

"Yeah, I know. Don't do anything you wouldn't do. You *are* a broken record at this point. That's not exactly a glowing suggestion, by the way. Speaking of what you wouldn't do . . . what do you really think about this letter? When I was talking to Pierre about closing the double homicides, he was questioning why my father would refer to himself in the third person in the letter, if it really is him. You think I need to be worried?"

"You mean do *we* need to be worried."

"No, I mean me. I'll be the one without a job if this goes south, not you two. He made that very clear."

"Personally, I have my doubts. Like I said before, I think everything we have on him at this point is circumstantial at best. You're the one who went to Pierre, asking to close the cases. What do you really think?"

"I think it could be just like any other letter law enforcement has received from murderers over the years. He's taunting us, playing tricks. In particular, he was taunting me."

"What does Cassandra think about it? You ask her since we talked the other day?"

"Not really," Asher said as he pulled out his phone. *Come down to Xavier's,* he texted her. *Need ya for a minute.*

"Seriously? You're texting her? She's right there in the other room."

"Yeah, I know. I can't be wasting valuable energy like that. No caffeine, remember," he said, holding up his decaf.

Cassandra popped her head out of her office and scowled at them. "A text message? Really?"

"Decaf!" Asher said again.

She rolled her eyes and remained in her chair, scooting herself into the hallway.

"Come on." Asher waved toward himself. "Nobody likes a slowpoke."

She continued to roll down the hallway, one double-footed push at a time, her middle finger high in the air like a flag of pride.

"I love the enthusiasm." Asher smiled.

"I hope my travels were worth it."

"Hold that thought," Xavier said.

Asher got into it. "The letter. What do you think about the reference to my father in the third person if he's the one who sent it?"

"Isn't it a bit late to be playing guessing games? You already went to Pierre, and he gave you exactly what you wanted."

"What do you think about it?" Asher repeated.

"Personally, I think you're right."

"Seriously?" Xavier said. "You were just saying how it's all circumstantial. What the hell?"

"Yeah, I know. But I've been thinking about it, and I think Asher is right. It's too big of a coincidence. Sure, the evidence is circumstantial, but when you put it all together as a single case, it's pretty compelling."

Asher turned to Xavier. "At least *one* of you has a brain."

"Well, Scarecrow here hopes you're right, or Pierre is gonna tornado your ass."

Chapter 68

As Damien entered Landry's Seafood House that day for lunch, his long, black coat was dripping with water from the torrential onslaught of rain. He pushed his hand back through his damp hair and removed his glasses as he approached the waitress behind the podium. The softly lit restaurant and bar smelled of fried seafood and beer.

"Hi, how many?" the waitress said in greeting.

"Oh, I'm meeting someone upstairs."

"Okay, you can follow me."

She escorted him up the old wooden stairs, which were outlined by a gold railing, to the second floor. It served as the primary eatery; the downstairs bar was vacant.

"Are you able to find the other guest?" she asked.

"I think I'll be okay."

The shimmer of Sofia's silver NOLA necklace caught his eye from across the room. She was seated next to a window at the edge of the restaurant, overlooking Damien's public office.

"Is this seat taken?" He smiled as he pulled out a chair across the table.

"Of course not." She gave him a smirk in return.

The restaurant had an old-timey feel, with the waitstaff formally dressed in black-and-white attire. The faint smell of alcohol made its way across the room, only briefly interrupted by a lingering aroma of shrimp and the chatter of nearby diners.

"It's good to see you again," she said.

"Yeah, you too. Speaking of, I'm glad you decided to stop by the other day. I was thinking maybe I scared you away with the flowers at work. Your call was a pleasant surprise."

"Of course not. I have yet to meet a woman who doesn't enjoy a fresh bouquet of flowers once in a while."

The march of mules and the roll of their carriages sounded from the street in front of Jackson Square. St. Louis Cathedral was framed in the background against a charcoal sky.

"It's a beautiful day, huh," she said.

"You read my mind."

"I don't know about you, but the rain calms me."

"I can definitely relate. That's how I feel about the riverwalk," he said, looking out to the water. "It's perfect, even in this weather."

The Steamboat *Natchez* was making its last call for the afternoon boarding as the daytime breeze and moisture escaping the clouds pushed against the window, accentuating the feeling of comfort, the sense of calm, Sofia felt with Damien.

"Can I get you anything to drink?" the waitress asked.

"Merlot for me, please," she said.

"And for you, sir?"

"Ice water. Please."

"I'll be back around for your orders."

"Wine for lunch, huh. I'm guessing you don't have to be back at the university after this?"

Sofia shrugged. "It's academia. I pretty much make my own schedule. Besides, academics aren't shy of the bottle. We need something to calm our nerves after dealing with all the drama and egos day in and day out."

"Is it the egos for you or someone else, perhaps?"

Sofia remained silent, only the corner of her mouth turned upward, hiding an unspoken "yes" beneath the tautness of her lips.

"Here we are," said the waitress after a moment. "One glass of wine and an ice water. Are you ready to order?"

"I think we'll take another minute." Damien spoke so abruptly, he almost cut her off.

"No problem. I'll make my way back around."

Sofia drew a sip from the maroon-filled glass as Damien stared out the window once more. "So, tell me," she said. "What's an inner-city guy like you, working these streets, doing interested in a college professor—much less one with my baggage?"

He laughed as if she had delivered the punchline of the world's raunchiest joke. "And what makes you think you have baggage?" he asked. "I like to think of it as nothing more than a life change. You're on your way out, I'm assuming, no?"

Her eyes floated upward in response to the directness of the statement, to his way of speaking so matter-of-factly.

"I'm no longer sure of anything on that front."

Damien looked through her with an intense glare that was impossible to divert. Then he rose from his seat, leaning forward across the table, approaching with the utmost caution.

"Is it okay if I am sure?" he said, and kissed her plush lips.

Chapter 69

assandra and Xavier might have delivered a split decision on whether Mauricio authored the letter, but Asher was sure of himself. Although he hadn't been close to his father, he felt his investigative skills were on point. As a matter of fact, he loved it when colleagues doubted him—it provided an internal drive that propelled him forward.

Asher returned to his office and began work on rounding out the case files for the double homicides. He needed to meet with Agnes to finalize the death certificates and confirm the manners of death, but it was nothing more than a formality at this point. As in many other counties, law enforcement investigators did much of the research into homicides—along with the medical examiner's office, particularly at the crime scene—but the chief medical examiner signed the death certificates.

It was after lunch when Asher heard a soft rap on his office door. Sofia popped her head around the corner. "Hey, am I disturbing you?"

"No, not at all."

"I brought a pick-me-up," she said as she held out a coffee, waiting patiently for him to take it off her hands.

"Thanks, but I already have some decaf." He pointed to the empty Dunkin' Donuts cup on his desk.

"Oh, okay," she said, but just waited with an extended hand. After a moment, he grabbed the cup and placed it to the side.

From her office, Cassandra could see Sofia standing in front of Asher, attempting to rope him in with amends to their broken relationship. Cassandra knew what he wanted, and it wasn't to stroke the regrets of an unsupportive wife. He glanced through the blinds and caught Cassandra, eye to eye, watching them.

"So, what are you doing here?" he asked Sofia. "You never come by the office."

"I just wanted to smooth things over and apologize for last night. I know I said some things that were spiteful, and I just wanted to say I'm sorry. I had no right making those accusations and saying what I did."

Asher leaned against the corner of his desk and folded his arms. His attention was fully split, aware that the current conversation, including Sofia's body language, was an act, both for the fake apology and for Cassandra openly watching from her office.

"Well, I'm not all that sure what you want me to say. Telling me that you'll do as you please doesn't exactly smooth things over."

"I know it doesn't fix everything, but—"

"You know, working with a forensic psychologist over the years has made me pretty good at one thing," he said as he made his way around to his chair behind the desk.

"Really? That's who you wanna talk about right now?"

"Reading people."

Sofia's eyes hardened, and her mouth fell flat. She attempted to force a counterfeit smile, but all she could do was stand frozen at the center of the room.

"One thing *some* people do when they feel a sense of guilt, a feeling of shame for their actions, is they turn that guilt outward and onto those around them. This makes it openly apparent that there's something more to what's being said. They become somewhat of a mirror."

She began to fidget with her hands as she cocked her head to the side. "And what's that?"

Cassandra could see Asher now seated behind his desk, talking to Sofia as if someone was getting a lesson from Pierre. She stood at the foot of his desk like a student begging for a bump in her grade just before the final.

"You tell me."

"There's nothing to tell, Asher. What are you accusing me of, exactly?"

He smirked. "Far less than what I've been accused of *by you* over the last few weeks."

"Oh, give me a break. I haven't accused you of anything."

"Sure, other than screwing my partner. Or, better yet, my 'work wife.'"

"That's not fair."

"You're damn right it isn't fair." He nodded. "But it is what I have to deal with at home, on top of all this bullshit." He picked up and dropped a stack of papers on his desk. "You realize what I've been trying to figure out, what I've been dealing with here?"

She remained immobile, a blank expression across her face.

"I've been trying to figure out why my damn *father*, of all people, is running around murdering couples who are cheating on their spouses. I've been having to walk around all day knowing that my dead father was killing people, and I don't have the first damn clue why. So I go to my boss, and I convince him that I've solved these cases, Mauricio is to blame, and all the while I don't have a fucking clue as to what's really goin' on. So, please, tell me exactly what I can do to ease *your* mind so I can assure *you* I'm not fucking my colleague. I would hate for you to lose any more sleep over your stressful situation."

"Asher, I had no idea," she said, walking around the side of his desk.

"You sure as hell don't." He stood up, shoving his chair into the desk. Then he threw on his coat and tossed the coffee into the trashcan. "But I'm beginning to think I might. If you'll excuse me, I need to consult my work wi—my colleague."

Chapter 70

*S*ofia walked out of the office and pressed the down button for one of the several gleaming elevators. *That's fine. If he doesn't need me, if he doesn't want my apology, that's fine. I can get ten more Ashers at the snap of a finger*, she thought.

The elevator chimed, and she stepped into the empty box as the steel doors began to close behind her. Before they could seal, a hand interrupted.

"Oh, hey Sofia," Xavier said with surprise. "I didn't see you back there."

"Hey, Xavier. Bottom floor?"

"Yep, thanks."

He sensed that something was off. She was leaning against the wall with her arms folded and a blank but intense stare at the wall of white, glowing buttons as if she were trying to press each one telepathically.

"You good, girl? Looks like you're about to erupt."

"You've been friends with him forever, right? How in the world do you deal with his temper and smart-ass comments?"

"Who, Asher?" He chuckled. "Well, his short fuse and sarcasm are what keep me coming back for more."

"I'm serious. I don't know how much more I can take. It's like this job is killing him. Killing *us*."

An abrupt jolt jostled the elevator as the number one lit up with an orange glow above the door, followed by another ding. As Xavier walked off the elevator, she grabbed his arm and pulled him aside.

"What do I do? It's like no matter what I say, I'm on mute. It just doesn't resonate. I can't do it any longer."

Xavier adjusted the strap to the computer bag slung over his shoulder and looked around the lobby, sure he was about to get caught up in drama he wanted no part of. "This sounds like something y'all need to talk about. I love ya, girl, but only you know what needs to change with the two of you. Maybe he needs some space."

After a moment of silence, they exited the lobby and stopped under the overhang of the building, dodging the blistering sun that was only exacerbated by the thick, wet air lingering from the rain.

"Look, don't tell him I said anything, but I'm worried he's getting a bit too close with Cassandra. Is there anything you've seen at work? Anything I need to be concerned about?"

Damien was watching them from his Jeep in the parking lot. "She better not screw this up," he mumbled under his breath.

"And you think stalking him is gonna help the matter?" Xavier said.

"I'm not stalking him. He brings her to my damn house nearly every day. Or she's picking him up for work when he can clearly drive himself."

"They're partners, Sofia. That's what they do. They *work* together. Like I said, maybe he needs some space."

"All I give him is space. That's all he asks for to begin with."

"Okay, so give it to him. Just make sure that space doesn't turn into neglect."

Sofia gave him a look as if he'd just insulted her mother.

"Neglect? What, you think I'm just gonna up and leave?"

"I didn't say that. I just don't wanna see him get hurt, any more than I want that for you."

They made their way into the parking lot. Sofia opened the driver's door of her car and tossed her purse onto the passenger side. Xavier went to his own vehicle nearby.

Damien slid down into his seat and pulled his hat down low. The sun was cutting across the cab, shining over half of his face, leaving the other side sunken in the Wrangler's shadow.

"I've got a feeling I'm not the one who's gonna get hurt," Sofia said to Xavier before getting in.

Chapter 71

The leopard's blue-green eyes darted from left to right. As Owen rounded the corner, the cat immediately became fixated on his presence.

"Here we are," Ivette said. "Meet you back here in a couple hours?"

The cat crouched, its shoulder blades rising above its back.

"Sounds good," he said as she grazed his hand with hers and walked away. "Remember, you need as much data as possible for your ethogram."

"Yes, ma'am," he said with a sardonic smile.

Owen had waited three years to take Dr. Broussard's animal behavior course, which had a research component based at the Audubon Zoo. She was the top expert in the field at UNO, and she had shown a unique fondness for Owen from the start of the semester.

The Amur Leopard paced from one corner of the enclosure to the other, sidestepping its surroundings and dropping below the hanging branches without breaking its gaze, showing perfect knowledge of its environment. The sounds of a waterfall within the enclosure drowned out any conversations from passersby.

Owen sat on the wooden bench directly in front of the pen and began to record the individual behaviors of the feline. He needed to catalog each action the cat made before proceeding with his semester project.

He leaned down to grab a stopwatch from his dark red bookbag, fumbling through the various pockets that were crammed with assorted items—scratch paper, a ruler, a calculator, gum wrappers.

"It's interesting to see how predators act when you put them in a cage," Damien said, taking a seat on the bench beside him.

Owen rustled, startled in his seat. "Um, yeah. Sure."

Damien took a sip of water and adjusted his sunglasses. "I assume you're here doing some type of study? I saw you writing in your notebook."

"Yeah, I'm here for a college course. What about you?"

"Oh, me? Not much. Just another lone wolf out and about. I do this sort of thing in my spare time."

The leopard began climbing up the larger of two tree trunks spanning the enclosure. The cat lounged at the top of a wooden bridge, resting its head on its enormous paw.

"You learn anything new?" Damien asked.

"Not yet. I've only been here a few minutes. I need to record everything I can for some preliminary work before I start my project."

Damien nodded. "It's great to see them up close, isn't it? But can you imagine what it would be like to see them hunt in the wild?" He put his arm over the back of the bench, his hand nearing Owen's shoulder. Then he turned to the man, leaning his head forward as he looked over the top of his glasses. "They can take down prey two to three times their size. Deer, wild boar—they make easy work of it."

Owen shifted in his seat, leaning against the armrest that trapped him between Damien and the bench's edge. "That's crazy," he said as a single bead of sweat ran down his temple.

"You pick them to study because of their rarity?" Damien asked.

"What do you mean?"

"Well, there's estimated to be less than one hundred—possibly even as few as thirty—left in the wild. What I mean is, they're rare," Damien added, crossing his leg toward Owen and leaning his head against his hand at the back of the bench.

"I had no idea," Owen said. "Hopefully, the zoos can keep them alive. It'd be horrible if they went extinct."

"Oh, I think they'll be fine," Damien said assuredly, looking up to the sky. "Leopards have evolved to do leopard things. Besides, big-time predators like to work alone, other than the occasional company of a female here or there. I'm sure you can agree, no?"

"Agree?"

"Yes. The company of a female is good from time to time, no?" Damien repeated sternly.

"Sure. I don't see why not."

"You see, it becomes a problem, however, when multiple leopards begin to encroach on one another's territory. They begin to fight over the females."

"Well, if there's only thirty or so operating across their range at a given time, I'm sure they can learn to share."

"Hmm." Damien grinned as he spoke. "I suppose we'll just have to wait and see."

$$Chapter\ 72$$

The sunlight crept through the minute cracks between the bedroom blinds, hitting the walls in thin slits that scattered across the dark room in a symmetrical fan. Asher had slept in to avoid crossing paths with Sofia before she left for work. The cases were finally closed, and he felt he had earned a day off.

After walking into the gently lit kitchen, he opened the cabinet above the coffee pot and fumbled around for a filter, jamming it into the pot with half-opened eyes. He ineptly poured one, two, three, four heaping, messy scoops of decaf under the lid, missing the pot altogether on the last scoop. Then he slammed the lid shut and dropped himself into the nearest chair, waiting through the excruciating seconds for a sip of dawn.

As he began pouring the first cup, he felt his heart begin to race, and a cold flash shot through his body from his forehead down to his toes as shooting pricks of pain filled his fingertips. The room began to spin, rapidly. The signs were all too familiar—perhaps even banal at this point.

I need to know whether he wrote the damn letter, Asher thought. *I can't afford to lose my job. My home is already a mess.*

He sat back down at the dining room table and rested his head on his forearm, his arm on the tabletop. *I've gotta stop this. Everything will be fine. There is no other answer. He had to have done it.*

It's where all the evidence points. I have the evidence to back me up.

His body began to tremble, his lips quivering. A single sip of coffee was now knotting his stomach, churning as it made one gurgling shriek after another.

Maybe Cass can ease my mind, reassure me that we haven't made a mistake. She's really been the only one on my side with this.

He pulled his phone from his pocket and placed it on the table in front of him. Then he dialed Cassandra on speaker while running his hands through his hair and fiddling with the full cup.

The phone rang once. Twice. Three times. He waited for a good ten rings at least, but there was no answer. The final ring sent another wave of icy cold down throughout his body as he ended the call, this time accompanied by a gut-wrenching queasiness.

"Come on," he mumbled to himself.

He dialed again. Ring after ring, he waited at the table, staring at her name across the screen. They passed at an utterly painful rate. Soon, he hung up once more and slid the phone away from himself. It fell into the chair at the opposite end of the table.

The sweat began to drip from his brow and down his cheek, hanging on to the five-o'clock shadow that edged his jaw.

He needed control. He needed to know it wasn't a fuckup. He needed reassurance that he wasn't going to lose his job. The nausea wrecked his stomach as he began to tremble more intensely.

A black box, Asher. Nothing can enter the black box. He tried to imagine the shape—the three-dimensional cube—over and over, but images of Sofia and the homicides continued to seep into his mind, one after another. His eyes were closed, but he noticed the sun beginning to crawl into the kitchen as the inside of his eyelids changed from black to dark red and back to black again. It was as if a strobe light were forcing its way into his mind.

"A single, black box. Nothing else," he repeated aloud. "One black box."

He stood up and rushed to the bedroom, leaving the still-steaming coffee on the table. *I've gotta get the hell out of here.*

He grabbed his pistol and placed it inside his waistband. Then he slipped on his shoes, grabbed his phone from the chair, and hurried out to the carport. He paused for a moment before opening the car door, looking out over the roof of the Vette, out to the rest of the neighborhood, which was covered in a morning fog. The truth was somewhere in all of that. It was muddled, but it was there.

He climbed into the car and started the ignition. As he backed out of the driveway, he had an eerie feeling. *There's no way Pierre is letting me off that easy.*

Chapter 73

Asher made his way to St. Charles Avenue, then drove toward the Pontchartrain Expressway. He downshifted into second gear, shoving the engine into high RPMs. The whistle of the blown 383 could be heard from half a mile away.

Perhaps the lakefront can turn the day around, he thought.

He exited at St. Bernard Avenue and headed toward Lakeshore Drive, just behind UNO and the Lakefront Arena. He drove along the waterfront, back and forth, multiple times before stopping at a small, lakefront parking lot behind Privateer Place—a student housing center on the north side of campus.

The lake was clear, with a lingering stream of fog blanketing the water not far from the coast, an ever-evolving shimmer of light dancing across the waves. As he stepped out of the car, he immediately felt a sense of relief impossible to find amid the bustle of the city.

Walking to a bench near the walkway, he sat alone, overlooking Lake Pontchartrain.

"Justin always answers," he said to himself.

He dialed the therapist's number as he sat cross-legged on the bench, closing his eyes in the morning breeze. A faint mist passed over him from the waves crashing against the cement wall only feet away.

Justin didn't answer.

Ring after ring, Asher could only think about how those who were supposed to be there for him were only there when they were required to be.

It's beyond ironic, he thought. *I thought your work wife was supposed to pick up on the first ring. No answer. Surely, your therapist who is responsible for your sanity will answer. Of course not.*

He began walking along the water's edge, watching the seagulls and a lone pelican land on the extended stretch of cement that ran the length of the lakeshore. He stopped and leaned against the waist-high wall, looking below at the waves crumbling against the rocks.

Either way it turns out, there's nothing more I could have done. If I turn out to be right, great. It's finished. If I'm wrong, at least I have Cass to back me up. There's no way Pierre lets us both go. He won't have a department to run.

He began walking back to the car, the sun rounding the clouds as it moved higher in the sky. He tried Justin once more in hopes of a reassuring conversation.

No answer.

As soon as his thumb hit the "end call" button, his phone began to vibrate, Cassandra's name flashing across the screen.

"Hey, you called?" she asked.

"Yeah, a little while ago."

"What's up? I didn't think we were goin' in today."

"No, I don't plan on it. We need a day off after the last couple weeks. I was just calling for something really quick, but I think I got it."

"Are you sure? We can meet up if you want. It's been a while since we've gotten together outside of work."

"Maybe sometime soon. I think I need to be there this

afternoon when Sofia gets home. There's some shit we need to handle. Thanks, though."

"Okay, well, call me if you need anything."

"Will do."

"Oh, Ash . . ."

"Yeah?"

"Don't worry about Pierre. We'll deal with it either way."

Chapter 74

The crème-colored, cinderblock classroom was filled with thirty students, and Owen always managed to acquire a seat in the front row. He loved watching her work, the way she commanded the class with a never-ending knowledge of animal behavior. He cherished her walk, back and forth from her computer to the whiteboard.

Her tan legs in that black skirt were second to none.

"That's all I have for today," Ivette said to the class. "I'll see you next week."

While the other students ambled out, Owen approached the desk at the front of the classroom. "Dr. Broussard, do you have a minute after class? I was hoping we could sit down and talk about my project."

She looked at her watch, then glanced around the room. Students were still leaving at a slothful pace.

"I'm ready for lunch, but if you wanna meet me up in my office, we can discuss things there if that's okay with you." She winked.

"I'll see you there."

It was just after noon when she arrived, computer bag thrown over her shoulder with an armful of papers. She leaned in to unlock her office door as the massive pile of work began to slide from her hands.

"Here, let me get that for you," Owen said.

Ivette transferred the work to his hands, which freed her up to unlock the door. He stepped inside before she closed the door behind him and set her computer bag on the desk.

The room had a stunning view of campus—the UNO Quad and library were visible from the corner office. The midday sun shone down onto the bright green, St. Augustine grass across the yard, creating an appealing contrast to the cloudless, baby-blue sky.

"So, you need to discuss your *project*, is it?"

Owen turned around and locked the office door before taking a seat in front of her desk. The room was filled to the brim with family pictures, academic certificates, and books, ranging from ecology textbooks to Lane's *Power, Sex, Suicide: Mitochondria and the Meaning of Life.*

"From the looks of it yesterday evening, you had things under control collecting your preliminary data. What's up?" she asked as she sat on the edge of her desk, facing him. She slipped off her three-carat, diamond wedding ring and placed it next to the computer keyboard before coating her hands with lotion.

"Yeah, I've got it under control. I really just wanted to see. you."

"Oh? And why is that?" Ivette asked as she uncrossed her legs and leaned back onto the desk.

"We never got to finish what we started."

The tip of her turquoise, slingback heel met his knee and slowly pushed his leg open. She ran the pump down the inside of his thigh and up to his groin. From the looks of it, he wasn't objecting.

"And what is that, exactly?" she asked.

"Why don't you come sit down right here," he said, tapping

his leg. "We'll talk about the first thing that pops up."

"You've got to be *kidding* me." Ivette burst out laughing. "That tacky bullshit doesn't actually work on women, does it? Oh, I'm sorry. I'm sure it does work on the *girls* around campus."

"You weren't opposed to my boyish charm before," he retorted.

"Maybe that's because your *boyish* charm is attached to some not-so-boyish attributes. Keep up the attitude, and you're really gonna get it."

She stood in front of the chair, hiking up her skirt to just below her ass. He could see the faintest glimpse of her black, cheeky underwear.

"You promise?" he asked.

"I don't make promises I can't keep," she said as she lowered herself onto his lap.

Chapter 75

efore she could unzip his pants, they heard a quiet knock on the door—three quick raps of the knuckles.

"Who the hell is that?" Owen said. "You have a meeting with someone?"

"No," she said, her voice delicately cautious. "No one ever bothers me when the door is closed."

Looking toward the door, she called out, "Who is it?"

No answer.

"Yes? Who is it?" Ivette repeated.

They looked at one another, not sure what to do. The shadow on the other side of the frosted door, however, didn't budge.

She jumped up and let down her skirt as Owen hurriedly crossed his legs and faced the desk.

"Who is it?" she asked one last time with her head to the door. She looked back to Owen, who was trying his hardest to act remotely normal.

The only thing to do was unlock the door, considering someone, anyone, could have seen Owen enter the office. As she turned back, the shadow was motionless, seeming insistent on receiving a response.

As she cracked opened the door, her forehead was met with

an icy, black silencer screwed to the barrel of a .45. Surprisingly, she didn't make a sound. She slowly stepped backward into the office with her hands up to her shoulders, managing to retreat all the way to her desk before Owen realized what was occurring.

"What the *fuck*?" he said in a surprised yet quiet tone.

Instead of a verbal response, Ivette's head shot backward as the jacketed hollow-point expanded upon entering the center of her forehead, fragmenting on impact. The empty casing was ejected from the port of the pistol and landed on a nearby bookshelf next to one of Ivette's favorite novels, *Sex at Dawn*. The faint smell of gunpowder emerged into the air as a pale stream of smoke escaped the barrel and disappeared, floating across the room.

Her body fell limp, and she collapsed where she was standing.

Owen climbed over the desk, fumbled, and slid across the papers strewn about there. He tried to open the office window before realizing it was permanently locked. Then he resorted to pathetic reasoning, explaining why his life should be spared, why it was such a big mistake to murder a student.

"Come on, you don't wanna do this, trust me. Please. You know how bad this will get for you if you kill a professor *and* her student? Come on. What do you want? Tell me what you want, and I'll make it happen. *Please.*"

The two-tone Springfield 1911 was intimidating enough with its long, five-inch barrel. Add the blacked-out, seven-inch silencer, and anyone standing at the opposing end would have no quarrel being quiet.

If I scream, I'm already dead, Owen thought.

His back was now pinned against the office window, his hands up, palms out. His blue jeans slowly became darker as urine flowed down the inside of his leg and formed a pitiful puddle between his feet.

"Please," he repeated. "I'll do anything. Just name it. *Please.*"

"Shut up."

"Okay, okay. I'm sorry. I'm sorry," he pleaded as he turned his head sideways in an attempt to avoid the pressure of the silencer against his forehead.

He was trapped. The only way out was back over the desk or through the silencer attached to the end of a .45-caliber pistol that was clearly capable of turning his head into a canoe.

"Look," Owen continued at a whisper, "what's done is done. We can both walk out of here, no questions asked. Just, please. You don't have to."

"It's too late for apologies. And you're right, what's done is done."

The hollow-point entered just above his ear and fragmented with no outlet. The second casing ejected and bounced off the wall, landing in the yellow puddle on the floor, which was now beneath Owen's head. His eyes remained wide, fixated on a pair of red-bottom shoes as the blood mixed with urine.

Chapter 76

"Hey, I'm glad you could make it," Damien said as he opened the door for Sofia. "Come on in."

"Thanks. I was trying to get here as quickly as I could, but I had one last thing to wrap up at the university."

"No worries," he said, shutting the door behind her.

She put her purse on the counter and turned, smiling and giving him a sidelong look. "Do I smell something baking?"

The combination of apple and cinnamon sugar was unmistakable; she closed her eyes and took a deep breath.

"You caught me. I'm a professional chef in my spare time," he said with a straight face.

"*Professional*, huh?"

"Well, I'll let you be the judge of that." He held out an apron. "Turn around."

"For me?"

"Apple turnovers." He pointed to the counter. "We still have another batch to make."

She turned her back to Damien as he slid the apron over the top of her head, tying a tight bow in the back before running his hands across her shoulders and down her arms. "There you are."

"How do I look?" she asked with her hands on her hips.

"Like a culinary *artist*."

He pulled the pan of puff pastry toward them and placed a cup of egg wash with a brush in front of her.

"So, how long have you been a pro baker?" She giggled.

"Oh, for as long as I can remember. My father was a chef. He used to cook nearly every night when I was young. He taught me pretty much everything I know."

He dipped the brush into the cup and handed it to her. "Just a light coat around the edges will do."

"Do you still spend a lot of time cooking with him?"

"My father? Not for many years. He passed away when I was a teenager."

"I'm sorry to hear that," she said as she placed the brush back into the cup. "I can't imagine what it would be like to lose a parent at that age."

Damien paused and leaned against the counter, staring at the gleaming pastry. "Next, we cut," he said before handing her the pizza cutter. "Six even squares." He traced with his finger.

Then he walked to a nearby drawer and fetched a can opener, along with a can of diced apples from the cabinet. He leaned over her shoulder to examine her work before nodding. "Not bad. Not bad at all."

"Thank you, Chef."

At that moment, the oven beeped. He took the finished turnovers out and placed them onto a cooling rack. The tops of the pastries were dusted with a crisp, white snow, complemented by a subtle, brown caramelization around the edges.

"Oh my god, that smells amazing." She gasped. "I hope mine turn out as good as yours."

"Now all you need are some apples and cinnamon, and we'll be ready to close 'em up."

He opened the can and handed it to her before setting a

small bottle of cinnamon onto the counter. She carefully placed the apples at the center of each square and dusted them with a touch of the brown powder.

"Perfect," he said. "Let's fold each one over, pinch the edges with a fork, and then we're ready for one last coat of egg wash and sugar on top."

"I have no idea how to do this."

He stood behind her, grabbing the fork with one hand while folding the pastry with the other. The tines lightly entered the dough, crimping the edges with a parallel pattern of four straight lines. "Just like this," he said. "See?"

He remained behind her, looking over her shoulder while holding her waist as she began closing the pastries. The scent of bourbon vanilla made its way from his beard up to her nose as a ripple of arousal shot from her neck down to the small of her back.

"Is that it?" she whispered.

"Perfect."

He leaned in closer and nudged her earlobe with his nose. The soft prickle of his beard ran against her cheek as his lips rested on her shoulder. Her focus shifted from baking to how deeply she didn't want him to stop, how much she needed him to continue providing what she was required to steal from her husband.

You have no idea how bad I need this, she thought.

Sofia turned around and leaned backward, her hands gripping the counter's edge at her sides. He moved in closer and ran his hands down to her thighs, picking her up and setting her onto the counter. Her legs wrapped around his waist.

"This okay?" he asked, his voice a mellow cadence.

Her arms were draped over his shoulders as he kissed the

front of her neck, working his way up to her chin, her rose-colored lips.

"More than okay."

As he picked her up and began walking down the hallway, she felt how hard he was, how sure he was with her. They entered the room, and he stopped in front of the bed before lowering her down onto the mattress, so gentle and slow it seemed impossible for him to have that much control.

He paused for a moment, taking her in, as he realized how perfectly it had all unfolded.

———

As she slept, Damien heard the buzz of her phone on the nightstand. Asher's name flashed across the screen.

I suppose you want her back, Damien thought.

He picked up the phone and swiped the green button, answering the call.

"Hey, you left work yet?" Asher said. All he heard on the other end of the line was a steady string of soft breaths.

"Sofia? Can you hear me?"

An inhale. Silence. Exhale.

"Hello? You there?"

Oh, I'm here, Damien thought.

Chapter 77

The following morning, Asher and Cassandra arrived at the office later than their usual time. There were no new cases to their knowledge, but Asher did want to discuss the letter a bit more with Xavier and Cassandra, and follow up with Agnes and Xavier to see if there were any last additions to evidence he could include in the files before moving on.

"So, it looks like you may have gotten a decent-quality sleep last night," Cassandra said to Asher, waiting for the elevator to reach their floor. "The missus finally come around to her senses and talk things over with you?"

Asher shook his head. "I wish that were the case. You're right, though. I did get some amazing sleep last night. But that's only because she never came home."

Cassandra's eyes grew wider. "*Wow*, didn't see that one coming."

"Tell me about it. I called her late into the evening around dinnertime, but I couldn't get her on the phone. I'm about at my rope's end, I'll tell you that."

She moved to the same side of the elevator, closer to him. "You know, you're always welcome to crash at my place if you need to. I know it isn't ideal with her already having issues with me and all, but the offer is on the table if you ever need to get out of there."

His eyes brightened as the elevator opened. "Thanks. If she comes back, and I can't handle it, I may take you up on that."

"Aw, shit," she said in anticipation as they stepped off the elevator and through the office doors.

The moment they entered the office, Pierre shot up from behind his desk and marched toward them, his face beet red with a tiny line of spittle escaping the corner of his mouth.

"Good morning, Boss. What can we do for you today?" Asher smiled with sarcasm, knowing there was nothing he could do to stop whatever reign of terror Pierre already had planned for the two of them.

"No, a *good* morning would be if I didn't have to clean up this epic fucking catastrophe the two of you have so reliably created!" the chief shouted.

They looked at him, baffled, neither with a single clue as to what he was so worked up over.

"Oh, you look confused, numbnuts. Why don't we step into my office so I can recap what I've been dealing with all morning while y'all were taking your good ole time getting into work today." He pointed to his office.

"I think someone has something to tell us," Asher whispered to Cassandra. They kept pace a mere two steps behind their boss.

As they made their way down the hall, they passed Xavier's desk. He was putting forth every effort to mind his own business and not get dragged into what was sure to be a painful meeting.

"Hey, buddy," Asher said to him, breaking the walk. "Would you like to join us? I think we're about to have a very lively, eye-opening experience. I would hate for you to miss it."

Xavier remained silent, slowly raising his middle finger.

"Oh, that's no way to treat an old friend," Asher said derisively.

"Have fun," Xavier responded.

Pierre stood at the door as they entered his office and sat in the two chairs in front of his desk. He slammed the door so forcefully the blinds fell to the floor. Asher raised his shoulders with surprise and glanced backward.

"Congratulations, you have single-handedly fucked up your last case," Pierre said to Asher. "Although, maybe I should credit *both* of you, since you agree on virtually everything." He looked to Cassandra.

"What are you talking about?" Asher asked.

He tossed a set of crime scene photos onto the desk in front of Asher. "*This* is what I'm talking about—another couple murdered at UNO yesterday evening, a professor and her student. Apparently, Daddy continues to knock off a few more from the grave."

"What the fuck?" Cassandra said as she leaned forward and grabbed the pictures from Asher's hands.

"How was she strangled?" Asher asked. "I don't see any ligature marks or what was used to strangle her in these pictures. Who took these?"

"That's because there is nothing. They were both shot," Pierre said.

Asher looked up at him as if it were his first day on the job. "No. Absolutely not. This isn't the same case. No way. All of our victims were shot and strangled in pairs. This is another case altogether. You're not putting this on me," he said as he tossed the pictures back onto Pierre's desk.

"I'll put it on whoever I want," Pierre said. "It's a couple, the woman was married, and you may wanna look at some of these again," he said, tossing a single photo back into Asher's lap. "The gun was left at the scene—a 1911. You're telling me that's a coincidence? I don't think so."

Asher sat, shaking his head from side to side. Not only was he wrong about his father, but now the killer was changing his MO.

"Let me make this short and sweet," Pierre said. "The two of you are suspended. Leave your badges on the desk on your way out."

"You're letting us go? Are you shitting me?" Asher said as he stood up.

"I'm *suspending* your asses. If that's not up to your liking, I can straight-up fire both of you if you'd prefer. Is that what you want? If I were you, I wouldn't be asking any questions. I don't even know why I'm only suspending you, but take it as a gift. Now get the hell out of here before I change my mind."

They placed their badges on Pierre's desk and began walking out of the office. Asher pushed aside the blinds on the floor with his shoe and opened the door.

Before he closed it, he turned to the chief. "I know you think I'm wrong, but my father was involved in this."

Chapter 78

Upon leaving the office, Asher and Cassandra drove southeast on Esplanade to the French Market to walk, talk, and blow off some steam after a more-than-surprising morning. The sun was making its way into the navy-blue and cotton sky, and they had the whole of the day before them.

The open-air market was buzzing with tourists, souvenir shops, Cajun cuisine, and blues music, with Albert King's "Born Under a Bad Sign" playing in the background. The smell of crawfish étouffée and jambalaya, tomatoes and rich spices, made its way out from a pocket-sized kitchen tucked deep within the center of the market, flanked by a small hat shop and freshly powdered funnel cakes.

"What's the plan?" Cassandra asked Asher as they walked down the center of the market, dodging bodies yet lured by the smell of fresh seafood.

"Plan? What plan?" he huffed. "Unless Pierre finds a reason to reinstate us, I assume there is no plan."

"So, we're just gonna give up, just like that? All of our hard work leading up to this is just gonna go to waste? I can't live with that. No investigator in their right mind would have passed on your father as a suspect."

"Then what do you suppose we do? It's not like we can run

around playing cops when we're no longer part of the unit—at least, not for the time being. You heard him, though. We're suspended, not fired."

Asher's phone rang, buzzing with the *Halloween* theme song as Michael Myers's picture displayed across the screen.

"Hey, Agnes. What's good?"

"Hey, sweetie. Where you at? You in the office?"

Asher whispered to Cassandra, covering the phone's speaker, "It's Agnes."

"See if you can get any info out of her," she muttered back.

He spoke into the phone again. "I wish. I'm actually walking through the French Market with Cassandra. We had an, uh, unfortunate run-in with Pierre this morning. He gave the two of us a bit of time off. I'm sure you already know why."

"*What?* How in the world can he afford to let y'all go? I guess he's officially lost it, huh?"

"Well, we're suspended for now, but we'll see where it goes. What can you tell me about the most recent murders? I'm assuming you and Xavier have already been at the scene. Pierre was showing us some pictures."

Cassandra nudged Asher's arm and pointed to a nearby menu written in blue and yellow chalk on a small folding blackboard. Boudin balls, crawfish étouffée, and seafood gumbo were three of the many choices.

"Isn't it a bit early for lunch?" he said, covering the phone once more.

"Hell no," she said. "What you want?"

Without hesitation, he pointed to the boudin balls. "Make sure you grab some remoulade sauce."

"Yeah, we were there late last night," Agnes said. "Based on the cause of death, I can't say for sure it's the same guy, but once you add in the fact a 1911 was found at the scene, it's a bit hard to say otherwise."

"That's what Pierre was saying. You find any ligature marks on the female at all? Anything?"

"Nope. She's clean. Just a single gunshot wound to the head for both of them. I hate to say it, but your guy's changing his pattern. It's definitely gonna make for an interesting case moving forward."

"That's what I'm afraid of."

Cassandra returned and placed an order of seafood gumbo and boudin balls, drizzled with orange remoulade sauce, on a table across from the kitchen. Asher dug in as he closed his eyes and savored the sweet but tangy and spicy sauce paired with the crispy boudin.

"You have any idea when y'all will be back at it? It's gonna be a rough ride without y'all working on this."

"No, I can't say when, but hopefully Pierre will come to his senses. If not, I might do some digging outside the office."

Cassandra nodded in agreement as she fished a spoonful of gumbo from the paper bowl.

"Y'all take care, and call me if you need anything."

"Will do, Agnes. Keep me posted."

He hung up and placed the phone next to his plate, leaning back as he shoveled another piece of fried boudin into his mouth.

"So, what's the plan?" Cassandra repeated.

"Find some beignets," he said through the mouthful.

From a table across the way, tucked behind a large sago palm, Damien watched. *That's cute*, he thought, as Cassandra wiped a touch of sauce from the edge of Asher's mouth.

Chapter 79

As they pulled out of the parking lot, Damien was close behind. His lifted Wrangler stood out among the surrounding vehicles, so he was sure to keep his distance while maintaining a close eye on Cassandra's SUV.

Inside the car, she and Asher were talking.

"Maybe I should stop by the office later and talk to Xavier," Cassandra said.

Asher looked at her with a single raised eyebrow as if she were crazy. "And that's gonna do what, get us *both* fired? Xavier isn't gonna have any more information than what we've already got."

"You don't know that. He could go back and look at the camera footage again or retrace our steps on the 1911 thefts. We never did get any leads on the firearms. I mean, they have to have come from somewhere."

"Yeah, whoever is doing this, *that's* where. The serial numbers were shaved down, so clearly whoever owned them doesn't want us finding out. But that doesn't necessarily mean they were stolen."

Cassandra made a hard left onto Dauphine Street, looking in her rearview mirror. "You see that?"

"What? I don't see anything."

"I think someone's following us."

"Where?"

"Five cars back."

"I haven't noticed anything. Take a left up here on Canal and see what happens."

All Asher could think about was the letter; it made no sense. Everything pointed to his father, but Mauricio was referred to in the letter. His father was dead, but the bodies were still piling up.

She turned onto Canal Street and made a quick right onto St. Charles. The Jeep continued straight onto Baronne.

Damien knew where they were headed.

"See, they kept going. Stop being so paranoid."

"Paranoid? We clearly don't know who or where this person is. I think it's safe to say I'm doing my job at this point."

"Yeah, yeah. Isn't 'doing our job' what got us into this mess in the first place?" Asher chuckled. "Keep driving."

"You don't plan on walking away from this, do you?"

"Walk away? No. Take a step back and assess? Sure. If you wanna talk to Xavier outside the office, go for it, but it won't be pretty if Pierre finds out. Me? I'm taking another look at that damn letter and what I was able to grab from Mauricio's place. There has to be more to this. It isn't all one big coincidence."

She made a left onto Washington Avenue seconds before Damien. Then she turned right onto Coliseum Street as he pulled to the side of the road about a block away, at the corner of Washington and Coliseum.

He was in clear sight of the SUV as she pulled up in front of Asher's home.

"Well, I guess I'll call you tomorrow if anything comes up. I'll talk to Xavier from a distance. I can't just sit around, hoping that the chief will figure this out. It's gonna drive me crazy."

"I get that. You do what you gotta do. I'll be here goin' through Mauricio's stuff, but I'll call you if I find anything."

"Sounds good."

He opened the door and stepped out of the Tahoe.

"Oh, Ash," she called after him.

"Yeah?"

"Good luck with Sofia. Like I said, my door is always open if you need anything. Don't hesitate to call."

Asher let out a heavy breath. "I haven't forgotten, trust me."

As Asher closed the car door, Damien turned left down Coliseum Street in the opposite direction. Cassandra caught a flash of the Jeep in her driver's-side mirror before she cut a U-turn.

part three
THE SPOUSE

Chapter 80

The next day, Asher got an early start sifting through what was left of his father's belongings. He didn't collect much from the apartment, but he thought there must be something he had missed in what he did have—some clothes, Mauricio's desk along with its contents, and the trunk he had found in the closet.

It was still dark, around 5 a.m., as he sat on the living room floor and began opening each of the desk drawers, fumbling with what little remained of his father's life. The top center drawer contained an old desk calendar, some pens, some pencils, and an empty glasses case.

He flipped through the calendar, which was from the previous year and contained no useful information for solving the murders: *Doctor's Appt., 10 a.m.; Oil Change, 2:30 p.m.; Cable Install, 11 a.m.*

None of it was what Asher needed.

"Come on. I know you have *something*. You didn't show up empty-handed," he muttered.

He opened the top left drawer, which contained nothing more than a framed photo that had been found on top of the desk in the apartment, along with an envelope. He was surprised to see that the only photo found in his father's apartment was of the two of them. They hadn't spoken in years, yet his father was reminded of Asher each day.

The envelope had no writing on the outside. He opened it and removed a single piece of paper folded in thirds, the handwriting modest and shaky, the black ink smudged, tattered. A lack of light made it arduous to read, and he could scarcely make out the salutation. "Dear Son," the letter began.

Asher stood up and moved to the sofa, clicking the small switch atop the black, swing-arm lamp positioned on the end table. He leaned onto the arm of the couch as he began reading the letter. His stomach dropped, and he felt his heart skip a beat, taking all but a shallow breath from his chest.

You are probably wondering why I have suddenly come back into your life. I was hoping to do this in person, but I was just diagnosed with stage 4 lung cancer and have only been given a short time. I hate having to put this in a letter, but I wanted to at least attempt to make amends with you and finally tell you what happened when we lost your mother.

Asher shifted his weight and folded his legs beneath himself, settling into what was already feeling like devastating news. He brought the letter closer, within sight, struggling to read the unsteady, tear-stained words.

Your mother was not alone when she died. She was found with my best friend, Mr. Jean Baptiste, who was my closest friend from school, late in my teenage years. I did not want your memory of her to be tarnished, so I kept the full truth from you to protect you. I realize that you may have figured some of this out for yourself, but what no one else knows is that Mr. Baptiste's son was also there when I discovered the two of them. I did not have the heart to tell the police about him for fear it would destroy his life as well. I guess I just wanted to protect you both.

I realize now that my reasoning was selfish, and you deserve the truth. I just wanted to be part of your life again if only to help in some small way. I have always followed your career and cases over the years, and I am so proud of the man you have become. I do not know if this will help but look in the trunk in my closet. There are two pistols left of my 1911 collection, along with some old photos of pistols that were stolen at the time of your mother's murder. The missing pistols have always bothered me, and I could never figure out where they went. It has struck me as terribly odd ever since I heard about your current cases in the news.

I am sorry to have to write to explain all of this, but please know that I loved you and your mother beyond words.

Please forgive me.

Love always,
Dad

Asher read the letter over and over, trying to understand what had kept his father from simply coming out and saying it from the beginning. Why all the running around and obscure requests to meet?

His hands began to sweat, adding another layer of wrinkled moisture to the already ragged letter. Lightheadedness made the room feel as if it were shifting, ever so lightly, beneath him. His heart was racing, each beat getting faster, skipping a thud here, a thump there. His breathing was labored, surface-level. He needed to stop it.

Grabbing his phone, he dialed Cassandra. *Come on. I really need you to pick up*, he thought. *Come on, damn it.*

"Hello," she answered with a groggy morning voice. "Who is this?"

"Hey, I need you to head my way soon. I gotta show you something."

"Isn't it like, early?"

"I don't know. The sun is up, isn't it?" he said, not considering anything other than the breakthrough.

"Uh, it's pretty fuckin' dark."

"Can you come over? I have something I need to show you, something we need to look into."

"Seriously, Asher? Right now?"

"You were just giving me shit about not giving up on this, so yes now. Get your tired ass up and meet me at my place."

"I'll be there in thirty."

Chapter 81

"This better be worth it," Cassandra said as Asher opened the door. "I'm all for an early morning, but this is, uh, *early.*"

He immediately took note of her casual a.m. wear—blue jean shorts, a white off-the-shoulder shirt hinting at the black bra beneath, and a vibrant green piercing above her eye that she wasn't allowed to wear to work.

Snap out of it, Asher, you have work to do, he thought.

"Oh, it's worth it," he said. "Just wait until you see this."

She walked in and collapsed onto the sofa, her feet on the coffee table, arms spread open in exhaustion. "Just when we think that we've closed this thing, that we've finally cracked another case, it doesn't end."

"Yeah, well, don't get too comfortable," he said, handing her the letter. "I have a feeling you'll appreciate the wake-up call."

She leaned forward and began reading the note, her eyes wide and jaw open already, even though she was only a couple sentences deep. She glanced over and looked to Asher as if she expected a narration of some sort.

"Keep going," he said.

Upon finishing, she tossed the letter onto the coffee table and sank back into the couch with an expression of unequivocal shock. "Okay, so who is he? Who's the son?" She threw up her hands. "This was a long time ago, right? Is he even around anymore?"

"That's a good question. That's why I brought *you* here. You're better at the whole stalking thing than I am. How long you think it will take you to find a name and address?"

She blew some air out through her nose. "You mean, *if* he's still around."

"Sure, if."

"Grab my laptop out of the car. I'll take care of the coffee," she said as she strolled into the kitchen.

"Why in the world do *I* have to fetch the computer?" he said with a cynical tone.

"Because I'm already in the kitchen." She smiled over her shoulder, pushing herself onto her tiptoes, reaching high for a coffee cup off the top shelf.

Soon, they were on the sofa talking, reminiscing over the case. She was able to complete a search and produce a short list of four persons of interest, each named Jean Baptiste, who had lived in the parish over the last several decades.

"So, where do we start?" she asked.

"Well, the letter says it was his best friend from school during his teenage years, so see which of the four Jean Baptistes went to the same high school as Mauricio during the same time period. From there, we can pinpoint which son we should be looking for."

She paused and glanced over. "You know we're gonna get fired for this, right? We're logging in to the department's search engine while suspended, which is insane that we can even do it. This is just flat-out brilliant."

"Let me worry about that."

"You know what high school your dad was at?"

"No, he never mentioned it."

"Okay, not a problem. Let me see what I can do," she said as she began typing frantically.

Asher heard the bedroom door squeak open, and Sofia walked into the kitchen in her robe. "I didn't know we were having company."

"Yeah, neither did I," he said.

Sofia turned around and walked back into the bedroom, slamming the door. "Sorry, I should've warned you," he said to Cassandra.

"No worries. I figured as much."

"Let's try and get moving on this as quickly as we can, yeah?"

"Agreed."

"Here." She pointed to the computer screen. "He was at Holy Cross. According to the alum directory, there's definitely a Jean Baptiste who went to school with him."

"Great," he said as he stood up in anticipation. "Now all we need are the names of any children and their addresses."

"Yeah, yeah. I'm working on it. Don't have a panic attack just yet."

"Oh, that's very funny. Why don't you just push me off a cliff while you're at it."

She stood up and pointed to the screen. "There. You're all set."

"Seriously? That's it? You've been working for like, all of a few minutes."

"The department hired me for a reason, Asher. I'm not *only* an annoying sidekick."

He looked at her and smiled. "All right, then. Let's get the address and get out of here."

"You aren't serious. You're actually wanting to go after this *right now*? Right this second?"

"What? You thought I was joking? We have a chance to figure this thing out, prevent even more homicides, and potentially get our jobs back. You think I'm just gonna sit around and let it go? No. Not to mention, you were previously all over me for not pursuing this further. Now you have doubts?"

"Okay, you're right. You're the lead on this—you take the reins. By all means."

"Thank you. Now before we get going, do you have a to-go cup?"

~

"Doesn't look like a psychopathic killer's home to me, what about you?" Cassandra said as they sat outside Damien's house, half a block down the street.

"Eh, they never *look* like anything," Asher responded. "That's the problem. If it weren't for them getting caught, they'd be living amongst the rest of us as the good ole neighbor next door. Those are the scary ones. It's not the screaming, bloody, savage slashers of bedtime stories you have to worry about but the everyday Jacks and Jills who offer you their spot in line at the grocery store just so they can watch you check out, follow you home, and torture you before your child comes home to find you hanging from a pipe in the basement."

"Well, when you put it like *that* . . ."

He shook his head. "I don't see anything. Let's run by Xavier's place and see if he's home so we can fill him in. He can update us on any new info he's got."

"Whatever you say. This is your crazy after all."

Chapter 82

As they pulled into Xavier's driveway, he was detailing the Camaro; much like Asher, he was a neat freak when it came to cars. The hood was open, and Xavier was polishing the chrome valve covers. The white rally stripes on the black hood, lifted up into the sky, stood out like a vast flashing indicator of contrast, gleaming through the layers of polish.

"Hey, hey," Asher said as they stepped out of the car. "You know, if you keep at it long enough, you're gonna polish the paint right off that thing."

"Probably. But it'll still look better than that beat-up rag of a Vette you got." Xavier threw the towel into Asher's face.

"Well, only one of you has good taste, I know that," Cassandra chimed in.

"What's up? I thought y'all were on hiatus for a while?"

"You know us," Asher said. "We can't keep still. You got a minute? There's something we need to show you."

"Yeah, sure. Let's have a seat."

They sat beneath a shaded table in front of the home, the benches covered by an awning to keep the afternoon sun at bay. Cassandra pulled out her laptop and opened a single file containing the consolidated information Xavier needed to review. "Here's what we uncovered this morning. We wanted to get your thoughts on this before we decide to move on the house. We weren't sure if you found anything else we should know about since yesterday."

"Before you *move on the house*?" Xavier said in disbelief. "Y'all just don't quit, do you? You know the kind of trouble you'll be in if you keep at this without Pierre's approval, much less a court order? Getting fired will only be the start of your worries."

Asher chuckled. "Yeah, we've considered it. We're too far in at this point to walk away, though. Besides, it's personal. Would you just up and step away if *your* father was involved?"

"Let me take a look, and I'll get back to you." Xavier reached for the laptop.

As he read the file, the stunned expression on his face said everything. Xavier was not one to be easily swayed or surprised. But the information in front of him was a blatant calamity on the team's part; the answer had been in front of them the entire time, quite literally on Asher's doorstep. "So it wasn't Mauricio, but he was willing to give you what you needed the entire time. Pierre is gonna have your ass, my friend. I hope you're prepared for the shit storm that's coming your way if you ever walk back into that office."

"I'll deal with Pierre the way I always have."

"Oh yeah, and what way is that?" Cassandra asked. "Laughing while he screams in your face?"

"Exactly. It's my go-to move."

"Well, best of luck with that," said Xavier, "but it looks like you've got a good reason to pursue this to me. It's just unfortunate it has to be done off the books. For the record, I'm telling you not to."

He handed the laptop back to Cassandra.

"Is there anything else we need to know, anything you've

found since yesterday?" she asked.

Xavier shook his head. "Sorry, but not really. I combed back through everything. The surveillance footage, double-checking any possible matches to the partial print, the records of firearm thefts y'all put together—I even made a few more phone calls to the decedents' spouses, everything. I can't find anything new. Whoever this motherfucker is, he knows what he's doing. It's clean work. I'd just love to know why."

"Wouldn't we all." Cassandra shook her head.

"Okay," Asher spoke up, "well I think we should keep an eye on the address for at least twenty-four hours before we decide on anything for certain, make sure the face matches our records. The two of you mind teaming up for that? I have something I need to tend to."

"Oh no," Xavier said, "you're not dragging me into this. I'm here for emotional support only."

"Seriously?" Asher said. "I'm not sending her over there alone. I need you on this."

Xavier looked at Cassandra with an I-hope-you're-right expression, eyes wide, mouth crooked. "Fine, but if this goes south, y'all *forced* me into this. That's my story, and I'm sticking to it."

"Of course. I wouldn't expect anything less." Asher gave him a satirical grin. "All right, then. I'll meet up with y'all sometime tomorrow, and we can decide what to do. Like I said, we'll give it twenty-four hours, then move on it if everything looks good."

"What do you have to do, anyways?" Cassandra asked him.

"I'm working a domestic case."

Chapter 83

As Asher walked through the door, Sofia was in the dining room, papers spread across the table with far too many sticky notes, pens, and folders. However, she was not alone. Her coworker, Byron, was also at the table, working frantically to piece together a grant they had been slaving over for months in an effort to meet an upcoming deadline.

Byron looked peculiar—medium-length, dirty-blond hair, a heavy scruff on his face, average build but tall. He appeared to have a grin lurking beneath the surface of his expression, although he wasn't smiling.

A jolt shot through Asher's body.

"Oh, hey. I didn't know we were having company," he said.

"Yeah, me neither," Sofia responded harshly.

Asher walked into the living room and placed his briefcase onto the coffee table, glancing back at them. They were smiling, something Asher hadn't seen from Sofia in quite some time. She caught sight of Asher out of the corner of her eye, quickly diverting her attention back to Byron once she noticed Asher's interest in the two of them.

Asher could smell the scent of freshly baked chocolate, either brownies or cookies, although he couldn't discern the difference. "Something in the oven?" he asked.

"Yep," she said.

Asher stared, looking at her while she was buried in paperwork and the company of a complete stranger, at least to him. He walked into the kitchen and opened the range, seeing the large, individual cookies spread across two pans, square chunks of double chocolate resting in pillows of rising dough.

"Hey, Byron Landry," Asher heard, a hand reaching out next to him as he stood up from the oven. "Nice to meet you."

He had a foreign accent, an acute intonation in his voice Asher couldn't place. He shook his hand and gave him a slow, curious nod.

"I'm one of Sofia's colleagues at the university. I don't believe we've met."

"Asher, her husband," he responded.

"I figured she was married, as much as she's always rushing off to get home in the evenings. Unfortunately, she hasn't told me much about you, though."

Asher turned his head in Sofia's direction, waiting to assess her response. She never looked up from the paperwork.

Before he could get a word in edgewise, Byron continued with a dark smirk. "Wow, that's a nice sidearm you got there. A 1911, huh? They *are* beautiful, not to mention reliable, am I right?"

Just then, the oven began to beep, signaling the cookies were done. "Oh don't worry. I'll get that," the man said as Asher's focus remained fixed on Sofia, who was still focused entirely on the table.

Byron grabbed an oven mitt from the drawer and pulled the pans from the red-hot oven, placing them on a cooling rack to the side of the stove before turning off the heat. "There we are," he said. "Anyone up for a bite? Perhaps some milk to top it off?"

"You know your way around my kitchen pretty well, huh?" Asher said, continuing to stare vacantly at Sofia. "We should have you over more often."

"Oh, nonsense. Everyone keeps the mitts next to the stove. We all know that now, don't we, big man?" he said, patting Asher on the shoulder.

As Byron removed each of the cookies from the parchment paper and placed them onto a plate, the light gleaming down from the hood vent caught him in profile—he was somewhat handsome, but his small chin and crooked teeth outlined a character Asher felt was up to no good.

"Here we go," Byron said as he held out the plate, offering up one of the giant chocolate disks.

"No, thanks," he said. "I'm more of a seafood guy, myself."

Byron grinned, his teeth as jagged as the Louisiana shore. "Suit yourself. Just know you're missing out," he said as the chocolate traversed his teeth and lips.

"Here you are, darling." He passed the plate to Sofia.

"Oh, thank you." She took a deep inhale. "They smell perfect. By the way"—she looked to Asher—"I'll probably be getting home a bit late tomorrow night."

Byron sat down in the chair next to Sofia, the plate of freshly baked cookies between them.

"You know, you've gotta lighten up, my friend," Byron said to Asher. "It isn't too often you have a guest in your home baking you dessert, catering to you. Are you sure you don't want one? I'm sure we can learn to share."

Asher began walking down the hallway as he removed his phone from his pocket, typing "B-Y-R-O-N L-A-N-D-R-Y" into the notes app. "You should be careful," he said over his shoulder. "Sharing can get you in a bit of trouble 'round here."

Chapter 84

The following morning was hot, a heavy moisture lingering in the air. When Asher woke, he found himself alone. Sofia had left for the university, and it was time he made heads and tails of her strange behavior.

As he drove onto UNO's campus, he parked across the road from the science building at the back of the student parking lot. From there, he could see the faculty lot between the science and computer science buildings, and consequently, he had an ideal view of Sofia's Camry. She was one of the few biology faculty whose labs were located in the larger science building instead of the biology building, due to constraints on available space at the time of hiring.

As he sat there, his mind began to race. He thought about what he was being forced into—stalking his own wife to understand her emotional absence from their marriage, while also pursuing someone in his professional life. All he hoped for was that Justin was right. Perhaps Sofia was merely caught up in her own stresses and problems. He doubted it, but maybe it had nothing to do with Asher.

She's up to something, he thought. *I'm not gonna sleep till I figure this out.*

After two hours, she finally walked out of the science building and got into her car. She drove out of the faculty parking lot and headed south on Founders Road before hooking a left onto Leon C. Simon.

The difficult part, for Asher, was his vehicle. The Vette wasn't ideal in the least when tailing someone, so he needed to keep an excessive distance between them. Luckily, he had significant experience with such tasks, and he knew this part of New Orleans like the back of his hand.

Elysian Fields took them south to Decatur, where Sofia parked in a public lot behind Café Du Monde. Asher parked at the opposite end of the lot, cutting off the Vette as quickly as he could so as not to attract attention.

The wet air struck his lungs as he stepped out of the car and crossed Decatur, walking down St. Ann Street on the right side of Jackson Square. As usual, an overwhelming crowd, a nonstop line of customers, waited outside the café. A small jazz band was playing at the corner of the eatery's pavilion.

Where the hell are you going? he thought.

He was sure to keep his distance, about fifty feet behind her, covered by the surrounding oak trees as she made her way into the square. The streets were bustling, and the square was filled with sightseers taking in the brilliant, blue morning.

Sofia walked around the square, looking from corner to corner, bench to bench, searching for something, someone. After a few rounds, she sat at the southeast corner of the lot and began making a phone call.

Asher walked with careful steps behind the trees on the outside edge of the square. The constant flux of people into and out of the area only improved his cover.

Who are you calling? he thought. *Let's play a little.*

Asher pulled up his contact list and pressed the green icon next to Sofia's name. "I bet you don't even answer," he mumbled to himself.

She paused her conversation and looked at her phone before pressing the screen. "Hello?" she answered.

"Hey," Asher said. "How's work?"

"Good, I'm covered up with paperwork on this grant. You know how it is."

"Of course. Just thought I'd see if you have any plans for lunch."

"I'm probably gonna eat here in the lab. I really need to finish this up if we're gonna meet this deadline."

He began walking closer. He wanted to see her expression.

"Okay, just thought I'd offer."

"Thanks, but I'm good," she said with an impatient roll of the eyes.

"I'll see you later, then."

"Bye."

As she switched back to her previous call, her exuberance was as clear as the skies above.

Chapter 85

Cassandra and Xavier had been outside Damien's home since 5 a.m., about a block away on Dauphine Street, not far from Esplanade Avenue. They'd decided to take her SUV—it was more spacious and less obvious than Xavier's Camaro. Besides, Xavier would have had a coronary if he discovered someone eating in his car on a stakeout.

"The two of you sure this is our guy?" Xavier asked. "You had more than one hit on your search, right?"

Cassandra paused her consumption of her bacon-egg-and-cheese wrap to indulge the other detective's paranoia. "I'm pretty sure, yeah. Of the four Jean Baptistes, there was only one who went to the same high school as Mauricio during the same time period, and this is the current address of his only son. So, yeah, I'd say this is it. If it isn't, what's gonna happen? Pierre's gonna suspend us a second time?"

"Him firing both of you is a worry I actually have. You realize that, right? I sure hope y'all are good on this. Otherwise, I'm gonna miss having y'all around."

"Oh, stop getting all sentimental. You know we'll always be around to put up with your ass."

"Where the two of you get y'all's confidence, I have no idea."

Right then, Damien walked out of his back door and through the side gate of the small but well-groomed yard. He grabbed the green trash bin and wheeled it to the road. From a sideways glance, he could see the Tahoe parked at the corner of the street. He didn't pause, however. Without a flinch, without hesitation, he placed the bin next to the curb, turned around, and walked back through the gate.

"Son of a bitch," Xavier said. "Is that our guy?"

Cassandra handed him a printout of Damien's driver's license. "You tell me." She squinted. "I'm horrible at that. You know I can never make a proper ID from a photo. Even worse, artist sketches are what my nightmares are made of."

"It sure as hell is," he said. "I'm texting Asher."

"Why? He isn't gonna want us to do anything right now. He told us to keep an eye on him for twenty-four hours and confirm he's here—nothing more, nothing less."

Damien walked back inside through the same back door.

Xavier grabbed his phone from the holder suctioned to the windshield. "It isn't gonna hurt anything to let him know what's goin' on. Besides, he may wanna move sooner if he knows for sure the guy's here."

We have a positive ID, he sent. *He's still inside. What are you wanting to do?*

Xavier tapped the phone on his leg, waiting impatiently for Asher to respond.

It didn't take long for the phone to light up, a blue beam shooting around the edge. *Like I said, we need to wait. We'll handle it after we meet up later. Just don't let him out of your sight.*

"Let me guess," Cassandra said. "We wait?"

"Yeah, yeah. I heard both of you. This is just a huge waste of time. We have the address, and we have an ID. What the fuck are we waiting for?"

"Well, he already screwed up once. I suppose he wants to make sure this is our guy before he messes up again."

"I get that, but sitting here and watching a house isn't gonna give us any information we don't already have. Besides, why doesn't he just bring Mauricio's letter to Pierre? That's the new information. That would be the smart thing to do. Instead, I'm gonna get fired right there with the two of you."

The front door of the home opened, and Damien stepped onto the porch. He looked directly at the Tahoe, smirked, and placed a pinch of Skoal behind his lower lip. He walked off the patio and climbed into his Wrangler, rolling down all the windows.

Ted Nugent's "Stranglehold" blared from the speakers.

"*This* is how we get new information," Cassandra said as she started the SUV.

Chapter 86

Cassandra pulled out onto Dauphin Street, several cars behind Damien. The traffic was heavier than usual, which proved difficult for a tail.

"Any guesses on where we're headed?" Xavier asked.

"Not a clue. Any info is good info at this point, wouldn't you say?"

His phone rang. It was Asher.

"Hey, man. Where you at?" Xavier asked. "We're on the move. Not really sure where we're headed, but we're on him."

"Goddammit," Asher said. "How long ago did y'all leave?"

"Just now. Why?"

"Well, it adds a whole other level of problems. It's bad enough we're doing this off the clock. If we get found out *and* screw this up, we're fucked. Don't let him out of your sight, but keep your distance."

The Jeep suddenly ran a stop sign and darted right down Dumaine Street, heading away from Jackson Square. Cassandra slammed on the brakes as a mule and carriage, along with a slew of pedestrians, stepped out in front of the SUV at the stop sign.

"*Shit.* Call you back, bud," Xavier said as he hung up the phone and tossed it onto the dashboard.

Cassandra sounded the horn and flipped on the undercover emergency lights, steering around the passersby. "Here we go."

They felt each and every bump from the infinite number of potholes along the old, ragged road. The one-way street was lined with cars and parking meters on the right-hand side and random obstacles on the left—street musicians playing homemade drum sets, dumpsters, restaurant chalkboards advertising the day's specials, and slow-moving tourists taking in the French architecture.

"He took a right on Dumaine," Xavier said. "Come on, we can't lose this son of a bitch."

"Yeah, yeah, I got it. Keep it together, would ya," she said as she slammed the gas and narrowly missed a group of tourists meeting on a corner for a walking food tour. They jumped to the side of the street as the Tahoe missed the tall green streetlamp on the corner by mere inches.

"Whoa, whoa, *whoa!*" Xavier yelled as he grabbed the assist handle above the passenger-side window. "You're gonna get us both killed if you don't slow the hell down."

"They're called 'oh shit' handles for a reason, hun," she said as she rolled down her window and began yelling ahead at the nonchalant pedestrians meandering in the center of the street. "Let's go, let's go. Out of the way!"

She stopped at the next stop sign, where she looked in every possible direction but came up empty-handed. They couldn't tell which way the Jeep had turned.

"Which way did he go? *Which way*, dammit?" she said.

"I have no idea. I'm seeing exactly what you see, woman!"

Cassandra turned left and slowly began creeping along, street by street, looking for the all-black Jeep. "Call him back," she said.

"Yeah, so we can tell him that we just did exactly what he told us not to do. Sure thing. Let me get right on it."

Again, Xavier grabbed his phone and dialed Asher. It rang and rang. "What the hell," he mumbled. "Come on, man. Pick up."

He answered after far too many rings. "Yeah, what's up?"

"We lost him," Xavier said. "He cut out ahead of us and ran a stop sign. The Wrangler he's driving isn't as slow as it looks."

"Y'all are in the city. What the fuck are *you* driving, a Pinto?"

"I'm not exactly in the driver's seat, man."

"What the hell does that mean?" Cassandra said. "You wanna drive?"

"No. Oh, no. This is your car, your party."

"Are you shitting me?" Asher said. "Y'all took the Tahoe? Oh, yeah. That's real smart. Leave the muscle car at home and take mommy's SUV."

"It's called being discreet," Xavier said. "Besides, if someone over here would learn how to drive . . ."

"Oh, screw you. You were just about to wet yourself. I don't wanna hear it."

"Fine," Asher said with frustration. "Just canvas the neighborhood, see if you can find him, then head back to Xavier's place. I'll be wrapping up here in a little bit. We'll meet up and see where to go from there."

Meanwhile, Damien parked in a small garage on Chartres Street and began walking to Jackson Square. Sofia—and her husband—were right on time.

Chapter 87

Damien approached the square from the opposite end and walked up to Sofia as she sat on the bench.

Asher slowly paced outside the yard, just beyond the railing, watching them meet. She jumped up and ran to the center of the square, throwing her arms around Damien in front of the equine statue of Andrew Jackson.

"Hey, I'm so glad you could make it." She gleamed. "I didn't know if you were working today, but I thought I'd stop by and see for myself."

Asher squinted. He couldn't make out the man's face, which was partially covered by sunglasses and the shade of a black hat, but he got the gist. "So this is him," he whispered to himself. "Come on, Sofia. You can do better than this."

They locked eyes and kissed as if they were kids in the back of the movie theater. Damien spun them around and grabbed the small of her back, running his hands down to her hips.

"So, what's the plan?" He smiled. "You stickin' around for a bit while I get set up? Or would you rather grab lunch first?"

"It's a bit early to eat. I thought I'd hang out and see how things work, if that's okay with you."

"Of course. Maybe you can even help if you'd like."

"Definitely!"

"Let's grab what we need from the Jeep, first."

They made their way back to the garage where Damien had parked. Asher followed not far behind, sure to remain in the cover of the burly trees. He needed to see exactly what his wife saw. He needed to know each and every way he touched her, kissed her.

He crept through the shadows. The route was paved with large, gray stones, offset and staggered in different sizes. The black iron fence lined the square on the outside of the trees. He moved between lampposts, not yet lit in the day's sun.

They walked down Chartres Street at the back left corner of the square, squeezing their way between a red-painted building and the black poles supporting the balcony. Two blocks later, they reached a parking garage adorned with a red, hanging sign with a large "P" and "Premium Parking" written in white.

Asher waited inside a designer clothing shop across the street, keeping a sharp eye on the garage.

Moments later, they emerged. Damien carried a modest, black briefcase and an easel; Sofia a folding chair and a small, wooden box. They made their way along the two blocks back to Jackson Square, walking to the far side on St. Ann Street.

Asher was close—a mere twenty feet behind.

They stopped just shy of the east opening to the yard, between a birch tree and a lamp post. Damien opened the easel and removed several pencil drawings and paintings on canvas. He placed some of them onto the cement ledge; others, he hung from the fence along with a sign: *8x10 prints: $50; 18x24 prints: $120.* The art was largely portraits and landscapes in pencil with the occasional colored painting.

Asher stood inside the doorway of a Louisiana state travel store in the adjacent building, watching.

"Well, why don't we work on a new piece," Damien suggested. "Here, have a seat."

He unfolded the chair and placed it against the birch tree. Sofia sat down in the shade and began to fiddle with her hair, tying it up in a messy, curly bun.

"I never thought I'd be drawn by a proper artist before."

"And I never thought I'd have the perfect model."

Way to be subtle, Asher thought.

The sun was making its way directly overhead. The pinpoint rays shot down from cracks in the trees before striking the stone walkway, the ground appearing to move as if they were walking on water.

Asher's phone rang.

"Hey, still no sign of him," Xavier answered. "Wherever he is, he's long gone by now."

Asher stepped farther inside the store. "Okay. Like I said, let's meet up later at your place and regroup. At least now, we have an address."

"Where you at?"

"I'm busy. Don't worry about it. I'll be done soon, and we can meet at your place."

He hung up the phone without a response.

"Now, if I can only figure out who *you* are," he muttered to himself as he watched the gentleman draw his wife.

Chapter 88

Sofia was dressed in black flip-flops, skinny crop jeans, and an army-green shirt, the sun dancing across her face and lap as she sat in the chair, posing for Damien. He stood behind the shabby easel, his hat now backward, drawing her in black and gray pencil.

"Am I okay here?" she asked as he began the rough outline of a sketch.

"You're beautiful," he said. "Turn a touch to the left, chin up, and we're good to go."

Asher slowly made his way out of the travel shop and began to step, inch by inch, beneath the breezeway of the building; his gaze never faulted. "She *is* beautiful, isn't she," he whispered.

A light breeze rustled the leaves along the walkway, a few more falling from the trees above between Sofia and the artist. Her hair blew in the wind, causing Damien to smile at the ever-changing portrait.

Asher noticed her expression, the way she was when Asher wasn't around. It hurt. It hurt deep. Seeing her in a bad mood or angry when they were together was one thing, but it was a whole new level of loss seeing her happy with someone else.

He stepped out from beneath the breezeway of the building and began treading toward a bench behind Sofia, facing the opposite direction. His sightseeing demeanor and the crowded street caused him to blend in with the background and become only another straggler in the city.

Again, he was only twenty feet away, and closing.

"So, how is it you get to take so much time off work?" Damien asked. "I mean, I guess I have such a flexible schedule because of what I do—I work for myself. But you have a boss, no? Don't you have someone to answer to?"

"Academia is a bit more flexible than your everyday job," she said. "It's pretty much like being your own boss. You're mostly free to do what you want, when you want, as long as you're putting out."

He chuckled. "That sounds like some of my past relationships."

"Oh, your exes were flexible?"

Another laugh. "You know, this is much harder when you constantly have me cutting up."

"Sorry, I'll behave."

"No, no. Don't you dare."

Fifteen feet out.

"I'm glad you came out to see me. I don't get many visitors working on the streets, other than customers. I've especially never been able to draw someone I've known before. It's a nice change of pace."

"Really? Who do you draw then?"

"Anyone. Who I pick for my work, or who picks me, even, isn't important. It's all about the story. What matters is the underlying message. Every piece of art can have a message, whether the artist wants it to or not. What that message is, however, is up to the viewer. The artist can have an idea in mind, but it's up to you to figure it out for yourself."

Ten feet.

"So, what's your message here?" she asked. "Or is this all in good fun?"

Oh it's definitely fun, Damien thought.

"Are you having fun?" he asked.

Sofia's smile faded to a more subdued expression, an expression of uncertainty. "Of course," she said flatly.

Five.

Asher felt his heart rate getting faster, his feet numb. He stared in the opposite direction, looking at a neighboring artist's work—a charcoal artist sketching the New Orleans landscape.

"Where are you going from here?" Damien asked her. "You have any plans tonight?"

She'll be home late, Asher thought.

"No, why? Do you have something in mind?"

"I always have someone in mind," he said.

Asher sat on the bench behind Sofia, facing the opposite direction. The wind was blowing at his back, and he could smell the rich aroma of coconut and hibiscus drifting from her hair. A lock dragged against the back of his neck. He took a deep breath, savoring the scent; it calmed his nerves, if only for a moment.

"Good," Damien said. "Perhaps we can continue this back at my place."

"I'd like that. Maybe I can cook you dinner."

Shrimp creole? Asher thought.

His stomach tightened. His muscles began to shudder. Asher gutted it out for a few more moments to see if he could catch his name, perhaps a clue, a hint, at where this man lived or how Sofia came to know him. But he got nothing.

Asher wasn't the type to make a scene or create confrontations if he could help it. No, he preferred to handle such evidence in the long term, when the time was right.

Poor guy, Asher thought. *He doesn't even know what he's getting himself into.*

Chapter 89

As Asher knocked on the door, the image of his wife flashed into his mind. Where did they go wrong? Who was the man? How did they meet?

All of these questions were going to have to wait. Asher needed to clear his mind of his career if he was going to repair his marriage.

"Hey, Xavier's out back," Cassandra said as she opened the door to Xavier's home. "Hope you're up for some barbeque."

"Oh, you know me. Always."

They walked out onto the back deck, which was adorned with string lights, Adirondack chairs, and a homemade, natural wood table Xavier built himself; woodworking was a hobby that kept him sane when he wasn't in the office.

Smoke flowed from the large barbeque pit, which also served as a smoker. The smell of applewood emanated from the seams of the grill as Xavier cracked open a beer and handed it to Asher.

"Sorry, brother. No wine today," Xavier said.

"No worries," Asher replied as he sat down in one of the wooden lounge chairs.

Xavier opened the grill, flipped a few burgers, and turned over a rack of ribs before lathering a thin layer of barbeque sauce across the meat.

"So, how's this all goin' down?" Cassandra asked openly. "We have a plan, or we just wingin' it?"

"Not as of yet we don't," Asher said. "The two of you are absolutely sure about the ID though, right? It's him?"

"Definitely," Xavier nodded.

"Something you need to think about—*we* need to think about—is what's gonna happen after all this is over if we do decide to move on this," Cassandra said to Asher, sounding concerned. "What are the chances the chief takes us off suspension versus fires us, where we end up with more issues than we already have? I'm not so sure that works out in our favor."

"Alternatively, y'all could go to Pierre with the new information. The worse he could do is ignore you. The two of you are used to that anyways," Xavier said.

"He doesn't want to hear any more from us, especially me," Asher said. "Besides, that's gonna take time. We don't have time. These couples are getting knocked off every few days. We can't afford to sit around and wait on this while the chief strokes his ego."

"Okay, just don't say I never suggested it."

"Let's plan on this," Asher said before taking a swig of his beer. "We meet outside of Baptiste's place at 7 a.m. We move on the house before he has a chance to get up and get moving."

"We don't know what time that is," Cassandra retorted. "We've only been on the house for one day."

"Like I said, we also don't have the time to sit around and wait," Asher said. "We'll meet one block down, at the corner of Dauphine and Barracks."

Xavier pulled the burgers and ribs off the pit and placed them in a large, metal sheet pan at the center of the table. "Dig in."

"I hate to ask now, but what are we doing, exactly, when all this is done?" Xavier asked. "So, we raid the house, grab Baptiste, and then what? We just walk into the unit and hand him over to Pierre? That's a little, uh, dramatic, no? He's just gonna thank us and give the two of you your jobs back?"

"The one piece of the puzzle you're missing is that *you* were not suspended," Asher said. "We were."

"Oh, yeah. So, Xavier figured this all out on his own and apprehended Baptiste by himself. Sure," Cassandra said. "Pierre won't bat an eye at that at all."

Asher slammed his bottle down onto the table and stood up. He began walking into the house before briefly turning back to them. "What do *you* two want to do? It seems like y'all are pushing back on this every step of the way. You tell me what to do if this is such a bad idea, then."

He continued into the kitchen, pushing the sliding glass door down the tracks and into the wall.

"I got him," Cassandra said.

"It's all you." Xavier waved a rib in the air.

She went inside.

"What are you getting all worked up over?" Cassandra asked as he paced back and forth in the kitchen. "All we're trying to do is look out for you, for *us*, and think about what's gonna happen when the smoke settles from all this. Aren't you concerned about how Pierre, how the media, will react to this? We'll hang if this doesn't go as planned."

"No, I'm not thinking about that. All I'm thinking about is doing my job and preventing the next set of homicides. All I *continue* to think about, nonstop, is the fact that I had these cases solved if I would've just talked to my dad. But I didn't. All I'm concerned with is ending this. Pierre can keep me suspended, he can fire me, he can write me up. I don't give a shit. None of that matters. Why can't y'all see that?"

Cassandra moved in closer, grabbing his arm.

"Hey. *Hey*, look at me," she said in a consoling voice, bringing her head down only to look up into his downward gaze. "We're not going anywhere. We got you on this. We just wanna make sure we're covering all our bases, just like we always do. Okay?"

Asher looked at her with apprehension.

"I just want it all to be over," he said. "I can't keep going like this."

"I know. I know. And it will be. Soon."

She reached out and grabbed the front of his shirt with two fingers, pulling him in close.

"We got you," she said while pushing a tuft of hair back behind his ear. "*I* got you."

Chapter 90

A light drizzle ruled the following morning. It was 6 a.m. as Cassandra parked in front of Asher's home and waited for him to step outside. She turned off the engine and listened to the rain dance across the hood of the SUV. Today was the culmination of much hard work, and it weighed heavily.

As he opened the front door, he looked more put together and ready than he had in weeks—beard short and clean-cut, wearing a leather jacket, a new pair of jeans, and black lace-up work boots. After shutting the door, he leaned down to the garden and plucked a single small sunflower from the soil. She saw the three extra magazines strapped to his left hip, his 1911 in the four-o'clock position of his back.

He calmly walked to the Tahoe as if the rain were nonexistent, as if each drop somehow missed him and was of no concern.

"You ready for this?" she asked as he closed the door and pushed the water back through his wavy hair.

"More than ready," he said while handing her the flower. "Sorry about yesterday. I know you're only looking out for me, for us. It isn't a bouquet, but it is for you."

She twirled the flower just below her nose, her eyes closed. She smelled the scent of fresh leaves, falling leaves, in a field of subtle sweetness. Cassandra placed her hand on his thigh, running it up and down as she smiled into the sunflower.

"Anything other than roses is perfect. And you don't need to apologize. We're all a bit on edge with this one," she said as she placed the flower on the dashboard behind the steering wheel. "Let's get this show on the road, shall we?"

"We shall."

As they drove east toward the French Quarter, Asher was fully aware that his career hung in the balance. Regardless of the outcome, their decision—his decision—would have dire consequences for all three of them. At the end of the day, he would either have his job back, paving the way for a confident discussion with Sofia, or he would be fired, setting himself up for what might be the end of his marriage as well.

He wouldn't juggle both any longer.

"Xavier on his way?" he asked. "We can't afford to wait around."

"He is. If anything, he'll beat us there. You know how he is."

They pulled up to the corner of Dauphine and Barracks, the home only half a block away, tucked back in the shadows of two older, rundown houses on either side. The sun was hidden behind a gray sky of continuous clouds pushing their way through the city. The neighborhood was dead silent; only the soft massage of rain could be heard kneading the grass. Occasional thunder rolled in the distance.

"Looks like you were a bit optimistic," he said as she put the Tahoe in park, Xavier nowhere to be found.

It was 6:55 a.m.

"You know him better than I do. He'll be here," she said as he looked at his watch.

Not a minute later, Xavier pulled in behind the Tahoe and flashed his high beams, signaling his arrival.

Cassandra leaned over the center console to the back seat and grabbed two kevlar vests. She handed one to Asher and placed the other one over her head and onto her shoulders. Then she slid her black raincoat over the vest, "New Orleans Homicide Task Force" printed across the back in bold, yellow letters.

Asher removed his leather jacket and velcroed the vest tightly at his side. As he looked in the rearview mirror, he saw Xavier doing the same. Asher's stomach began to tighten, his hands shaking. A wave of tingling pain made its way down his body as if to provide one last chance for him to back down, to change his mind. He could just as easily turn around and head home, no questions asked. It was that easy.

And that hard.

The rain wasn't letting up. If anything, it would provide a sense of cover, a dampening of sound as they approached the home.

Asher's phone rang.

"Hey, y'all about ready?" Xavier asked. "I'm good to go."

"Almost," Asher replied. "We need to be clear on how this is gonna go down."

"Go for it."

"Cassandra and I will take the front door. Xavier, you'll take the back. Just wait on us to move first. If all is good, you can meet us inside."

"We doing this without notice?" he asked.

"We'll knock up front, but I'm not sitting around waiting for things to go sideways. We knock once and then move."

"Sounds like a plan," Xavier said.

"We'll do this as quietly as possible, but make sure you're prepared. He will be."

Asher hung up the phone and placed it in his front pocket. Then he removed his pistol from the holster and hit the magazine release, double-checking himself. He placed it back into the magwell and pulled back the slide, chambering a round. The pistol jerked forward, the high-pitched, metallic sound inciting a loud ringing in his ears—a ringing that was all too familiar.

"You good?" He turned to Cassandra.

"It's been a long time coming," she said as she released the slide of her pistol, the sound of metal stopping metal as the gun lurched in her hand.

"Let's do it," he said.

They stepped out into the morning rain and onto the broken, uprooted sidewalk. The home was steps away, and he had no idea.

Chapter 91

Asher unholstered his pistol as he tiptoed up the stairs and onto the front porch. Cassandra was one step behind, her gun drawn as she squinted in the early-morning rain.

Xavier strolled down the driveway, past Damien's Wrangler, and unlatched the side gate of the white picket fence. It made a loud shriek as he pushed it open, causing Asher and Cassandra's heads to swivel. Xavier put his hand up to signal that it was okay. Squeezing himself through the small opening he had made in the fence, he proceeded down the brick walkway to the back of the home.

No lights appeared to be on inside; the windows were pitch black. Asher moved to the left side of the front door and leaned against the wall, Cassandra to the right.

"You good to go?" he whispered.

She nodded, signaling that she was ready for him to knock on the door. The silence was devastating, the air heavy.

Without a word, without warning, he knocked on the door, loud enough for anyone who may have been inside to hear.

Nothing, not a sound.

He slowly turned the doorknob, then looked to Cassandra with raised eyebrows.

It was open.

Was it really that easy?

It turned effortlessly as he pushed open the door and pulled his head back outside, against the house. He peered around the corner with his pistol aimed into the center of the living room, waiting to see if anyone would emerge. The room was stark black save for a small, peach-colored hint of light making its way from an obscure location farther into the house.

His heart skipped a beat. The palpitation took his breath away, the beat pausing before thumping harder to catch up as it continued to race. He could feel his pulse in his neck. The lightheadedness was setting in, and the room shifted back and forth, left to right, right to left. Asher felt unsteady. His feet moved beneath him.

Get it together, he thought. He wiped the sweat from his forehead as a single drop invaded the corner of his eye, burning, blurring his vision.

Asher stepped through the front door and into the living room. The home was lit only by a faint stream of light escaping a bedroom door at the end of the hallway. The hardwood floors creaked as he stepped farther into the room. He paused, glancing back over his shoulder to Cassandra as she entered through the front door and turned on her flashlight. She placed it beneath her pistol, pointing it in front of Asher, and nodded for him to proceed.

Xavier was at the back of the home, his pistol aimed at the door where it would open should he need to enter the home quickly. He made sure to keep his head out of view of the window.

The gentle landing of rain on the grass was the only sound he could hear.

Asher moved through the living room and into the kitchen

on the right side of the hallway, leading with his pistol. It was empty. He stepped fully into the room, providing a moment's clarity before proceeding.

Cassandra turned the corner to an empty bedroom on the opposing side of the hallway, adjacent to Asher. The room was clear. They stared at one another across the hall, knowing they had the remainder of the home yet to search.

Then, they heard a scream—a woman's cry—echo from the back of the home.

Asher pushed his head into the hallway, glancing around the corner with his gun. His stomach plummeted as a hot flash shot through his body. His face ran numb.

There Damien stood at the end of the hallway, holding Sofia by a fistful of hair, her head back, chin up. His pistol was shoved against the base of her head, behind her ear—a Rock Island 1911, a perfect mirror of Asher's gun.

"I thought you'd never get here." Damien smiled. "Took ya long enough."

Thinking on his feet, Xavier made the decision not to move through the back door. He could hear voices from inside the home but not through the walls. They were coming from an open window. He treaded lightly down the side of the house and noticed a window tilted open, the rain dripping from its edge.

"Ash," Sofia murmured.

Damien pulled her head back more forcefully, and she winced.

Asher squinted, trying to make out the face of the man holding his wife at gunpoint. After a few seconds, it all came into focus.

It was the same guy.

Xavier walked through the mud alongside the home to

reach the open window. He had a clear view as it all unfolded: Cassandra had Damien at gunpoint, but Damien had Sofia. Asher was out of sight, however, across from Cassandra on the opposite side of the hallway.

Xavier inched open the window, careful not to alert Damien. He lifted his pistol, but Sofia was between the two of them. He needed to wait or figure out an alternative angle.

No one else knew he was there.

"It's time to talk," Asher said. "Looks like you've already met my wife."

Damien chuckled. "In more ways than one, my friend. More ways than one."

"I don't think she needs to be involved in this. Why don't you let her go, and we can figure out a way to make this all go away."

"You see, that's where you're wrong. She *wanted* to be involved in this. She *chose* to be involved in this, just like you did."

Xavier still didn't have a clear shot. No matter how he looked at it, Sofia was in the way. *Come on*, he thought. *Just move her to the side, and you're done.*

"Besides," Damien continued, "two on one isn't a fair game."

"You're absolutely right," Asher said. "You never stood a chance."

"Sorry, hun," Cassandra said to Asher. "I think he was referring to you."

Chapter 92

Out of the corner of his eye, Asher saw the rifling—twisting and glinting—from the barrel's edge of Cassandra's pistol, now aimed at the side of his head. Even in the dark space of the home, her inner savagery could be seen.

"Aw, what's the matter, *Ash*? You look upset," Damien mocked. "I started to think you had it all figured out."

For a moment, Sofia stopped fighting. Her jaw went slack, mouth open, as she looked at Cassandra with bewilderment. Asher's gaze shifted to a place of disbelief as his eyes ran down to the floor, up the wall, and over to Cassandra's look of satisfaction. He shook his head and looked back to Damien.

"Now, you see, what *really* upsets me about all of this," Damien said, as if it were another day in the office, "isn't our current situation. I mean, after all, this was bound to happen." He shrugged. "But I just can't wrap my head around the fact that you refuse to fuck my wife. What's the problem? She too much for you?"

Cassandra grinned as she brushed a stray piece of hair from her eyes. She leaned her head to the side and pushed her lips together, forming a pitiful look.

"Just look at her," Damien continued. "How could you not take advantage of that? She *threw* herself at you," he said as

Cassandra winked and smiled the smile Asher knew and loved all too well.

Only for a moment, an I-told-you-so expression flashed across Sofia's face. She knew, deep down, that her gut feeling about Cassandra had always been right. She'd never been able to put a finger on it, but she knew perfectly well.

The expression didn't last long, however. She quickly realized it was her husband who had fallen victim to Cassandra's ploy. And she was riding passenger on the same crazy train.

"*Your* wife, on the other hand." Damien laughed. "That shit spreads like butter. I can see, now, why you married her—sexy, confident. She even smells the part," he said as he pressed his nose against her hair and drew a deep breath.

Sofia lunged forward in an attempt to break free. "Oh, no, no, no." Damien grabbed her hair yet again, pulling her back so vigorously, her feet were swept out from beneath her as she fell to the floor, the pistol now aimed at the top of her head.

"I will admit," he continued, "she isn't the brightest. Some guy just shows up at your work with flowers, and with a snap of the fingers you forget your husband ever existed. Sounds like the two of you have some issues to work on. Or maybe that's just how she likes it—on the side. Your mother certainly did."

Asher shook his head in disbelief. He gripped his gun tighter, his fingers throbbing red and white. The black, open sights of the pistol shook, pulling back and forth across Damien's head. Asher's nerves were showing.

Maybe there was nothing wrong all along, Asher thought for an instant. *Maybe our marriage problems were merely their problems.*

"You got it figured yet?" Cassandra said with a smile.

"I think he needs some help, baby," Damien said.

"I *never was* your partner," she said with a bogus frown.

Asher could see Damien grinning, satisfied, as she spoke.

"I told you she was no good," Sofia mumbled from down on the floor. "I told you from day one she was a mistake."

"Shut the hell up," Asher interrupted. "I think you've done enough at this point." His mind was darting all over the place. He no longer had his bearings on who was what.

Cassandra and Damien began to laugh, looking at each other with utmost pleasure.

"You see," Damien said. "That's all it takes. One wrong word, one sideways glance, and you're set off like a dog on a leash. You think you have this all under control, but you've *been* controlled since day one."

Xavier had a clear shot now that Sofia was on her knees in front of Damien. But he couldn't see Asher. He was listening, however, and couldn't believe what was unfolding. He had a clear view of Cassandra *and* Damien.

"What the hell does my wife have to do with this?" Asher asked.

"Quite frankly, I don't think you know what *anyone* has to do with this," Cassandra said. "You still don't get it."

"You think your wife deciding to cheat on you was all one big misfortune?" Damien said. "You think you were lucky enough to have a supportive, consoling partner who was just sitting by, waiting to jump you? You know what led you here today was the result of some hard-earned investigative work, don't you? Think again, Detective."

"The only reason you're here is because we brought you here, both of you," Cassandra said. "All those years back, I was just an eager, young psychologist with a dream of working law enforcement." She chuckled as she bit her lip and shook her head. "No. I was the wife of a man whose family, whose father, was taken from him all too early in life. The sad part?" she whispered. "Lead homicide detective *Asher Huxley* couldn't put it all together."

His wide eyes conveyed his disagreement with what his ears had registered. "No, it doesn't add up. You joined homicide before I did. I was still on forensics back then."

"Oh give me a break." She scowled. "We were working the same cases, running in the same circles. Besides, once you joined the unit, we ended up here—partners." She looked into his eyes. "You still don't know how your mother died, do you, *Ash*?"

Damien raised his hand as if he were the excited schoolboy in the front row, itching to get the question right. "I just can't take it anymore," he said, overly enthusiastically. "Pick me, pick me!"

Asher's heart was pushing hard against his chest. His pulse throbbed deep within his throat. His vision narrowed, and all he could see was Cassandra's lioness eyes at the end of the tunnel.

She leaned in, her pistol pressed beneath his chin. "I'll give you a hint," she whispered into his ear. "I'm not the one you need to worry about."

Damien winked as Sofia heard the double click of the pistol's hammer behind her head.

Chapter 93

It was eleven years prior, three years before Cassandra joined the homicide unit, and Damien was late for his appointment. He signed in at the front desk and found a seat in one of four chairs in the dark, simplistic waiting room. An abstract finger painting of a remote marshland sat crooked on the wall across from him, a stack of three magazines on the coffee table at the center of the floor.

He had switched therapists as frequently as clothes, and the loss of his father had been weighing heavily. He was in search of something new, someone who cared and would be willing to provide solutions.

"Mr. Baptiste," the nurse called, holding a clipboard and blood pressure cuff.

After meeting with the nurse for check-in, he walked into the office and was met with the soft and gentle handshake of Cassandra.

"Hi, have a seat." She pointed to the chair in the corner of the room. Her hands were smooth, warm. Her smile was crystal clear and snow white.

The room looked as if she had recently moved in, although he knew that wasn't the case. Her diploma hung behind the computer screen, the remainder of the walls bare.

She radiated experience and was one of the few members

of her practice who knew how to hold a conversation, not like the majority of practitioners in her field, who interrogated their patients and made them feel as if they were on trial before someone who dangled their future in front of their tired, anxiety-ridden eyes.

"So, how are things going?" she asked.

"Rough," he replied as he shoved his thumb into the palm of his hand and cracked his knuckles. "I've decided to switch providers given some changes I'm going through and heard through some close friends that you were highly recommended."

"Thanks for reaching out," she said, looking him in the eyes. She noticed how sharp, how seductive, his blues were—waves of slate swirling in a black-centered sphere. "If you don't mind me asking, what is it that caused you to switch providers?"

She crossed her legs, and for a moment, his mind drew a blank. He'd never been caught off guard like this—the Christian Louboutin heels, the tight skirt, the white blouse. He mirrored her by crossing his legs to hide the fact it had taken all of ten seconds for him to become aroused.

"Well, my previous psychologist was more of a sit-and-listen kind of person rather than someone who cared enough to hold a conversation. I've been with far too many therapists who just wanna ask questions and listen. That's not really what I'm looking for."

"So what is it you think you need, exactly? Is it someone who can help you by doing something in particular?" Her eyes ran across his body as she bit her lip. His muscular chest led to his veined, cut arms. A chill shot through her body and down between her legs as the hairs on her arms stood erect.

"I'm looking for someone who can tell me what to do, someone who can give me some sort of direction to help with depression."

Cassandra nodded. She liked the sound of that. Given the context, she knew what he had meant. But she couldn't help but let her mind wander elsewhere.

Tell you what to do? she thought.

"To be honest, I have enough friends. There's plenty of people in my life who feel like they need to give me advice when all I want them to do is listen. My psychologist, on the other hand, is someone I need to hold a conversation with, someone who can give me advice and tell me what to do, not just listen."

"Well, how our sessions will run is really up to you. I don't tell my patients what we need to talk about, or even do, during our sessions. I leave that up to them. So, if conversation and recommendations for dealing with things is what you feel you need to get out of this, then that's what we'll work on."

"Sounds like I'm in the right place."

"I have a gut feeling you are," she said before pausing, acknowledging her level of comfort. "Like I said over the phone," she continued, "today is really just an intake appointment, where we can get acquainted with one another, determine what you're looking for, and have a solid plan for when you begin your regularly scheduled appointments. Is there anything other than what we've already discussed that you want to bring up?"

"Not in particular. I think if we can focus on the practical side of things to help me cope, that would be great. I do appreciate you taking me on as a new patient."

"Of course. We can get into the details next time, but they can schedule your next appointment at the front desk on your way out." She stood, extending her hand.

Damien gave a sideways, mischievous glance. "Actually, I

was hoping *you* could tell me when we would meet again," he said as he took her hand and didn't let go.

"I'd have to check my schedule and get back to you on that."

"Of course. Coffee sounds great," he said with a straight face.

She giggled and twisted her lips to the side with a blush. She didn't object.

"Call me when you have a day in mind," he continued as he let go and began to walk away.

"*Me?* Call *you?*" she said, laughing.

"Like I said, I need someone to tell *me* what to do," he said over his shoulder.

Chapter 94

"What is it you want, then?" Asher said, anger filling his voice. "You waited all this time to get us here, so tell me. What is it you want?"

Damien smiled and looked to Cassandra as if he couldn't believe Asher was asking such a question. "Damn, Asher, come on. You still don't get it do you? There *is* nothing you can do to fix this. I'm amazed that after all of this, you still think there's something that can be fixed."

A flood of despair ran deep in Asher. For the first time since the case began, he felt no hope. He had put himself into a situation with no exit. It didn't matter what happened in the end, because he now saw that the likelihood of both he and his wife walking away was nonexistent.

Someone was going to pay, whether he liked it or not.

"The only way you can fix this," Damien continued in a slow, deliberate tone, "is if you go back and keep me from strangling your mother. I'm guessing the probability of that happening is slim."

"Or better yet . . ." Cassandra grinned.

Damien finished her sentence. "Keep your mother from fucking my father."

Asher's eyes fell to the floor, his face expressionless. "What the hell are you talking about?"

"What? You think it was all random? Why do *you* think I did it?" Damien paused. "I was there, Asher. I saw it with my own two eyes. Your mother single-handedly ruined my family. Ruined *me*. It's too bad about your father, though. I was starting to think the chemo was working."

Xavier wasn't sure what to do. His gun floated, back and forth, between Damien and Cassandra. He wiped the rain from his face and squinted, straining his eyes to see Cassandra buried deep in the hallway, her silhouette outlined only by the white door frame in which she stood. *What the hell is this?* Xavier thought.

"There's no way you pulled that off by yourself," Asher said. "You expect me to believe your father sat there and watched you kill my mother? You're insane."

"You're right about that. I am a bit fucked in the head," Damien said with a blank expression, running his hand through his beard. "My father, on the other hand, stepped away. Just for a second. It's fascinating how quickly someone will pass out with your hands around their neck, if only for a moment. And it only takes a few seconds more for them to stop breathing all together."

Even with the pistol at the back of her head, Sofia made one last-ditch effort to escape him. She darted to her feet, but too slowly. Damien grabbed her by the collar and pulled her back toward him, wrapping his arm around her stomach as she kicked and squealed. He shoved the pistol against her right temple.

Xavier no longer had a clear shot of Damien. His gun remained on Cassandra, her chest between the two white-dot sights glowing with a hint of green in the dark morning rain. The droplets beaded on top of his gun, forming clear bubbles that balanced, staggered, one in front of the other.

"All I want to know is what this has to do with me," Asher demanded, his voice shaking as he struggled to keep himself on his own two feet. His vision was blurred, his field of view thin. His arms felt weak. The pistol seemed to weigh a ton. "What my mother did has nothing to do with me *or* my wife."

"Oh, it doesn't? I'm sorry. We can all go home then," Damien said wryly.

"Well, shit." Cassandra shrugged. "This is all one big mistake."

"Besides," Asher said, "you don't think your father had any fault in all of this? It was all my mother, huh? That's pretty convenient considering what happened in the end, your father wanting to kill himself instead of look at his own son again."

Damien's mouth clenched and came to a point, his lips cinched. "My father *paid* for what he did, just like your mother."

"No, your father was too chicken shit to handle what he had done, so he ended it himself. Nothing more than a bitch move, in my opinion. I bet that eats at you every day and night, doesn't it? You killed the one woman your father loved, and now you have to walk around pretending like it doesn't bother you. Perhaps that's something you should speak to your psychologist about. Sure would fuck *me* up."

Cassandra and Damien looked at one another in disbelief at what Asher had just uttered, given his predicament.

"Hell, if you really think about it," Asher continued, "*you* killed your father. If it wasn't for you, he'd still be alive. *You're* the reason he's dead."

Asher suddenly noticed a small glint of light scatter across the ceiling, coming from another room, out of sight. Something metallic in the otherwise darkened home. *Xavier*, he thought.

The black box appeared without warning, clear as day. Nothing should enter the black box. What did needed to be removed.

"Last chance," Asher said.

Cassandra chuckled. "What? You think you have the upper hand here? You have nothing, no one. You're done."

"Sorry, hun. Wasn't talking to you," Asher said as Damien's face invaded the empty box.

"Excuse me?"

"Time's up," Xavier whispered.

Chapter 95

The bullet entered Cassandra's chest several inches below her right collarbone and exited her shoulder blade. She dropped her pistol and fell to the floor as if someone had connected with a right hook. She was down but not out. It was a clean exit, and she was out of sight, on the ground, within the dark bedroom before Xavier could fire another shot.

Before Asher could react, Damien squeezed the trigger. The .45 made a clean pass through Sofia's head, continuing into the adjacent sheetrock, sending a fine dust into the immaculate home. She dropped where she was standing, motionless, her head all but touching her feet on the floor.

Unfortunately for Damien, both shots had given Asher a split second to respond, and Damien instantly knew he had made a mistake.

The man's head filled the black box, and Asher knew how to address unwanted thoughts. He smoothly pulled the trigger, sending a single round through Damien's head before landing two shots at center mass in less than a second. The opposing wall was promptly decorated with a heavy shower of burgundy, contrasting with the monochromatic, turquoise painting of St. Louis Cathedral now with three holes, one above the other in a precise, vertical line.

"I can't see her!" Xavier yelled from the window at the side of the home. "Where's she at?" All Xavier could see was a dark hallway, along with Sofia and Damien's bodies lying on the floor.

Asher looked to the doorway across the hall. It was empty. He moved across the way, only to see an empty room with a small pool of blood on the floor, trailing to an open window. Surprisingly, her gun was left on the floor of the room. He looked out of the window and saw Cassandra running between neighboring houses in a dazed stupor.

"She's out back!" Asher called.

Cassandra pulled herself over the waist-high, chain-link fence at the back of the yard, falling to the ground on the other side as she clutched her chest in pain. The rain continued to fall, only hampering her escape.

Xavier darted from the side of the home through the backyard garden and toward the fence. "Come on, girl. Don't make me!" he yelled while raising his gun as she began to stand up in the neighbor's yard. Blood smeared across the top railing but was quickly washed away in the light rain. For a split second, they locked eyes. She sat there, panting in hopes he would somehow, someway let it go.

Xavier fired two shots—one hitting the vertical, steel pole of the fence and the other missing altogether as she rocked from side to side. She stammered to her feet and continued between the two houses behind the yard.

Asher, meanwhile, back in the house, ran into the hallway and slid to his knees, cradling Sofia's unmoving body in his arms. On one hand, the detective in Asher saw clear as day there was no chance for her to survive. Her left profile was unrecognizable. On the other hand, the husband in him was going to do anything to bring her back. He laid her flat on the floor and began CPR.

Every cell in his body knew it was hopeless, yet he fought through the motions out of pure will.

His mouth was painted in crimson as he met his wife's lips for the last time. He breathed into her but received nothing in return. Her only movement was the rise and fall of her chest as he completed one compression after another. He sat, empty, as he held his wife's body, feeling the warmth of his skin being pulled away by her chill.

He hadn't held her in weeks, and this would be the last time.

Outside, Xavier hopped the fence and darted after Cassandra. She pushed her way down a grass alley between homes, shoving trash cans aside, clanking and banging against one another. His large build made it difficult for him to run for any extended period of time. As a result, the two were surprisingly on an even playing field, although Xavier had time on his side.

She crossed the street and ran behind another home, the backyard shielded by a small garage on the side of the house. By the time he had reached the backyard, he couldn't tell which direction she had gone in. Left ran into another chain-link fence, but straight ahead was an alleyway with no one in sight. To the right lay another home with no entrance to the backyard. He jogged down the alley but found no blood on the wet ground. No Cassandra.

"You've gotta be shitting me," he huffed, hunched over with his hands on his knees.

As he reached the next line of houses, an elderly woman startled him as she spoke from her screened-in back porch. "Excuse me, can I help you?"

"Yeah, did you see a woman run through here just now? It's an emergency," he said as he held up his badge.

The lady, unmoved by his question, was oblivious. "Sorry son, but I haven't seen anyone. Are you okay?"

"Yeah." He nodded, out of breath. "I'm fine."

"Do I need to call someone? Are you sure?"

He held up his hand and shook his head, the rain dripping from his chin.

Xavier made his way back to Damien's house and walked through the back door. Asher was sitting on the floor in the hallway, holding Sofia with her head draped over his arm. He rocked back and forth as he brushed her hair from her face.

"Shit," Xavier said.

He too could see that any effort to revive Sofia was a moot point. But he called the paramedics anyway as Asher cradled her, refusing to let go. The tears raced down Asher's face and carried with them the last of her.

Xavier crouched next to him and placed his hand on his shoulder. "I gotcha, man. I gotcha."

The three of them had seen their last moments together. Just as Asher had lost a spouse, Xavier would never again see that cherished piece of his best friend.

Asher turned to him with red, bloodshot eyes. "Where is she?"

"I lost her," Xavier said with disappointment as he struggled to catch his breath. "She's bleeding like a stuck pig, though. She'll either show up face-down in the street or at a hospital."

Chapter 96

hree days had passed, and Asher had only gotten up to use the bathroom and make funeral arrangements. It was morning, and he lay in bed staring at the ceiling for hours while replaying the raid in his head, trying to remember each and every move while simultaneously fighting to forget the image of his wife on the floor. The individual dots of popcorn moved across the white landscape of the roof—shooting, arguing, chasing. But in the end, they all returned to their original state, providing no answers and no direction forward.

The anxiety had dissipated. His body, once riddled with pain and unease, was now numb. Today was Sofia's funeral, and somehow he hoped to stumble across a shred of motivation that would push him out of bed and onto his feet.

The sun had long since risen, and the rays lit the room on their own accord. Sofia's brown hair tie remained on the nightstand, her hair still intertwined among its loops. He could smell the remnants of coconut lingering on the adjacent pillow, her blouse draped across the corner of the bed. Asher had slept in an otherwise empty bed for far too many nights, but the last three were different. They were permanent.

He sat up and rested his legs over the edge of the mattress. He could see, out of the corner of his eye, the small blue light flashing on his phone. The text messages and missed calls were becoming overwhelming. But he needed to make it through the day before he worried about the rest of the world.

Her baby-blue slippers were by the door, perfectly aligned in place, as always.

A soft knock sounded from the living room.

Asher pushed himself up from the mattress and arched his back. He grabbed his pistol off the nightstand, pulling back the slide just far enough to peek at the round he knew he'd find in the chamber.

He knew what to expect, opening the door, but he now had a tickle in the back of his mind that was new—new, but familiar at the same time.

"Who is it?" he said while stepping to the side of the doorway.

"It's me."

Asher opened the door and received a big bear hug from Xavier, along with a pat on the back. "You hangin' in there?" his friend asked.

"Yeah. I'm still here."

"Good. Today's a big day, huh? There anything I can get you?"

Asher shook his head. "Other than sleep, not really. It's gotta happen one way or another."

"What you averaging per night? You don't look so hot."

"Last night? About four or five hours. A few more hours than I was getting a couple nights ago."

They made their way into the kitchen, where Asher opened the fridge. "Water?" He gestured. A look—a culpable look—washed over Xavier's face, his eyes pinned to the floor.

"What's up?" Asher asked, still holding out the bottle. "You good?"

"You said this was gonna happen one way or another. I just wish it wasn't."

"Wasn't what?"

"Happening. At all. I've been thinking a lot, over the last couple days, about how things played out. I wonder if it should've gone differently."

"Don't. Let's not go there," Asher said, his tone somber but supportive.

"I just can't help but wonder if I should've—"

"Xavier. Don't." Asher continued to shake his head. "The end result has nothing to do with you. All of us were in a bad position, and someone had to do something. For all we know, it could've ended a lot worse if you hadn't stepped in."

Xavier took the water and sat in a chair at the kitchen table.

A few two-by-three pictures of Sofia were spread across the table—one of her and Asher in Jackson Square, one of them at the Audubon Zoo, another one of only her at the lakefront, with Asher's car as the backdrop.

"You bringing these along?" Xavier asked.

"Yeah. Figured I'd leave some with her, take a couple for my wallet. Doesn't feel right keeping them all to myself."

"I hear that." Xavier leaned over and pulled out his wallet. "Here. Leave this one for her." He placed an old, wrinkled photo of the three of them onto the table. It was from years back, not long after they all met, when they brought in the new year with a barbeque at Xavier's place. She and Asher were sitting arm in arm at a picnic table with Xavier behind them in an apron, showing off his spatula skills.

"You sure?" Asher asked as he picked up the photo and leaned back against the counter, looking deep into the picture with a subtle smile. "This is a good one."

"Yeah. It only feels right to leave something behind. Besides, we both have the memories."

"Well, I appreciate it. And I'm sure she would, too." Asher set it next to the other photos on the table.

"You know how many people are showing up? Between family and colleagues, I guess it should be quite a few, no?"

"Yeah, I'm sure there'll be a number of people from her work, but relatives more than anything. There's a lot of family members from out of state we haven't seen in a while."

"Sounds like a plan." Xavier grinned. "You about ready?"

"Yep, just need to grab these"—he stacked the pictures on the table—"and we should be good to go."

Asher put on his sports coat, and together they walked to Xavier's car. It was a beautiful, green morning, the fog beginning to lift from the grass and drift around the rooftops. Before opening the car door, Xavier leaned over and picked up a pecan nut that had fallen from the tree in the front yard. "You know, my grandparents used to have a pecan tree in their backyard. I remember, as a kid, walking outside and sitting under the tree, eating one after another. It's one of those memories that hangs around no matter what."

"I bet you love spending time at their place, then."

"Actually, it got wiped out in Katrina. Now I just come here and bug you," he said while cracking open the shell. He split the fruit in half, sliding one portion to Asher across the roof of the Camaro. They looked at one another over the car as they savored the buttery, sweet crunch.

"Well"—Asher gestured to the tree—"consider it part of the family."

Chapter 97

"I'm assuming Pierre is gonna be there," Xavier said as they drove to the cemetery.

"I guess so. He's in the loop now, so it'll be interesting to see what happens if he shows up. We've only talked twice since the other day. Although, I know *you're* at the office pretty much all the time, so you probably have a better idea about what he plans on doing."

"Yeah, I think he'll come around. After all, you saved the department from even more humiliation than we've already had to deal with."

Asher ran his hand over the smooth, black dashboard, slick with Armor All, and looked into the back seat. "You know, this old piece of crap really isn't that bad."

Xavier chuckled. "Of course it isn't. You're just used to driving that beat-up rag you call a muscle car. I've been tryin' to get you to take it for a spin ever since I worked on the interior some more. It's a whole new car, man."

"We'll have to put 'em side by side sometime soon. It's about time we settle things once and for all, huh?"

"Anytime, anywhere." Xavier smirked.

As they followed the hearse along the winding roads of the cemetery, a flock of blackbirds was rustled from an oak tree at the center of the yard. The shadowy pairs of wings made their way upward into the lifting fog and disappeared, scattering between distant treetops.

The day was serene, placid.

Sofia's only wish—as she'd jested in passing—was to be buried beneath an old tree, as close as possible to its shade and "away from the crowd." As a biologist, she knew well what happened to the deceased over time, and she preferred for her remains to serve a pragmatic purpose and be returned to the earth rather than remain static indoors, only to be pined over.

The one sound emanating from the otherwise tranquil yard was the flapping of the black awning beneath a bald cypress at the far corner of the cemetery, an opening for Sofia's casket at its center, isolated from the surrounding headstones. Intertwining strings of Spanish moss hung from the cypress's branches and reached to the ground, forming a green-gray curtain surrounding the burial.

As they approached the canopy, Pierre and his wife, along with a couple of Sofia's family members, had arrived early. In a surprise to Asher, Pierre approached him with an extended hand as he arrived.

"I wasn't sure you'd make it," Asher said.

"Contrary to what everyone thinks," Pierre said, "I'm not *completely* heartless. Besides, you guys are part of the family, no? It's only right we show up for one of our own."

Asher shook his hand and sat next to the podium at the head of the service. The stillness of the day's events put him at ease, even more so than he'd thought possible. As attendees trickled in, almost everyone approached him—family members, work colleagues, even acquaintances of Sofia whose names he couldn't recall.

The one person he was surprised to see, however, and did

not receive a greeting from, was Byron. Much as before, Asher sensed a disconnect with him, a sense of unease. But he wasn't going to let such an occurrence ruin the day's service.

Near the end of the ceremony, when most of the attendees had left, Pierre walked over and sat next to Asher. They rested in silence for a moment, thinking about the undeniable influence Sofia had had in their lives. Out of nowhere, Pierre did the unthinkable.

"Here," he said as he handed Asher his badge. "You've earned it."

Asher cracked a half-baked smile and grabbed the badge, running his thumb over the silver metal, considering what it meant to be back on the unit. It was a part of his life he wasn't sure he could bear losing in addition to his wife. Although, he also wasn't sure how he would continue to serve in the position given his current loss and state of mind.

"You sure?" he asked, his voice hesitant. "I wasn't expecting this, especially now."

"Yeah. I've given it a lot of thought over the last few days. I decided that losing you, in addition to what you've already been through, would be more than any of us could handle. Yeah, I'm sure. You solved the cases. In the end, you did your job, even though you went about it all wrong. Just promise me one thing."

"What's that?"

"You finish it."

Asher didn't respond. He didn't know what to say, or if he should say anything at all. Such a statement was filled with a heavy weight, loaded with expectations but also appreciation.

"As much as I hate to admit it," Pierre continued, "you're the only one who's qualified, given the circumstances. I only want you to remember one thing." He leaned in close.

"Let me guess—this is my last chance?" Asher whispered.

Pierre winked and patted him on the leg. "See? You're already up to speed. It's good to have you back on board." The man rose from his seat and buttoned his jacket as his wife grabbed him by the arm. "Take as much time as you need. Although, I suspect you won't take long."

Xavier filled the now-empty chair next to Asher once their boss had left.

"That looked good. I'm guessing you're back?" he asked.

"Yeah, I suppose so."

"You don't look too excited. You sure this is a good thing?"

Asher nodded as he slid the badge into his coat pocket. "Yeah, I'm just not looking forward to my next case is all."

"Why is that?"

"Well, let's just say I have some catching up to do."

The last of the family and friends trickled away, and soon only Asher and Xavier remained. Asher plucked a single flower—a red rose—from the bouquet rested at the center of the casket. He placed the pictures beneath the flowers and said his last goodbye.

Chapter 98

Asher woke up the following morning feeling slightly better than he had the several days prior. Even if it was only a smidgen of progress, it was progress.

He went through his normal morning routine, then sat in the sunroom, soaking in the sunrise with his cup of decaf in the hammock. He swung back and forth, watching a downy woodpecker hop across the fence in the backyard, white feathers shimmering against the black background of its wings. They were Sofia's favorite. She would watch the birds fly between the trees, morning and evening, as the sun made its rounds behind the neighboring rooftops. It was much like the people in his life—Asher watched them come and go, not sure when, or if, they would return.

Some, of course, could not.

⁓

Asher placed the birdfeeder just outside the window of the sunroom but in view from the hammock. He clipped a high-energy suet of feed into the hanging cage and retreated onto the porch. He had no plans, was in no rush. One cup of coffee turned into two, then three.

A pair of downy landed on the feeder, nibbling at the solid, yellow brick of feed. One bird sprang toward the other with its wings open, pushing it away, only for it to return and try yet again to find its place at the feeder. This behavior continued until the first bird got the message and flew away. The second continued to eat alone, then followed suit. The pair would mate and remain together, a monogamous couple. Asher wondered how they did it. How did one continue to drive away the other, yet they returned to feed together day after day? After all, not all woodpeckers were exclusive to their partners.

He didn't plan on returning to the office for several days. He was better, but he felt he needed the time. As soon as he returned, he would be thrust back into the stress he so desperately wanted to escape. But it kept him up, on his toes. If not for the stress, he wouldn't know what to do with his time. His own mind would get the better of him.

Asher left the house and drove to the Quarter. As he walked down Decatur, the ambience of brass horns and hooves meeting cement flooded him with appreciation, but also uncertainty. He was *the* leading homicide detective in one of the most unique cities in the world—and now he was desolate, widowed, and partnerless. A sense of worry radiated throughout his body, sitting quiet in the background, scratching at his chest. But he walked forward anyway.

As he rounded the corner, he saw street artists working back to back, surrounding Jackson Square. Painters, musicians, performers, and jewelers lined the iron fence. One individual in particular caught his eye—a charcoal artist drawing black-and-gray landscapes. The man's work was familiar. His portion of the fence was adorned with every size of canvas conceivable, each of which displayed a photorealistic depiction of the city in its natural state, most of them drawn from pure memory.

Asher sat on a neighboring bench and watched him draw, wondering what it was, exactly, that had driven her here. What had driven her away from home? Or better yet, which came first? Was it her growing disinterest in him, or was it his worry and work-related stress that pushed her away?

None of it really mattered, though. Not anymore. Sofia would never walk the city streets again.

After making his rounds of the square, observing the art in progress, he crossed Decatur and began walking toward Café Du Monde. If there was one fact natives of N'awlins were sure of, it was that any time was a good time for beignets and coffee.

A blues street band was playing to a crowd of onlookers at the corner. He dropped a five-dollar bill into the guitar case as he passed, the singer tipping his black fedora in response. The city was fresh with new beginnings, the perfect destination for a clean start.

La vie nouvelle.

The café was buzzing, as it was virtually seven days a week. Peach walls flowed into terracotta tile floors littered with powdered sugar. Small, round tables were staggered throughout the building below bottle-green and white stripes above the kitchen, which matched the outside awning. Indoor and outdoor seating flowed, subtly, one into the other as waiters wearing white paper hats and black bowties shuffled between the minefield of table tops with their large, black serving trays.

Asher was seated inside but near a set of French doors and windows looking out to the sidewalk. The sun shattered in bright, lemon rays as it reflected off the aluminum napkin holder at the center of the table.

"Hi, what can I get you?" the waiter asked.

"Ice water and an order of beignets. Thanks."

Chapter 99

Asher pulled out his phone and began scrolling through the morning news. Page after page was nothing but misleading, divisive stories. He was quickly reminded as to why he rarely paid attention to the media. The world was coming apart at the seams—nations invading one another under false pretenses, billionaires suing over social media empires, individuals condemning one another over personalized identity politics. It made Asher's world look like child's play, and he had walked through some of the most disturbing homicides imaginable.

He could already envision the headline of his own story: *NOPD Loses Control as One of Their Own Jumps Ship.* He didn't need to scroll any farther and see the true headline for himself. His imagination was harsh enough.

Putting away his phone, Asher leaned back into the chair, glancing outside to the passing crowd as the street band covered B.B. King's "The Thrill Is Gone." A couple danced at the edge of the street, the husband dipping the wife as she laughed, her bronze hair hanging to the ground. The singer joined them on the curb, swaying in rhythm with the music as the couple made their way into the street.

The waiter returned with Asher's order. "Here you are." He

placed a large, dark coffee and a small box onto the table.

A black box.

"Is there anything else I can get you?"

"Sorry, I think there's a mix-up. I had a water and an order of beignets."

"Yes, sir. The lady at the register said this is what you really want. She insists."

He glanced over to the counter but saw no one. Without pause, the waiter walked away from the table as Asher stared, blankly, at the box.

"Well, here's to knowing ya," he whispered to himself.

As he lifted the lid, he paused, frozen from head to toe. A single French cruller stared back at him. His eyes made another sweep of the café but came up empty. For a moment, he considered his options.

Then he chuckled under his breath before standing. He pulled the doughnut from the box and placed it between his teeth as he pushed his chair into the table. He leaned into the café door, back first, and walked out into the fresh air. As he dropped the box into the trashcan, he took a lavish bite of the warm, twisted glaze.

The yellow-red light swept over him as he paused, smirking, in the morning sun. Chin up, eyes closed, he sipped his coffee. Bitter—just the way he liked it.

About the Author

KB Fisher is a Louisiana native originally from Greater New Orleans. He lives with his family in the Southeast United States.

One of the most valuable things a reader can do for an author is to provide an honest review of their work. Please visit the book's review page on either Amazon.com or Goodreads to do so.

Website: authorKBFisher.com
Email: authorKBFisher@gmail.com
Twitter: @authorKBFisher

9 7989 8802 0 0004